# A GRAVE END

# A GRAVE END

## WENDY ROBERTS

**W🌐RLDWIDE**

TORONTO • NEW YORK • LONDON
AMSTERDAM • PARIS • SYDNEY • HAMBURG
STOCKHOLM • ATHENS • TOKYO • MILAN
MADRID • WARSAW • BUDAPEST • AUCKLAND

# W⊕RLDWIDE™

A Grave End

A Worldwide Mystery/May 2020

First published in 2019 by Carina Press.
This edition published in 2020 with revised text.

Copyright © 2019 by Wendy Roberts
Copyright © 2020 by Wendy Roberts, revised text edition

ISBN-13: 978-1-335-29978-9

This edition published by arrangement with Harlequin Books S.A.

For questions and comments about the quality of this book, please contact us at CustomerService@Harlequin.com.

Harlequin Enterprises ULC
22 Adelaide St. West, 40th Floor
Toronto, Ontario M5H 4E3, Canada
www.ReaderService.com

**Printed in U.S.A.**

Recycling programs for this product may not exist in your area.

# ACKNOWLEDGMENTS

Thank you, dear readers, for following Julie's journey.

# ONE

THE BONES OF the dead don't care where they rest. It's those who are left behind that are driven by a need to bring the bodies home. My job is to use my dowsing rods to help find missing remains, and hopefully, give some peace to the living. It wouldn't have been my first career choice, but I didn't choose the departed. The dead chose me.

I sat at the kitchen table with laptop open staring at a number of emails received about the same case over the past few months. From the very first message months ago, I thought there was no way I was going to take this case. The emails were from a man in Blaine, Washington, my old hometown. His daughter-in-law had been killed, and although his son was doing time for the murder, the body had never been recovered. The fact that the missing body was someone from my old hometown was the major part of the reason I didn't want to touch this case. But over the past few weeks I'd grown more curious.

"Good morning, sweetheart."

Garrett walked into the kitchen and I lifted my face for a good morning kiss. He smelled of soap and shave cream.

"Are you taking a new job?" He joined me at the kitchen table.

"Maybe." I frowned and shook my head. "It wasn't my first choice but now I think it might be time I talked to someone and got some firsthand information."

"This isn't the one where the guy is in prison, is it?"

"Yes. The other day I finally replied asking for more information but this morning I received a reply saying the dad had died of cancer so I didn't have to bother."

"Now that they don't need you, it's making you more curious in taking this on?"

I opened my mouth to say that wasn't the only reason, but Garrett's phone rang in the other room and he jogged off to answer the call. I returned my attention to the messages on my screen.

When Garrett returned he had his leather duffel bag slung over his shoulder.

"Going somewhere?" I got up and went to him.

"The case I've been working…" He dropped his bag on the floor and circled his arms around my waist. "There's some follow-up I've got to do out of state. I'll be a couple days."

"Damn. I was hoping you'd be home this weekend." I rested my cheek against his chest.

"You had big plans to stain the deck, right?" He planted a kiss on the top of my head. "I promise I'll get to it."

This wasn't about the deck. I needed to talk to him about something, but it wasn't the kind of thing I could bring up as he was on his way out the door. I'd already put if off a few days so I guessed a couple more wouldn't hurt. He kissed me goodbye in a way that left me breathless and aching for him long after his car backed out of the driveway. Wookie whined.

"Daddy's only going to be a couple days," I told the dog, giving his head a reassuring pat.

I returned to my computer and printed off some information. It was going to take a number of hours to drive to visit this potential client, and even though I was still on the fence about taking this case, I hoped the long drive would help me clear my head about a lot of things.

THE FERRY LINEUP for the Edmonds to Kingston route wasn't too long. I put my Jeep in park and settled in to wait for my crossing. A dark knot of October clouds were knitting together and a gust of wind caused some leaves to dance across the hood of my car. I was scrolling through my phone when it rang in my hand. It was my best friend, Tracey.

"It's a beautiful fall day, isn't it?" She skipped the hellos. "So I was thinking who better to get together and bake cookies with than my bestie. I bought dough for four dozen cookies and I will eat every single last one of them myself. I need you to save me."

"I'm about to drive onto a ferry so you're on your own."

"You're doing a road trip and didn't call me?" She sounded hurt and then added, "Or is this a romantic getaway with Mr. FBI?"

"Nope, Mr. FBI is away and I'm checking out a potential client." The ferry was beginning to load so I started my Jeep. "How about I stop in and we can do the cookie thing when I get back late this afternoon?"

"Deal."

After I disconnected the call I drove onto the boat. The ferry ride was only a half hour, which was just enough time to walk up on deck. The salty air whipped across Puget Sound, tore through my hair and misted my face. This October day was set to bring an assortment of torrential rains and breaking sun that mimicked my mixed mood.

The ferry began to dock and I returned to my Jeep, my cheeks still stinging from the cold. Playing an audio book on positive thinking, I continued my journey. Fifteen minutes after I drove off the ferry, I was driving across the Hood Canal Bridge. Although I didn't like to walk across bridges, driving on them didn't usually give me an issue. But driving on a mile-long floating bridge caused my nerves to ping.

It was the thought of this case that caused my hands to still be gripping the wheel too tightly twenty minutes later. I stopped at Fat Smitty's and grabbed a chocolate shake and a hot dog but I still had a couple hours to go. It really was a beautiful drive, the kind Garrett and I would've loved to do together, but the destination left a sour taste in my mouth.

At the Ozette Corrections Center, a line of people were already waiting to be processed into the prison for visiting hours. Although I'd found bodies that helped put people away, this was my first time being inside one of these facilities. I was about to have a sit-down with a convicted murderer so it was no wonder my stomach clenched as I signed in and went through screening that rivaled the most thorough airport security. I sat in the waiting room with dozens of others.

My name was called and I was brought into the large visitor room. Dozens of inmates in their beige uniforms sat at tables across from their guests. There was a play area on the far side for kids, and at the other end of the room, a bank of vending machines. It only took me a couple seconds to spot my potential client. His face had been in all the papers.

Roscoe Ebert got to his feet and waved me over. I wound my way around other people to take a seat across from him at a large table.

"Jesus, I thought you'd never come." He nervously scooched his chair closer to the table. "You got approved as a visitor months ago. Every week I've been waiting."

"Listen, Roscoe, the only reason I'm here is because your dad must've sent me a dozen emails begging me to take your case."

"So you waited until he's dead to agree. Nice."

"Your sister told me that cancer got him. Sorry for your loss." I felt guilty for not telling Roscoe's father that I'd at least interview his son, and that guilt had brought me this far but that didn't mean more.

"Dad kept thinking he could beat it, and for years he did."

"Your sister told me I didn't need to bother—"

"Kim didn't tell you not to bother 'cuz she thinks I'm guilty. She just doesn't think you can help."

"She might be right. Look, I figure I'd honor your dad's request and at least come talk to you. That doesn't mean I'm going to go looking for a body. I'll get your take on things but just because I'm here doesn't mean squat."

He leaned back in his chair and frowned. Roscoe Ebert looked lean and mean and wore the expression of a man not used to being told no. He had a large neck tattoo of a dagger piercing a bloody heart. Another tat was a large Chinese symbol with thick black strokes that was centered on his forehead. "Fine. Get me something from the vending machine before we start. Doritos and a Coke."

"I didn't bring any cash."

"Seriously? Oh my God, dude!" He scrubbed his hand across the stubble on his shaven head. "Who the hell comes to visit and doesn't bring cash?"

"This isn't a social call."

"Yeah, well, I'm only allowed one visitor at a time so you being here means that someone with actual snack money is being turned away for you."

I doubted there was a long line of people waiting to see Roscoe Ebert but I needed to take charge of this meeting so I scraped my chair back loudly and got to my feet as if to leave.

"Nah. Sit down." Roscoe flashed me a quick smile filled with rotting teeth and waved to my chair. "I was joking. Jesus." I remained standing until he cleared his throat and added between clenched teeth, "Please."

I took my seat and folded my hands on the table. "Tell me everything that happened."

"You already know the case, right? It was in all the freakin' papers and I'm sure my dad and sister—"

"Yes, your dad told me everything and I checked out the papers, but I need to hear it from you." I tapped the table with my finger. "From the beginning."

He pulled his chair even closer to the table.

"You remember Alice, right? You two went to the same grade school, I think."

"Yes."

My memory of Alice was the main reason I came

today. We hadn't been friends but once when getting changed for PE class in fourth grade, I'd caught sight of bruising up and down her back, and another time at recess I saw a bruised imprint of a large hand on her upper arm. When she'd caught me looking at her arm she tugged down the sleeve of her T-shirt in an attempt to cover the mark. I'd met her nervous gaze and slowly rolled up my own sleeve to show a map of purple and green. We'd shared a look between us that needed no words for connection. I might not have known Alice the adult but I was here to honor that beaten child.

"So this is how it went…" Roscoe closed his eyes and tilted his head as if trying to bring it all to mind. "Alice was a few years younger so I didn't pay her no attention growing up. I moved out of Blaine after graduation. Went to work for an uncle at a garage in Portland but when the garage closed I moved back home, and when I saw her again it was like love at first sight, you know?" He grinned dreamily as he opened his eyes. "She had this flaming red hair that was like fire, and more freckles than you could ever count. I was fixing transmissions at the shop next to the convenience store where she worked. I went in to the store every break I had to buy something. I'd buy a soda or a magazine or a chocolate bar just to get a look at her. Finally I got up the guts to ask her out and she turned me down flat."

He laughed at that and then continued, "One day, I went home after my shift and I spent an hour in the shower scrubbing all the grease off my hands, and then I put on my go-to-funeral pants and a button-down shirt. I sprayed on some cologne and even stopped to buy one red rose at the market before I drove to her work and asked her out again. This time she said yes."

"How long before you got married?"

"A couple years. I wanted to wait until I could afford a place of our own. Dad said I could have a piece of our land to call my own so I bought a used singlewide and we called it home. It's just down the road from—" He nodded his chin at me to indicate his trailer hadn't been far from where I grew up. "It was kind of a dump but Alice fixed it up nice. Borrowed a sewing machine from my ma and made all the curtains herself. Kept it sparkling clean. Made me homemade meals every night. Perfect, you know?"

"And then…?"

"Things went bad." His look soured. "You know what it's like. Everything is peaches and cream and lovey-dovey in the beginning, but then all the little things start to bug you. She wanted me to work more hours so we could buy more stuff, and in the meantime she was working hardly at all. Her hours got cut and instead of looking for more work, she just sat around thinking of all the stuff we should buy." He held up a hand in case I was going to be upset about that comment. "Hey, I wanted stuff too so don't go thinking that was the worst thing. We argued but I still loved her, you know? We were still doing it on a regular basis." He gave me an oily smile, but I kept my expression impassive.

"And?" I wanted him to get to the point.

"It's simple. She wanted kids. We tried but it just didn't happen. At first we were cool about it. Just kept saying it would happen in time but it didn't. After a couple years she was freaking out and we went to the doctor. It was me. No swimmers." His eyes grew hard. "Things were different after that. She got depressed. I kept feeling like it was all my fault. She wanted to try in vitro with someone else's seed. You know how much that shit costs?" He blew a raspberry through his lips. "We couldn't afford it. My dad offered to pay. He wanted a grandchild but I refused to take his money for that. He was already helping us out. No matter how many ways I explained that to Alice, she would not let it go."

"So, you killed her."

"No. I did not." He pointed a finger in my face and his face grew dark. "Since Alice was like a dog with a bone about getting pregnant, I went and got her a puppy. A black Lab that she right away named Jet. She loved that dog like crazy. We both did. It gave her something to do. Something to focus on besides getting pregnant."

I thought about how Wookie came into my life and was my best friend during tough times.

"Dogs can be great companions."

"Exactly." He nodded. "Don't get me wrong, Alice was so bad at training the damn thing so all of that fell on me but I didn't mind. Jet was a quick learner. After a couple months I could take that dog anywhere off leash and he'd never take off. If I told him to stay, he wouldn't move. He loved to ride in my pickup with his head hanging out the window." Roscoe's eyes grew damp and he cleared his throat loudly. "Sorry. I miss that damn dog."

*But not your dead wife.* It wasn't lost on me that Roscoe didn't get emotional until he'd brought up the dog.

"I heard that Alice loved Jet too."

"Sure, but not the same. She loved him more when he was a cute puppy and not so much when he was tracking in mud and fleas." He sighed. "Anyway, the dog wasn't enough. We split."

It was a matter of court record that Roscoe and Alice had fought over custody of the dog at the time of her death.

"When I walked out, Alice went nuts about keeping custody of the dog."

"I can see that. The dog was hers. You'd given it to her as a gift."

He snorted.

"Jet was for both of us. Sure she went all goo-goo over him at first but she never once took him to the vet or picked up his crap. She liked cuddling him in her arms but would chase him with a broom if he got hold of one of her shoes. I was the one the dog respected." He thumped his chest. "Jet wouldn't even come to her if she called him. I'm telling you the dog had zero interest in her."

"Must've pissed you off when the judge said you had to share him."

"Damn straight." He put his palms out. "But you know what? I was angry about that in the beginning, but I knew it was just a matter of time before she stopped wanting Jet so much. It had already gotten to the point where she'd ask to bring him back to me after five days instead of seven because she wanted to go out drinking with her girlfriends and was worried Jet would eat another pair of shoes. So I knew soon Jet would be back with me full-time so I was pretty chill about it."

"But the night Alice was killed, witnesses said you two had a big fight over the dog. If you were so chill, what was that about?"

"I was out with Blossom and—"

I straightened in my chair and tilted my head to make sure I'd heard correctly. "I'm sorry, you were out with who?"

"Blossom. This chick I was just kind of seeing at the time."

"Tall? Busty? Black hair down to her ass?"

"She cut her hair shorter a while back, but yeah, that's her. You know her?"

Blossom had received that nickname in high school because she had a penchant for flower-print shirts. I couldn't even remember her real name, but I recalled how cruel she could be to a poor kid like me who was lucky to get clothes from the thrift store. I also remember Alice trying desperately to fit in with Blossom's mean-girl crowd.

"We went to school together. What's her real name?"

"Damned if I know." He rubbed the crease between his eyebrows as if that would help but then he gave up. "We went out only a couple times before all this happened."

"Okay, so you were out with Blossom and then…?" I tried to get my mind back on Roscoe's story so waved my hand for him to continue.

"Yeah, Blossom and I were at the pub and she stepped outside for a smoke. Then she comes back inside and tells me that Jet is locked in a car across the street and she can hear him barking. So I'm thinking, what the frig is that all about?" He crosses his arms with indignation. "I go outside and sure enough, there's Jet in the back of Alice's car. The minute he sees me he goes ape shit, right? He's howling and pawing at the glass."

"This was winter though. November, if I remember. And it was cool out but not below zero or anything, so Jet wasn't in any danger."

"He was freaking out." Roscoe leaned forward, palms down on the table between us and whispered, "I wasn't about to just leave him like that, so I busted him out."

"Broke the window of her car and took him."

"Yup." He grinned proudly. "The car alarm went off and Alice came out of the coffee shop and lost her frickin' mind. She was screaming so loud I thought her head would explode. Of course, other people came out of all the businesses around there to see what the hell was happening. I took Jet over to my truck and locked him inside and then I told her she'd have to take me to court if she ever wanted to see the dog again. I didn't scream at her or anything. I was totally chill. I know witnesses said we had a big fight in the middle of the street but, dude, that's misleading. Alice was shrieking like a maniac, but I was totally mellow on account of I knew I was in the right. She knew it too and that's why she freaked." He smiled.

"And then you killed her. Over a dog."

"I'm telling you I did *not* kill Alice!" Roscoe yelled.

A guard came up to us and asked me if everything was okay. I told him I was fine and then the guard gave Roscoe a warning to keep his voice down.

Roscoe cleared his throat and lowered his tone.

"Would I ask you to help find her body if I was the killer?"

He had a point, except dealing with murderers was seldom logical. There were lots of crazy killers who were publicity hounds. They loved the attention they got, and in this situation, finding Alice's body would bring his name into the forefront of the news again. Maybe he was the kind who got off on that. He wouldn't be the first creepy killer who found that titillating.

"Maybe you just like getting your name in the news."

"Screw that! I'm telling you I don't know what happened to her." Roscoe's voice was a plea.

"Who was she at the coffee shop with that night?"

"By herself. Reading a book. She did that." He shrugged. "I don't know how Alice ended up dead that night and how I ended up here doing life for murder one. I didn't do nothin'."

"They found her blood in the back of your pickup. The murder weapon was a fancy sword that you kept on display in your trailer and it was found in the grass next to your truck."

"Yeah, but no body." He blew a raspberry through his lips. "How often does someone get convicted of murder without there even being a body?" He shook his head slowly. "If it weren't for bad luck I'd have none at all."

"It wasn't just a little blood," I pointed out. "It was enough blood to say that your truck was definitely the crime scene. And what about the thumb?"

"Yeah. The thumb. That's messed up." He drummed his fingers on the table and then leaned in. "How stupid do I look? If I was going to kill someone, do you think I'd leave a bloody mess and a body part in the bed of my pickup? And I paid nearly seven hundred dollars for that Wakizashi Emperor Series Sword. Saved for months to buy it and hung it on the wall because it was a work of art."

"So someone used *your* sword from *your* house and she bled out in *your* pickup but you're innocent."

"I know how it looks." He narrowed his eyes. "And that's why I'm here. They think I went nuts but no matter how pissed off I was at Alice, I wouldn't've killed her. I still loved her." His furious look was a challenge for me to say otherwise, and when I didn't, he continued, "Besides, I'd never be so stupid as to use my own sword! And I'm too much of an idiot to take a hose to my truck to clean it off and hide or toss the sword? Just leave all the evidence there sayin' 'come get me and lock me up'?" He folded his arms tight and thrust his chin at me. "I was set up, man. That's why I need you."

"If you were set up, you need a lawyer. Not me."

"Nah, I need you to find Alice's frickin' body. You find her body, then they're going to have to do the whole CSI thing and get DNA off it, you know? And any DNA on that girl ain't gonna be mine. Find her and I'll be set free."

"It's been two years. If her body was easy to find, the police would've found it by now."

"No kidding. That's why my dad said we needed to reach out to you. This is your thing, right?" He waved a hand at me. "Using those metal sticks of yours to find dead people is your jam. I bet you have those things in your car right now. Everyone in the area knows how you work with the FBI and you're all over the state finding bodies. Back home you're a freakin' superhero. You're ready to find dead people anytime, am I right?"

I did have my rods and pack in my car but that sure as hell didn't make me a superhero.

"Yes, my dowsing rods help me find bodies, but I have to know where to start. I can't be crisscrossing all over the country or even all across Washington State. I don't have that kind of time, and even if I did, you don't have that kind of money to pay me to work that long or that hard." I wagged a finger at him. "I've already spent over five hours just to get here and talk to you. Now I'll spend hours more to get home. That's time I could've spent helping someone else find the body of a loved one."

"You didn't have to come out here, dude. We coulda done this little meeting by video visitation. Dad told you that. Don't know why you wanted to have this talk face-to-face." He shrugged. "But money isn't a problem. My dad set aside enough to take care of you before he died. After Alice died his cancer got worse. Maybe he just lost the will to fight it. Anyway, he changed his will then so that a reasonable amount be spent to try and find Alice and set me free."

"But I heard your mom is in a care home. That's not cheap."

"Sure, Kim is struggling to pay the bills but there'll be enough left after paying you to help fund Mom's care in the home, so it's all good. It's what Dad wanted. You go looking for Alice and you'll get paid for all your time, including this visit."

"Did Alice have any money of her own? Any insurance you would've inherited from her?"

"Of course, the cops looked into all that already and the answer is nope. She died with less than a hundred dollars in her bank account." He drummed his fingers on the table. "So now you've talked to me face-to-face, you gonna do it or not?"

I'd wanted to sit across from him and get a vibe of whether or not Roscoe Ebert was a murderer. My hope was that coming here would give me a feel about whether or not helping a convicted criminal and returning to the town of my infamous upbringing would be worth the time and torture. Turns out it wasn't as clear-cut as I'd hoped.

Roscoe rubbed the dagger tattoo on his neck and I met his gaze.

"I'm still going to have to think about it."

For the first time I saw a flash of sadness in his eyes. Then he looked away and frowned.

"You do whatever you have to do. Either way, let Kim know so she and my ma ain't sitting around hoping on something that's not gonna happen." He blew out a loud breath. "Guess I ain't got nothin' but time anyway. You go ahead and think about it and make sure you're thinking long and hard about poor Alice. Her body is out there somewhere and even after two years she ain't at rest in a casket. If you don't want to do it for me, you could do it for her."

If I did choose to take this case, Alice would be my only reason. "Tell your lawyer I want a copy of your trial transcripts. I've read what the newspapers say, I want to read everything brought up in court."

"Done. I'll call him today and tell him to send them to you." He smiled. "I knew you'd take this case."

"I'm going to check to see if it's worth my time first," I told him, shaking my head. "I'll let them know my decision." I pushed my chair back, started to get up, then sat back down. "By the way, who has Jet now?"

"Kim." He leaned back in his chair. "She's moved into my trailer. There's lots of land and Jet likes to run."

"Are you still in contact with Blossom?"

He shook his head. "She wrote me once after I was locked up. I never replied." He turned his palms up. "Didn't see the point."

"I'll get back to your sister as soon as I've made a decision."

"Good. And, dude, if you need to come back here to chat again, I don't mind." He gave me two thumbs up. "Just be prepared to buy me some Doritos, you know? A guy has to get his kicks somewhere."

I got up and told the guard I was done. Once I was back in my Jeep, I made a few notes on my phone about everything I'd learned from Roscoe. Coming here did not give me any firm sense on the case. I felt no immediate gut feeling that he was innocent and no compulsion to help him. But I did hate that Alice's remains weren't properly buried. I rubbed the back of my neck and sighed. I'd think about it on the long ride home.

As I started the Jeep, I glanced over at the backpack containing my dowsing rods sitting on the passenger seat. I'd actually had two reasons to travel to this part of Washington State, and I was about to start on the second reason. A few days ago I'd received a message through my website from a frantic woman who was looking for her daughter. The daughter, Rachel Wu, had driven from university to visit a friend in this prison but neither she nor her car had been seen since. The mother said that she had a feeling in her gut that her daughter was dead. The young woman was a known drug addict and she also had a number of DUI convictions. Although she'd been sober long enough to return to university this term, the mother spoke to Rachel on the phone not long after she left the prison and she sounded out of it.

While up this way, it wouldn't hurt to drive the area with my dowsing rods to see if I could locate Rachel Wu. As I placed my rods on my lap, a movement a few steps away in the prison parking lot caught my eye. A guy in his midtwenties with corn-yellow spiked hair and thick glasses waved to me as he got into his car. I glanced over my shoulder to see if he was waving at someone else, but there was nobody else nearby. I met a lot of people in my line of work and didn't remember them all, so I tentatively waved back as I steered out of the parking lot and on the main road.

Once off prison property I pulled over and reviewed what Mrs. Wu had told me about her daughter. In a nearby park Rachel had been known to hook up with fellow drug users. Mrs. Wu herself had found her daughter passed out behind the wheel of her car at that location last year. I put the address of the park into my GPS and drove ten minutes to the location.

I didn't spot Rachel's described Smart car in the parking lot or on any of the side roads nearby. Still I drove the area slowly, watching for any twitching of my dowsing rods in my lap, but nothing. I looked at the map on my phone and checked a few other nearby areas but there was no sign of Rachel Wu or her car.

I tossed the rods on the passenger seat and hit the

main road. After I'd been driving nearly two hours, the rain became a torrent. Even with my wipers on high, it was difficult to see the road, so all the drivers slowed down. Just as I was coming out of a sharp curve in the road, I was surprised by the sound of my dowsing rods abruptly swinging to the right in the passenger seat and clanging against the door. With a frown I pulled to the shoulder, and the rods continued to turn like a compass to point in the direction I'd just come. The rain tapered to a drizzle as I leaned over my passenger seat and peered out the window in the direction of the ditch where the rods indicated. All I could see was tall grass down below but the rods never lied.

"Damn it. There's a body down there."

# TWO

I TURNED OFF my Jeep and put my hazard lights on. From where I sat, there was no indication that a car had gone off the road or there'd been any other kind of accident, but there was definitely a body down there waiting to be found. I grabbed my rods from the passenger seat, climbed out and locked the Jeep behind me. Walking to the edge of the steep shoulder, I stared down and craned to see if there was any hint of what lay below. All I could see was that the weeds were tall and wet, and the trench looked deep. Although the rain had now almost stopped, the embankment looked slick and I wished I'd brought my hiking boots.

As cars whizzed by, the mud sprayed from their tires misted over me. I walked a few steps behind my car and the divining rods in my right hand eagerly tugged me forward. Just as I was about to begin my descent, a small white car pulled off the road and parked on the shoulder a few feet behind me. The young man who climbed out of the car was the spiky yellow-haired guy who had waved at me in the prison parking lot.

"Hey," he called out, pushing his glasses up his nose as he walked toward me. "Are you okay? Is there a problem?" He looked beyond me to my Jeep. "You got a flat?"

"No. I'm fine."

He took another step in my direction and I took a step in retreat, taking my phone from my pocket. He took the hint and stopped walking closer.

"I'm sorry, do I know you?"

"Raymond Hughes." He smiled and waited expectantly but I didn't offer any kind of recognition. He added, "Everyone just calls me Ray."

"You waved at me in the prison parking lot…" I looked at him questioningly and traced the screen of my phone with my thumb. Sure, he looked like a normal clean-cut guy with a baby face and soft brown eyes but I was prepared to call for help quickly if needed.

"You're Julie Hall. I recognize you from all the papers and stuff. I'm kind of a follower really." He glanced sheepishly at his feet.

"Oh."

Well, this was awkward. Standing on the side of the road waiting to go find a body was not exactly a place I wanted to start my fan club.

"Anyway, a friend of mine is a guest at the Ozette Corrections Center and when I saw you there I thought, well, look at that." He shook his head and chuckled. "I was kinda shocked because Roscoe has been telling everybody for months that the dowsing girl was coming to help solve his case and set him free, and I guess nobody ever believed him, but there you were in the flesh. I offered him my services, but he declined and—"

A car whizzed by and speckled us in muddy spray. We both took a couple steps farther from the roadway.

"So you know Roscoe?"

"Not personally. Bobby—the friend I was visiting—he's Roscoe's cellmate." He took a step around the hood of his car and peered down into the weeds. "There's a body down there?"

When I didn't answer right away he pointed to the dowsing rods in my hand.

"I just figured on account of you have your rods out." He stuffed his hands in the pockets of his hoodie and rocked back on his heels. "I could help you out, if you want."

"I don't need any help." My tone was more curt than I intended so I added, "But thanks anyway."

"Sure. No problem." He shrugged and gave me an easy smile, showing the kind of perfect teeth that came from expensive dental work. "It looks pretty steep though." He hooked his thumb in the direction of his car behind him. "How about I just wait up here in my car until I make sure you make it back up the hill safely."

"Okay." I slowly nodded. "That's kind of you. Thanks."

He told me it was no problem and once he was back inside his car I stepped off the road and into the wet grass. The tall weeds were slick and after a few feet the angle of the embankment increased. I found myself sliding downward like my feet were on skis. My arms were windmilling at my sides to keep my balance, and I nearly dropped my rods.

Once I regained my footing against a large rock halfway down, I drew in a deep breath and began to walk again. I angled my body to avoid a thorny bramble of blackberry bushes. The lowermost part of the trench was nearly twenty feet down from the roadside, and there was a small creek that probably grew into a torrent in spring. Now that I was down the embankment and on flatter terrain, I stuck out my dowsing rods and followed their lead.

The tall redroot pigweed grew thick like a wet curtain and as high as my chin, and I pushed it aside with my rods as I moved forward. When those weeds thinned, clumps of field horsetail brushed my knees. So thick was the brush that I almost bumped into the car before I could see it. There on its side surrounded by thick brush lay one of those tiny two-seater Smart cars. The vehicle had obviously missed the turn and tumbled into the ditch. My rods crossed to form an X as I approached the driver's door.

"Damn. It's gotta be Rachel Wu." I drew in a calming breath before I pushed the weeds away from the window and leaned in for a look.

A large airbag obscured most of my view but I could make out the body of a young woman slumped to the side in the driver's seat. Her black hair hung like a sheet obscuring part of her face. What I could see wasn't pretty. This wasn't a recent accident. Decay and bugs had found her. To be sure, I pushed a shrub away from the license plate and compared it the number Rachel Wu's mother had given me. It was a match.

I released a vivid stream of curses as I stumbled back a few feet and then closed my eyes against a wave of nausea that was quickly followed by the desire for a drink so fierce that I could almost taste it. I did a deep breath calming exercise I'd learned from Dr. Chen, then slowly made my way back up the steep side of the trench to the road. I was surprised when a hand reached out to help me once I was near the top.

"I heard you swearing so I'm guessing you found

what you already knew was there," Ray asked as I ignored his hand and took the last step up to the roadside.

I nodded. "Not pretty. Guess she ran her car off the road." Dragging shaky hands through my hair, I tried desperately to push down the craving for booze. "Thanks for sticking around to make sure I made it back up okay." I took my cell phone out of my pocket. "But I'm going to call the authorities now. No sense in you hanging around and getting all caught up in the activity."

I made the call to 911, and while I gave directions to the location, a cool breeze picked up. My clothes were soaked and I shivered. I pocketed my phone and noticed Ray was still standing there.

He held out a bottle of water. "Thought after that climb you might be thirsty."

"Thanks but I have lots of water in my car." I pushed back the wet hair from my eyes and then something occurred to me. "You said earlier that you'd offered Roscoe your services. What do you do, Ray?"

"I'm a bit of a psychic." He toed the ground sheepishly with his foot. "Nothing like you, of course, but I get the occasional call to help find lost ones." He walked back to his car and I watched as he opened the console, took something out and then returned to me holding out a business card that read *Raymond Hughes—Psychic Medium, Private and group readings!*

Beneath his phone number was an email address and website.

"Interesting," I said, unclear of what else I should say when meeting a self-proclaimed psychic. I moved to hand him back the card but he told me to keep it.

"Maybe we'll work together sometime. I know you get swamped with requests. As a matter of fact, I emailed you a while back myself and you didn't reply."

"Sorry." I cringed as I stuffed his card into my pocket. "I'm really not very good at keeping up with my emails. I get so many…"

"No worries." He pushed his glasses up his nose and smiled.

Also, I've had to be a bit more careful about who I replied to. A while back I'd had some emails from a "fan" that started off kindly enough but after a few messages had taken a creepy turn, I'd had to block him. Lesson learned.

"Since we're in similar lines of work, if you ever need a hand, give me a call." He smiled. "Like I said, maybe we can work together sometime."

"I prefer to work alone, actually."

"I respect that." He nodded enthusiastically. "And I completely understand because it's hard to work with others when nobody can even begin to understand what we do, right? I know what it's like to have people not understand my line of work. Believe me."

He laughed easily and I found myself smiling back.

"Sometimes it's helpful to have a like-minded person to bounce ideas off of, not to mention the fact that we could be sending each other referrals," Ray added. "Like this one. I told the Wu family to contact you and they did."

"Wait. You knew I was looking for Rachel Wu? You told Mrs. Wu to contact me?"

"Yes, she was on the news making a plea for people to help her find her daughter. I reached out and offered my psychic services. After giving her a reading, I felt strongly that her daughter had passed, and she felt the same way, so I told her she may want to look into contacting you." He smiled. "I'm glad she did. Feel free to call me if you ever need help with a case and want some input."

"Thanks. I appreciate the offer."

He wiped his hand on his pants and then stuck it out for me. "Do you mind?"

I thought he was asking to shake my hand. I transferred my rods into my left hand and stuck out my right. Immediately he wrapped both his hands around mine and gave a gentle squeeze. His eyes were closed and his face tilted to the gray sky.

"You're worried about Wayland," he muttered.

I yanked my hand from his and stared openmouthed. "What the hell?"

"Sorry." He cleared his throat. "Just felt the urge to give a quick read and that's what popped into my head." He hooked his thumb in the direction of his car. "I'm going to head out. You've got my card so—"

"Yeah. I've got it." I hurried back to my Jeep, climbed inside and locked the doors. After I started it up, I cranked the heat. As I watched Ray drive away, I hugged myself to infuse some warmth. Even with the seat warmer and fan on high I was chilled to my soul.

*You're worried about Wayland.*

The words were like a jolt of electricity and they triggered a vision in my head.

*The pub was dimly lit and I sat in a dark booth in the corner. There was a glass of wine in front of me and I was so hammered that I tried to push it away so as not*

*to drink more. Some of the wine sloshed on my hand as
I moved the glass, and I brought my fingers to my lips
to lick away the sweetness.*

The memory brought on a wave of nausea that caused
me to briefly clutch my stomach. Wayland Canteen was
a drinking establishment a couple miles from my house.
About six months ago, I'd had a setback. I hadn't had
a drink in a long time but one day the dark, quicksand
thoughts of my abusive childhood clamored so loud inside me that I'd sought solace at the bottom of a bottle. I
wish I could remember the details of that night because
it felt like I was forgetting something important, but I'd
been blackout drunk and it blurred away the night. As
a recovering alcoholic, I had a laundry list of shame,
but right now that night topped the list.

After the Wayland incident I did the mental work.
I returned to seeing my psychiatrist, Dr. Chen, on a
weekly basis. I journaled and meditated and listened
to self-help audio books until I could recite them verbatim. I also doted on Garrett and did housework like a
nineteen-fifties housewife as I tried to atone for my sins.

When Ray Hughes grabbed my hand and said the
word *Wayland*, it was like he reached right inside me
and brought all that sin out for the world to see. I shuddered and guiltily fumbled with my phone to dial Garrett. He picked up on the first ring. I told him about
my visit to Ozette Corrections Center and about how I
hadn't decided yet about taking Roscoe's case to find
Alice's body.

"What else is going on?" Garrett asked. "You
sound...upset."

"Yeah, I was just going to tell you I found a body on

my way home. A few minutes before the Hood Canal Bridge. My rods moved so I pulled over and went to look in the ditch. I found my client's daughter. Looks like Rachel Wu drove off the road, and she's been there awhile." The words came out in a rush.

"Are you okay? You called it in?"

"Just waiting for the law to arrive," I told him. "I'm fine."

"Are you sure?"

I could hear the worry in his tone and felt the shame of putting it there.

"I'm absolutely positive." I infused my voice with confidence to wipe away his concern. "Just a little cold and damp from wading in the wet weeds."

I wasn't okay. Ray reaching into my reprehensible soul had shaken me, but I didn't share with Garrett about meeting Ray or what he'd picked up from clutching my hand. I didn't want to bring up my disgraceful night from a few months ago, but I knew what Garrett was thinking—what he was probably always thinking: would I reach for a drink again today?

"After I'm done here, I'm stopping in to visit Tracey. We're going to have a cookie-baking marathon." There was forced cheeriness in my voice.

"That sounds great."

I could hear him exhale worry and I felt awful for putting it there in the first place. He kept me on the phone a little longer until a police car pulled up behind me and I told him I had to go. We ended our call with our usual I-love-yous.

I introduced myself to the officer and explained how I found a body using my dowsing rods. He didn't look skeptical or even pepper me with questions. Over the past few years I'd built a considerable and constructive reputation in Washington State and most of the law knew me.

We walked in the rain toward where I'd gone down the embankment into the ditch. I pointed to give him an indication of where he'd find the car and warned him about the slippery slope going down. I offered to go with him, but he insisted he'd be okay.

A minute later I heard crashing in the bushes below and guessed the officer must've lost his footing down the slope. By the sound of his cursing I figured he was all right. A little while later I heard startled and more creative swear words and guessed he found the car and the body. It wasn't long before the officer had scrambled his way back up to the roadside. He was now sweaty, his knees muddy and his face more than a little pale. He only gave me a brief nod as he walked over to his vehicle and got on his radio.

The rest was a repeat of what I was used to. Other officers arrived followed by the investigative unit. I told my story a couple times and provided a complete statement and all my contact information before I was allowed to leave.

All the persons who arrived spoke about the same assumption: it looked as though the driver didn't make the turn and her car rolled down the embankment. Also, based on how the body looked and the fact that the brush and grasses weren't bent or crushed in any way leading to the car, she'd been there a few weeks at least.

By the time I was driving onto the ferry, the sun was going down, revealing streaks of pink between the clouds. Even though the air was cold I once again stood on the deck of the boat, relishing the numbing of my face and hands during the half hour crossing of Puget Sound. I called Rachel Wu's mother and told her about finding her daughter. The woman's broken sob on the line hit me in the gut.

After, as I hit the road in Edmonds, it wasn't just the face of the dead woman that was filling my thoughts. I was also running through what psychic Ray had said to me.

*You're worried about Wayland.*

His words soured my gut the rest of my journey home. It wasn't until I was pulling into my driveway hours later that I remembered that I'd planned on stopping at Tracey's to bake cookies.

I called her and tried to get out of it by telling her I'd already been gone too long and needed to make sure Wookie got out for a walk. She listened patiently about finding the victim on the side of the road and made all the appropriate sympathetic noises.

"You need a distraction and baking these cookies will help."

"I really don't feel like visiting. Can we do it another day? I'm tired from driving all day."

"I'll come to you. These cookie pucks can travel. Set your oven to three fifty. I'll be there in fifteen minutes."

With a relenting laugh I ended the call and took Wookie for a jog to the green space at the end of our street. Tracey was waiting on my front steps and talking with my neighbor, Preston, when I got back. Tracey was my age but had the heart of someone much younger and today sported lime-green tips in her hair that made her look even younger.

"Garrett mentioned he was going out of town for a couple days," Preston said with an easy smile. "Thought I'd just check to see how you're doing."

"I'm fine."

My tone was clipped. Preston was a fellow FBI agent, and while he and his husband were nice enough, I suspected he was checking on me for Garrett and making sure I was sober. I hated that it was necessary.

"If you don't mind…" I nodded to Tracey. "We have cookies to bake."

"I'll drop some off before I leave," Tracey told him cheerily. "As long as we don't eat them all."

"Somehow I doubt we're going to eat them all."

As we stepped inside the house, Tracey paused to pat Wookie formally on the head and he eagerly licked her hand in return. There had been a time when Tracey was so terrified of dogs she wouldn't come inside my house, but after Wookie risked his own life to save her, she'd accepted my rottweiler and all his slobbery kisses.

"Who knows how many cookies it's going to take to get that look off your face." Tracey kicked off her shoes and made her way to the kitchen. "You're strung so tight it looks like you're about to snap."

"I'm just…" I thought briefly of telling her about my encounter with Ray, but that would mean sharing my shame regarding my Wayland drunk, and I'd hidden that from my friend. Instead, I gave her a few more details about finding the body off the road and blamed my uneasiness on that incident.

"That's horrible that someone would die like that and

lie in the ditch without anyone finding them for so long. Who knows how long that car would've been there if your rods hadn't sounded the alarm?"

She tsked as she searched my cupboards for a cookie sheet and finally found one. It was new. When Garrett and I set up house together it was one of the things I bought but I hadn't magically turned into a baking genius despite the tools that sat waiting.

"You think she fell asleep at the wheel or was drunk?" Tracey removed the price sticker and then washed and dried the pan.

"No way of knowing."

I walked over to help her line the pan with the frozen circles of cookie dough and then I changed the topic by talking to her about my visit to Ozette Corrections Center.

"It sucks that you have to go up to Blaine to search for the body." Tracey slid the tray into the oven and set the timer. "I know that's going to be hard because you hate going to the area where you grew up."

"Exactly why I haven't agreed to do it."

"Oh, you're going to do it all right." She scooped up my cat, Fluffy, and began snuggling the cat against his will. "You never talk about a case unless you've already made up your mind you're going to do it."

She was right. Somewhere Alice's body was abandoned minus her thumb. She deserved to find her way home.

# THREE

WE SAT AT the table eating cookies that were still warm and gooey from the oven.

"You've got a real worried look on your face," Tracey said around a mouthful of cookie.

"Not worried. Just curious…"

I pushed the cookies away because the sugary sweetness was turning my stomach. Or maybe the queasiness was Raymond Hughes. I decided to risk bringing up the meeting to Tracey without sharing the part about Wayland.

"Do you believe in psychics?"

"Well, I believe in you." She playfully punched me in the arm. "Aren't you a psychic?"

I'd never thought of myself that way. Sure I found bodies using dowsing rods and that was a pretty weird and unique talent, but it felt different.

"What about the kind of psychic medium who can grab your hand and tell your future?" I swallowed. "Or your past?"

"Last year my mom and I went to get a reading from this old lady in Bremerton. For fifty bucks she'd tell you your future."

"And?"

"She told my mom she was going to take a long

trip and she told me I was going to join a gym and get physically fit."

"Oh." I laughed a little because her mom hated to travel and Tracey had a connective tissue disorder that made working out nearly impossible. "I guess your psychic was a flake."

"You could say that." Tracey bit into another cookie. "But my mom did go to Hawaii with my aunt at Christmas and I guess you could call that a long trip. Also I go to physical therapy a couple times a week and you could call that a gym." She shrugged. "So who knows? Maybe it's all in how you hear it."

I rubbed the back of my neck and frowned as I thought about Ray and his knowledge of my binge at the Wayland Canteen.

"If you're thinking of going to see a psychic, then take me with you." She got up from the table and began putting most of the cookies from the cooling rack into a large paper sack. "I'd love to get a reading where I'm told I'm gonna meet someone tall, dark and handsome. Or even someone short, blond and average."

Tracey had broken up with her boyfriend a few weeks ago and was feeling the sting of loneliness.

"You'll meet someone. You don't need a psychic to tell you that."

"Maybe." Tracey yawned and stretched. "I'm going to drop these cookies off to Preston on my way out. I left a dozen for you and Garrett."

"Aren't you taking some for yourself?"

"I've still got a bunch in my freezer." She cringed and patted her stomach. "But I've eaten enough now that I'm not even tempted by those." We hugged at the door and she rubbed my back. "If you need someone to go with you when you drive to Blaine, just say the word."

I thanked her and after Tracey left I opened my laptop and googled Raymond Hughes psychic medium. He had some good reviews and a somewhat active social media account. His website was simple, giving contact information for readings. I clicked on his bio and a large picture of him popped on the screen and his brown eyes seemed to bore right into me. The hairs on my arms prickled and I quickly closed the screen.

I opened my emails and searched until I found the ones from Kim Ebert, Roscoe's sister, and the earlier ones from his dad. I read through all half dozen of them pleading for me to take her case to help free Roscoe from prison. In one of the emails Kim had given her phone number and address. Even though it was already late, I picked up my cell phone and sent her a text.

This is Julie Hall. When would be a good time to meet and talk about Roscoe's case?

I'd fallen asleep in front of the television when a text reply chimed on my phone. Kim messaged that she was home most days because she was currently unemployed. She sent a second text giving her address and asking if I'd decided to take the case. I didn't send a text reply.

That night as I was climbing into bed, Garrett called and I told him that I was driving up north to meet with Roscoe's sister in the morning.

"Oh." He cleared his throat. "You going to take Tracey with you?"

"No."

We both knew that going back to my hometown would be triggering. Still, I hated the worry in his voice and detested that my inability to remain sober had put it there so I added, "I'm going to be okay. I have a phone session with Dr. Chen in the morning."

"Okay. That's good."

I asked about his case, and even though he couldn't share the details with me, he talked about his new partner, who was vegan. We laughed about a restaurant they'd tried and how Garrett had ordered something vegan that had turned out to be so good he was thinking of converting both of us to a meat-free diet.

As I stretched out in bed and listened to his voice through the phone, I felt happy to have him in my life. The deep baritone of his voice caressed my ear and caused all my tense muscles to relax but after the call was over, I hated myself for the things I left unsaid. I'd failed to tell him about Raymond Hughes and his impromptu reading, and another thing that weighed heavy on my mind. I didn't feel like I could speak out loud about that even to myself yet.

The morning came with the snout of a rottweiler in my face and Wookie's insistence that I get out of bed. When a hundred-thirty-pound dog wants you to do something you should just give in. I opened the patio door and let him race out into the backyard to pee.

"Good morning, neighbor!"

I glanced over to see Preston and his husband, Phil, sitting on their deck having their morning coffee.

"Morning." I gave them a nod.

"Thanks for the cookies." Phil smiled.

"You're welcome."

"Phil's got stew in the slow cooker," Preston mentioned. "There's plenty if you want to come for dinner."

"No." I took a breath and forced myself to take the sharpness out of my tone. They were good to me, and if Garrett had asked them to keep an eye on me, it was only because I'd brought it on myself. "Thanks but I have plans." I smiled and told them to enjoy their day.

I stepped back inside and left the door open for Wookie to return after he was finished. I liked my neighbors but I'd been raised on a farm outside of town and then lived in a singlewide trailer on that property as an adult. Sometimes my introverted little heart longed for a space between my closest neighbors.

By the time I'd shooed Fluffy off the counter so I could make myself some toast, Wookie was back inside. I filled both the critters' bowls and paused to enjoy a rare and brief moment of affection from Fluffy when he purred and wound between my feet to show gratitude for his food.

I had a Skype counseling session with Dr. Chen. I'd been seeing her for enough time now that I could hear her words even in her pauses. When she didn't comment on the fact that I was taking a case near the place where I grew up, I felt a need to fill the void.

"I'll be fine. Really. It's not a big deal."

"Did you ask someone to go with you? Garrett? Tracey?"

The comment rankled.

"They're both working." I glanced away from the screen and then back. "I can handle it. Besides, we both knew I had to go back to work eventually."

Again, she let a silence stretch between us.

"I'll check in with Garrett or Tracey while I'm there if I feel even the least bit…" Like the quicksand thoughts would swallow me whole. "Like I'm not okay."

"It's important to let your support system be there for you." Her voice was velvet and her face concerned. "Have you talked to Garrett yet about—"

"No." I cut her off. "Not yet. I will." I cleared my throat. "He had to go away for a few days for work."

I wrapped up the session by assuring her that I'd do some meditation exercises before I hit the road. Dr. Chen was the mother I never had except I never saw her outside of her office or video chat, and I paid her a couple hundred bucks each time for her concern.

The promise to meditate was only a white lie. I packed up my backpack and filled up my water bottle from the tap. Once on I-5, I pointed the nose of my Jeep north and tried not to think about going home.

Home.

The word caused a full-body shudder.

As I drove, I turned up the volume on a self-guided meditation, ignoring the parts that told me to lie down and close my eyes since that wouldn't be wise while barreling down the highway.

In stark contrast to how I felt inside, the October clouds became thinner the closer I drove to my destination and soon I was reaching for my sunglasses. A few miles before entering the town I took a westbound exit that delivered me to the acreage of farmland that spread between the highway and the ocean. I knew the area as well as I knew every scar on my body caused by living there.

I took a right on a gravel driveway only a couple

miles from the farm where I grew up. On either side of
the road were acres of harvested cornfields, the dried
brown stalks a desiccated army of thousands stretch-
ing as far as I could see. Next to the singlewide stood
a wooden outbuilding that might have been a garage
or large shed. The paint was curled and peeling and it
listed to one side. The trailer itself looked in marginally
better shape but dirt and moss clung to the once white
siding like a blotchy green skin.

As I parked near the tired trailer, my throat grew
tight and my belly soured.

"You've got this."

I turned off the Jeep, stuffed my keys into the pocket
of my hoodie and strode toward the trailer. Dried, leggy
petunias sat in pots going up the stairs. The door was
opened a crack before I could raise my fist to knock.

"Hi, Julie. C'mon in, just watch the dogs don't make
a run for it."

I opened the door just wide enough to angle my body
inside while blocking one large dog and one small with
my leg.

"I guess you're Kim?" I shouted over the loud yips
and yaps of a Chihuahua and then bent to give the small
dog and a black Lab each a scratch behind their ears.

"Yup, I am," she told me. To the dogs she yelled,
"Go to your beds!"

Roscoe's sister was around five feet tall with soft
rolls around her middle and a two-inch white skunk
stripe down the part of her dyed black hair. A thick
greasy smear of red bedecked her thin lips.

"Let's have a seat."

I glanced around for a place to sit. I'd lived in a singlewide trailer on farmland for a number of years and I wasn't put off by the disarray I saw here or the cheesy decor. In fact, even though dark memories threatened, the place felt familiar. Kim lifted a pile of laundry from a corner of the couch and dropped it on the dirty shag carpet. I sat on the cushion she'd made available and Kim sat in a worn recliner. The first thing that struck me was the age difference. Roscoe looked my age of thirty but Kim looked a hard fifty.

"So you're Roscoe's sister." My eyes flitted around the room, resting on one colorful troll doll to another perched around the trailer. Apparently Kim collected the bright-haired trolls because there must've been a couple dozen of them.

"Half sister." She grabbed the lever on the side of her chair and raised the footrest. "Mom's first husband, my biological dad, died. She remarried at forty and then—oops!—along came Roscoe."

She laughed, exposing yellow teeth marred by smudges of her ruby red lipstick, then nervously scratched at a scaly rash the size of a dollar bill that ran from her collarbone up the side of her neck.

From across the room the dogs were watching us and whining.

"You and Roscoe have the same last name. Your stepdad adopted you?"

"Yeah, and my mom thought it would be good for family unity if I took the name."

"I'm sorry to hear about the passing of your stepdad."

"Cancer is evil." She sighed. "There was one good thing that came out of it though—he became a better person. More about family…or at least more about Roscoe." She nodded to me. "That's why he contacted you."

"Is that Roscoe's dog, Jet?" I pointed to the black Lab.

"Yup."

At the sound of his name the black Lab bounded over, followed quickly by the Chihuahua. Both jumped on the couch next to me, the Lab sniffing and the small dog yapping. I patted their heads and tried to turn Kim's attention back to why I was here.

"I guess Jet is the reason this all started," I began. "Roscoe broke into Alice's car, took the dog, and a lot of people witnessed the fight in the middle of town."

"I guess." She nodded and scratched at her neck more, flaking off some of the scales to reveal angry red skin. "You might say it's all the dog's fault. Stupid mutt." She reached for a can of Coke and took a long drink. "Now all I do is dog-sit those two for fifteen dollars a day. I was working as a cook but a car accident last year hurt my back." She put a hand to her lower lumbar as if to prove it.

"Is that where Roscoe kept his sword?" I pointed to a couple of hooks on a wall that seemed about the right distance apart.

"Yup. Of course, it's in evidence now."

"Roscoe claims to be innocent, and obviously, your dad…stepdad…believed that too, since he was the one who first emailed asking me to find Alice to try and get evidence to free your brother." I waited for Kim to also proclaim Roscoe was innocent but she seemed really focused on a hangnail on the corner of her thumb so I continued, "Blood was found in Roscoe's pickup along with Alice's thumb. How do you think that happened, if your half brother wasn't the one who killed her?"

"Obviously anyone could've taken his truck." She gave me a look that said I was dimwitted not to see that. "Everyone who knew Roscoe also knew that he left the keys to that truck under the floor mat. He came home. Passed out with Jet in the back bedroom. Meanwhile someone must've taken his truck and killed Alice. We never lock our doors here so…"

"Someone came inside here and took his sword too." She only nodded.

"Why would someone kill her?"

"Like I would know?" Kim snorted. "I heard she was humping anything that moved while they were married so maybe some guy got jealous."

I frowned because I hadn't heard that Alice had cheated. "That could still implicate your brother. Especially if he had hopes of reconciling."

"Well, I guess if I'm honest the cheating thing was just a rumor. You know how this town likes to talk. Second, there is no way those two were ever getting back together." Kim shook her head vehemently.

"How about we start from the beginning?" I asked her to tell me everything she knew, starting with Roscoe and Alice meeting and getting married. By the end of the story the dogs finally got bored with sniffing, licking and yipping at me and jumped off the couch. The Chihuahua made a nest in the pile of laundry. Nothing Kim said was different from Roscoe's story. In fact, some of her phrases were verbatim, which immediately gave me the sense they'd rehearsed their story.

"Why did the police immediately show up here the next morning?"

"Well, her car was still at the coffee place in town. When the shop owner showed up the next morning, he recognized Alice's car parked out front and saw her purse and keys were inside. Sure the back window was broken because Roscoe broke it to get the dog out but the car was still drivable so I guess the guy thought it was weird." Kim shrugged. "He called the police because he thought it was strange. Cops checked her basement suite and she wasn't there. Then they came here because, of course, by then they'd heard about the big hullaballoo in the middle of the street over Jet. When they saw the blood and the thumb in the bed of his pickup, he was arrested on the spot," she said, wrapping up the story. "Roscoe never knew what hit him."

"I'm guessing Alice knew who hit her."

Kim's eyes got hard. "Roscoe's the kind of guy who catches spiders and sets them free outside. His dad tried to take him out hunting when he was little but he just cried. He's as tame as a kitten."

"So you think he's innocent."

She opened her mouth to say something and then closed it again. I waited. Finally she said, "I don't know what to think. All the evidence sure points to him, doesn't it? I guess everyone has their breaking point."

I thought about the man I'd met with the tattoo of a knife stabbing a heart on his neck and the Chinese symbol on his forehead.

"I try not to judge a book by its cover," I began. "But his tattoos…"

"Yeah. Yeah." She shook her head. "Bad choices considering…you know."

"You know that the Chinese symbol on his forehead means death."

She nodded.

"If everyone with stupid tattoos was guilty of murder, a whole lot of us would be in jail." She cackled then rolled up the cuff of her sweatpants to reveal a faded and stretched tat of ballet slippers that said *princess* underneath. "Do I look like a ballerina or a princess?"

"Point taken. I guess if someone were to ask me what kind of tattoo you'd have, I'd say a troll since you obviously like them."

"You're right!" She smiled brightly. "I love those damn things. My ma got me started collecting them when I was a kid. Something about their stupid rubber bodies and bright hair just makes me laugh." She picked up a green-haired troll from a nearby table and gave its hair a rub. "So you going to look for Alice so we can free my brother?"

"Honestly, I don't know where I'd even begin. You really don't want to pay me to walk all over Washington with my dowsing rods."

"There's money set aside for you to try and find Alice. My stepdad made sure of that."

"Roscoe said whatever was left would go to the care home, which you're paying for. So that money would be going to you instead, right? Wouldn't you rather take it for yourself instead of paying me? Or did you already get money from your stepdad too?"

"Never saw eye to eye with the man so I have no interest in his cash. My stepdad always gave Roscoe money. If his son had a hankering for a new expensive toy, his daddy would buy it."

I watched her face but there didn't seem to be any resentment there. "That didn't bother you?"

"I've always fended for myself." Kim rubbed again at her neck. "If you're looking for my help on where to start looking, I'm afraid I haven't got a clue. My mom had a stroke a couple weeks before then so I was with her in the hospital that night. Now she's in a home with only me to visit her." She pouted. "You do whatever you feel is right. I don't blame you one bit for not wanting to get involved. It's a mess."

"It's not that I don't want to help. I just need a clue where to start looking."

"Well…" She frowned. "Seems to me that you being from around here, you'd know just as well as anybody else where a body could be buried."

I resisted rolling my eyes. "Whoever killed Alice could've dumped her just about anywhere, including into the ocean. The currents could've swirled her out to sea where she was eaten by an orca."

Kim shrugged. "Sorry. I wish I could be of help but…" Her voice just trailed off.

I told her my rate and how much I'd need for a deposit. She didn't even flinch, which made me ask, "What if you spend all your stepdad's inheritance paying me and there's not enough money to keep your mom in the care home? Even worse, what if I find Alice and it only proves Roscoe is guilty?"

"My stepdad wanted you so, far as I'm concerned, it's him hiring you and whatever happens happens." Her lips pursed in a harsh slash of red. "Sure I got some bills to pay and Mom's expenses are high, but the man put the money aside to pay you so I'm guessing that's what I'm gonna do."

I looked around at the ragged old furniture and stained carpeting. What I was getting paid could go a long way on home improvement but it sounded like her decision was made.

"Okay, all I can tell you is that I'll ask around, talk to people who knew Roscoe and Alice and see if I can get any idea of where to start looking for Alice's body." In essence I was promising to spend even more time in the hometown that brought back sick memories. My subconscious was unsettled by the idea. I quickly added, "I'll give it a week. If I'm not making any headway at all after that, I'm calling it quits. That way you're not just throwing money away. Deal?"

"That sounds fair." She gave a sharp nod.

"What about Alice's family? Do they know you've hired me?" I got to my feet and walked to the door.

"Her dad's dead. Her mom moved to Florida with some new guy and never came back."

As I slipped my feet into my runners, Kim added, "You don't remember me, do you?"

"From back when I lived out here? I'm sorry." I searched my memory. "I've forgotten more than I could ever remember about this area." Dr. Chen would've said I was repressing those memories and she would be right.

"I was your babysitter!" Kim exclaimed with pure glee.

I blinked in surprise and looked Kim over with fresh eyes but no memory came.

"Oh, it was only a time or two." She waved it away

with a swat of her hand. "You were only about eight and your grandma and grandpa were going away on some overnight fishing trip so you slept over." She pointed to where I sat. "You slept on that very couch you were sitting on!"

She cackled loudly at that and my stomach rolled.

"Sorry. I don't remember ever having a babysitter."

"Oh hell, I prolly shouldn't've even brought it up on account of what happened and the way your grandparents were."

She tsked and watched me closely. Her eyes were hopeful that I'd say something about my traumatic upbringing and malicious grandparents. Their notorious reputation had fueled the gossip mill in this town for years. A comment from me about that time would be currency for her around town for months. It wasn't going to happen.

"After you e-transfer me my deposit, send me an email listing all the names, numbers and addresses of anyone who had any contact with Alice." My tone was businesslike now. "I want to know the names and contact for all her lovers, coworkers, and anyone else you can think of."

Kim agreed and I stepped through the door. As I was going down the steps, an old Honda stirred up the driveway dust and came to a rest a few feet away.

"That'll be Blossom now," Kim said from behind me. "She'll be here to get the dogs."

"She cares for both dogs?" I asked over my shoulder.

"I just dog-sit while she works." Kim opened the door wide and both dogs bounded outside and over to the car.

Then Kim went inside and shut the door, not bothering to greet Blossom as she climbed out of her car.

The Blossom I remembered was one of the queens of high school but the woman patting the heads of the two dogs in front of her looked nothing like royalty. The dark hair that dusted her butt in school was now cropped to her shoulders in an uneven home haircut. Her face was void of makeup, and the dark circles under her eyes aged her well beyond thirty.

She noticed me then, straightened to her nearly six feet, planted hands on her hips and stood mouth agape, exposing a missing eyetooth. "Oh dear Jesus, is that you, Beanster?"

She was the only one who'd ever called me that, and all these years later it still rankled. An old high school friend had given me some jellybeans, which I'd jammed into the pocket of my sweater. Walking down the hall, Blossom had bodychecked me into the lockers, causing me to drop an armload of books. As I bent to pick them up, the jellybeans spilled from my pocket and rolled everywhere. She called me Beanster after that.

"Blossom." I gave a hard nod to the black Lab she was loading into her back seat. "Didn't know you had Jet. Roscoe told me that Kim had the dog."

"She did for a while but after she hurt her back she asked me to take him on account of he's got too much energy for her."

"But she dog-sits?"

"Yeah, she watches Jet and Chichi while I'm at work. Kim likes the bit of cash and Jet doesn't eat my shoes when I'm at work, so we both win." She laughed.

"Where do you work?"

"Over at the motel." She nodded with her chin in a vague direction, then looked away as if embarrassed. "Housekeeping."

The girl in school with the most expensive and current fashion was scrubbing toilets. I wanted to find some joy in that but I didn't. I didn't follow my classmates or neighborhood on social media but sometimes word of someone reached my peripheral anyway. Now one of those things jogged my memory.

"Didn't you own a secondhand shop on Martin and Third Street?"

She nodded. "Named it Blossoming. Cute, huh? I loved that stupid little store. Didn't you hear? The whole building went up in flames last year. It was just starting to make a profit too. All my inventory turned to ash, and I'd just let my insurance lapse. It sucks." She scowled at the ground, and for a second, I thought I saw tears in her eyes, but they were replaced with a look of determination. "I'm going to reopen just as soon as I get enough cash behind me."

"That's good. You always did have an eye for fashion."

"I know, right?" She looked proud even in her grubby jeans and stained T-shirt.

"Tell me about the night of Alice's death."

A couple of fat raindrops fell, and she shielded her eyes with her hands as she looked at me. "Why? You gotta know what happened, right?"

"I'm just trying to hear it from everyone's point of view."

"Okay." Blossom stuffed her hands into her jeans and proceeded to tell me everything about that night.

How she and Roscoe had been at the bar and when she'd gone outside for a cigarette, she could hear Jet barking in Alice's car so she mentioned that to Roscoe when she went back inside.

"Never shoulda said a word to Roscoe because the second he heard the dog was across the street in Alice's car, he went ballistic, and well…" She shrugged. "You know the rest."

"Did you leave with Roscoe after the fight?"

"Nah, he wanted to take off and bring the dog home but I still had friends drinking inside so I stayed with them and got a ride home afterward."

"When did you hear about the blood in the pickup and Roscoe being arrested?"

"I was sleeping in when Kim called me after lunch. She was freaking out. Most of the town was."

I remembered how things got around town when something dramatic happened. "So everyone gathered for coffee or beers to chat about it, I guess?"

"Not me, man." She shook her head. "The whole thing creeped me out. I was dating a murderer? Someone who chopped off a girl's thumb?" She placed the back of her hand to her forehead as if to faint. "I couldn't handle. I talked to the cops, gave my statement, then disappeared for a few days. I was smoke in the wind."

"What about your store?"

"I let my staff run it while I was gone. I needed the break." She shifted her weight from one foot to the other.

"Kim mentioned she thought Alice was having an affair. Any idea who she was sleeping with?"

"She said that?" Blossom glanced sideways at the

trailer. "Take that with a grain of salt, know what I mean? Kim can be a bitch."

"So you don't think Alice was messing around behind Roscoe's back?"

"Alice didn't have it in her. She was all sweetness and light. Definitely not the cheating type." She wagged a finger in my face then. "Hey, do me a favor and don't be telling Roscoe I've got Jet. He'd lose his mind."

"Why would he care?"

"Dunno. He just would. Guess after all he did to get the damn dog, he wants to keep him in the family, but I've grown kinda attached to the stupid hound." She tucked a greasy strand of hair behind her ear. "Not that Roscoe's getting out any time soon to come and check."

"So you think he's guilty?"

"Don't you?" She gave me a smirk.

"Guess I'm hoping to find Alice's body and see if that proves anything." I caught movement in the window of the trailer. Kim was watching us. "Any idea where I should start looking?"

"Oh, I don't know." She burst out laughing and reached through the window of her car for a pack of smokes. After she had one lit, she drew in a deep drag and blew out the smoke in a long stream toward my face. "If I had to guess, I'd say he just rolled her off a cliff somewhere. One thing about Roscoe is he's a lazy SOB. I can't see him digging a deep hole, know what I mean? He'd have to actually break a sweat. He's the kind of guy who'd drive ten miles to go to a drive-thru just cuz he didn't want to walk inside a burger joint to get his food."

Washington had over three thousand miles of coastline. If he pushed Alice's body off a cliff I was going to need an army of dowsers to find her.

"Any place in particular he liked to go? A fishing hole somewhere? A park he liked to visit?"

"We went out only a couple of times so I couldn't tell you."

"Anyone who might know?"

Blossom puffed away on her cigarette while she contemplated my question. "Talk to Barb over at the diner. She went down to visit him a few times." As she flicked an ash at her feet, she tilted her head and eyed me curiously. "Never thought you'd come back here after all that shit with your grandparents."

"It's in the past." The words came out smooth as silk even as my gut clenched.

"You were just over there, right?" She gazed off into the distance. "Maybe two fields over?"

Blossom was trying hard to open that wound but I wasn't playing. She opened her car door and slid behind the wheel.

"Can I get your phone number in case I have any more questions?"

She rattled off her number and I immediately sent her a text message so she'd have my number too.

"Let me know if you think of anything."

"Tell you what, next time you're up this way you can buy me a coffee and I'll see if I can dig up all of Roscoe's secrets to tell you." She giggled at that. "Not that he was exactly a deep person with a closet of skeletons, but I could ask around."

"I appreciate that. I'll also go talk to Barb."

"You do that." She started up her car. "Might wanna bring a Bible with you."

She drove away and I noticed Kim's eyes watching me through a part in her drapes. With a quick wave, I turned my back on her and climbed into my Jeep. Less than three minutes later, as if drawn by an evil magnet, I was parked on a country road staring at the land where I'd grown up. Gone was the little white farmhouse, long ago bulldozed because nobody would've lived in it after knowing the horrible history. Gone also was my single-wide trailer that had been parked in the back forty. But the new owners had worked and harvested the land. Deep down it surprised me that anything could grow in a place that held such evil.

Abruptly a wave of nausea rolled through me and I opened the car door just in time to vomit.

The land might have been stripped naked of its buildings, but a malevolent vibe still seemed to rise from it and engulf me.

# FOUR

PART OF ME wanted to get on I-5 and head back home and never return, but I also wanted to at least talk to Barb at the diner as Blossom suggested. I drove away from the road of my quicksand memories and headed into town.

You could practically see the Canadian border from the diner. I'd eaten many meals here and worked at the gas bar just a stone's throw away. As I pulled into the parking lot to park behind the restaurant, it felt more like coming home than it had a right to.

Before going inside I felt a powerful need to wash away the ugliness in my head and to touch base with someone who was lightness in my life. Garrett answered his phone immediately. I told him about visiting Kim, running into Blossom and driving to the old homestead.

"How are you holding up?" His voice was so filled with concern I had to bite the inside of my cheeks to keep from crying.

"Besides losing my breakfast, I'm good." I laughed.

"Do you need me to come home?"

And the very fact that he would drop everything at his FBI job and run home to be there for me was all that really mattered in this world.

"Nah, I'm going to be okay. I talked to Dr. Chen before getting here and she double-checked that everything between my ears was staying together." I tried to keep it light because I hated how much he worried about me. I detested even more how necessary his concern was and that I had to rebuild his trust after failing a few months ago. "I'm stopping for a bite to eat before heading back home."

"Send me a text once you're home, okay?"

I said I would and we ended our call with air kisses.

Stepping inside the retro diner felt like a tumble back to my earlier life. You could tell the difference between the locals in the place and any Canadians day-tripping across the border. The town residents looked up from their meals and coffee cups to stare unabashed at me and follow my walk across the restaurant, while those from across the border didn't know or care. I slid into a vinyl booth in the back and looked down at my phone so as not to make eye contact with any of those curious gazes.

"Coffee?" a young waitress asked. I didn't recognize her and she obviously didn't know me either.

I was grateful for the small reprieve. "Yeah. And a grilled cheese. Is Barb working?"

"She's on her break. I'll send her to say hey once she's back."

I thanked her and then reached across to another table to get the newspaper. It was more about hiding my face than reading the local news but by the time my sandwich arrived, I lowered it to see most people had become bored with my arrival.

I was halfway through my grilled cheese when a waitress began walking toward me. She was maybe sixty, stocky and wore her gray hair in a tight ponytail. When she was a couple feet away, she stopped. I could see the exact moment she recognized me and weighed her options to turn heel and walk away.

She stiffened her spine and came to me instead. "I'm Barb. You asked to see me?"

"Yes, I'm—"

"I know who you are and I know what you do." She leaned in, putting palms on the table. "I'm a God-fearing woman, Julie Hall, and I don't take to no satanic voodoo crap, ya got me?"

"I hear you loud and clear." I held up my hands in a symbol of surrender. "I'm only trying to help Roscoe Ebert and I understand you visited him."

She gave me a sharp nod. "I did. Drove all the way there to read him the scriptures a time or two. Tried to get him to repent."

"No luck?"

"Sometimes the devil has such a deep hold on a person they can't see the light of the Lord standing right in front of them."

The way she looked at me said that she was the light and I was the devil. This idea was not something new to me.

"Do you think Roscoe's innocent?"

"I'm neither judge nor jury." She picked a piece of lint from the front of her uniform.

"Oka-a-ay." I was getting nowhere here. "Did you know Alice?"

"Of course. She actually worked here a month or two. Was always late so eventually she was let go."

"She worked here? Was she close to any of the co-workers? Is there anyone else here I should talk to?"

"I have no idea who that girl spent her time with. It was none of my business."

"Okay." I tried a more direct tactic. "Do you have any idea where a killer may have stashed her body?"

She shook her head hard. I reached in my purse and pulled out a business card. "If you think of anything Roscoe may have said that could help find Alice's body, or even if you think of an area that could even have a remote chance of being the spot where she could be, then please contact me."

"If I think of anything I'd be sure to contact the police instead of the likes of you." She left my business card on the table when she turned and walked away.

I left the card sitting there in case she changed her mind but that was doubtful. Half my sandwich remained untouched on my plate. I paid my bill and left a good tip before heading back to my Jeep. I put my keys in the ignition and noticed one of the cooks standing by the back door having a smoke. I hopped out of the Jeep and walked toward him.

"Hi, I'm Julie Hall."

"Yeah, I know who you are." He dropped his smoke to the pavement and it sizzled out in a puddle.

"So you know I'm looking for Alice. I understand she used to work here."

"Yup." He looked up at the clouds and squinted. "Not for long. A few weeks maybe."

"Was she close to anyone at that time? Did she socialize outside of work with anyone else?"

"Nah, she was so shy and quiet it was like working with a mouse." He snorted and then his face got somber. "Not that it's a bad thing to be quiet. I don't like to speak ill of the dead."

"So she didn't take coffee breaks with anyone, or chum around before or after her shift with any other cooks or waitresses."

He shook his head.

"What about customers? Were there any regulars that insisted on sitting in her area so she'd have to serve them?"

"No, it was the opposite. Regulars stayed away from her section on account of she was slower than the other girls. She was polite to the customers but, you know, not overly polite."

"So you never saw her with anyone outside of work."

"Nope. She was a loner. Kept to herself. She was nice enough but not talkative. Not one bit."

I thanked him for his time and then returned to the Jeep. I drove through town stopping briefly at the corner of Martin and Third Street to look at the charred remains of Blossom's thrift store. You could still make out the name Blossoming in faded red letters above the door. I got out of the car and briefly walked down the street. The familiar buildings and the feel of the small city were a distant pull of memory and nothing more. I was relieved. Maybe I could do this. I could look for Alice's body in this area and be just fine as long as I didn't drive near the farm where I was raised.

"I'll give it a week," I muttered to myself and got back in my car.

As I pulled away from the curb, my phone rang.

"This is Dana. I was your waitress and I saw your card."

"Oh. Hi, Dana, did I forget something?" I glanced over at the passenger seat and saw my purse so that wasn't it.

"Nothing like that." She lowered her voice. "Some of the customers were talking to me about what you do and I think that's kind of cool. I haven't lived here long so I didn't know you were, like, famous or somethin'."

"Definitely not famous." I had to resist the urge to laugh. "More like notorious."

"Anyway, they said you were asking about that whole Roscoe and Alice thing and that you're gonna be searching for Alice."

"Do you have information on where Alice's body could be?"

"Not exactly, but I remember Barb saying one time after visiting Roscoe and trying to save his soul that she wouldn't be surprised if Roscoe just dumped her body over in the community garden. You know, the one on Seventh?"

"Did Roscoe have a garden plot at the community garden?" The guy I met in prison didn't exactly look like the gardening type.

"No, but Alice did, and after she was killed, I heard Roscoe actually paid a friend a few bucks to go and make sure her garden was taken care of."

That was definitely odd.

"Do you know the name of the friend who was helping at her plot?"

"No, but maybe one of the other gardeners knows. There's almost always someone around there."

"Okay, thanks for the information, Dana. I appreciate it. Did you happen to work at the diner when Alice was there?"

"She wasn't here long. I took a month off work to tend to my ma on account of she'd had hip surgery. Alice came and went during the time I was off."

"Could you talk to the other employees and some of the regulars? Find out if anyone remembers Alice hanging out with anyone in particular or see if someone has information they'd like to share."

"Sure, I can do that and if you, like, want me to do any other sneaking around outside of work and asking people stuff I can do that, you know. I don't mind."

"Just be careful. What if Roscoe really is innocent? That means there's a murderer on the loose, right? I don't want to put you in danger but if you happen to hear anything I'd appreciate the information."

After we ended the call I did drive over to the Seventh Street community garden. An elderly man was on his knees pulling weeds. Any vegetables had long since been harvested, but still I walked carefully through the rows so as not to step on anything as I got close to him.

"Hi! Do you happen to know which plot belonged to Alice Ebert?"

He glanced over at me, taking a slow look from my feet up to my face and pausing a minute on the backpack slung over my shoulder. "In my day we used dowsing to find water, not bodies."

My reputation had once again preceded me. "It's possible the rods are good for both."

He harrumphed and got to his feet. He pointed a muddy finger toward the corner of the plot of land. "Hers was on the very edge there but you're wasting your time. Cops dug it up a while ago and didn't find Alice. Even after that nice young man came and spent all that time tending to the plot."

Dana had mentioned Roscoe paying someone to take care of Alice's garden.

"Who was the nice young man?"

The old man looked up at the sky, then slowly shook his head. "Don't know if he ever did say his name. Maybe your age. Shaggy hair, beard and a little slow but had good manners. He was always saying 'yes, sir' and 'no, ma'am' like he was raised right."

That could've described just about any hipster in a hundred mile radius. I tried to ask more questions but he dismissed me by stating that was all he knew, then he lowered himself back to the ground and kept on with his weeding.

"I liked his hat," the old man muttered as he yanked out a thorny weed.

"What kind of hat was it?"

"Old school Mariners cap from back in the late 1970s. That royal blue with the yellow M on it. Had a hat like that myself back in the day."

I carried a Mariners cap in my backpack with my rods and I pulled it out now and placed it on my head.

"Don't think I've ever seen one like the one he was wearing," I remarked. "This is the only one I've ever had."

He looked up at me and grunted something before reaching for the next weed.

I knew it was a long shot since the police had probably been thorough, but still I got my rods out of my pack and began to walk with them throughout the community garden. It took less than half an hour to walk a grid of the plots, and my rods didn't waver even once. As I was stuffing them back into my backpack, the old man muttered, "Told ya."

I walked over and handed him my business card. "What can you tell me about Alice or her family?"

"Her dad was an ass and now he's dead. Her ma couldn't get out of this town fast enough once he was gone. Alice was a sweet girl. She got on good with Roscoe's ma, who was quite frail, although won't do you any good to talk to her on account of she can't talk since her stroke."

"If you think of anything more to tell me, or the name of that nice young man, could you give me a call?"

He didn't reply but at least he took the card and stuffed it in his pocket.

As I walked back to my Jeep, I noticed a police cruiser parked behind me, and the officer climbed out of her car.

"Hello." I gave her a bright smile, which was answered by a contradictory frown.

"Can I ask what you're doing?"

"Just taking a walk through the garden." I pointed behind me.

"Looked like more than a walk to me." She was maybe fifty with a tight ponytail and parallel creases between her eyes that deepened as she scowled at me. "Who gave you permission to do that?"

"Given that it's a community garden, I didn't know I needed to ask permission." I kept my words even, though my blood was beginning to heat.

"I know what you do, Ms. Hall. One of the neighbors across the street mentioned you had those rods of yours out and were bothering Mr. Cole in the garden."

"He didn't seem so bothered but I'm on my way so—" I walked past her car toward my Jeep and she followed.

"You think the law here are just country bumpkins that didn't think to check Alice's garden plot?" she hissed at my back as she followed. "You think we haven't turned this entire town and half the state upside down looking for her body?"

I pressed my key fob to open my door and turned to face her. "Look, I'm not trying to step on any toes. If anything, I just want to help. If I did find her body, your department would be the first place I'd call."

"Who hired you? Was it Roscoe? He was a bad seed from the day he was born and—"

"Kim hired me. His sister and dead father." I opened my car door and met her gaze with a firmness of my own. "Finding the body should do nothing but cement the case against Roscoe so, in the end, I'd just be helping your department. Like I've done in the past."

"We don't need your help. You don't live here anymore. I suggest you go back to your new home and stay there."

"And I suggest you talk to most of the other law in this state who would argue differently when I've found bodies for them." My words contained just enough heat to show I wasn't backing down, but a wave of nausea soured the back of my throat.

The radio in her car garbled out some message.

"People liked Alice. She was a kind person who never should've gotten messed up with the likes of

Roscoe Ebert. Just so you know, if you're going to be trespassing around these parts there's a good chance someone is going to call me." She turned and walked back to her car.

I waited until she pulled away and was long gone before I got inside my Jeep. My hands shook as I turned the key. Meeting the officer did give me an idea. I placed a call in to a homicide detective I knew in the area who I'd worked with in the past. I left a message for Detective Larry to call me, then I steered the Jeep into traffic.

I headed south on I-5 and was suddenly overcome with fatigue. I tried playing music and making a call to Tracey but I was still struggling to stay awake. The stress of the day had stolen all the energy I had, and at Tracey's good suggestion, I took the next exit and parked in the back lot of a strip mall for a nap.

My phone rang an hour later, shocking me awake. I grappled for it, dropped it on the floor, then finally took the call. "H-hello?"

"Hi, it's Ray."

"Ray?" I frowned, my brain struggling to catch up.

"Ray Hughes from the side of the road where you were body hunting yesterday."

"Right. Ray." I pulled my seat up from a reclining position and cleared my throat. "How did you get my number?"

"We exchanged business cards, remember?"

I didn't.

"Sorry, I'm a bit out of it today." I reached for the water bottle in my cup holder and took a sip. "What can I do for you?"

"I just wanted to give you an update about Rachel Wu."

"An update?" I took another drink from my water and wondered what he could possibly have to talk to me about.

"I had a dream about her. My dreams can be quite illuminating. Sometimes they're visions and often they—"

"You had a dream about Rachel Wu?"

"Yeah, in my dream it was like she was reaching out to me and telling me to contact her parents again so I found their number and gave them a call."

"This must be really hard on them." I cracked my neck.

"Yes, when I talked to them they were obviously grieving but they were very grateful to you for finding their girl. I'm meeting them this afternoon to give them another reading. Free of charge, of course, after all they've been through. They asked me to get in touch with you and see if you could join us."

I cringed. "That's really not my thing, Ray. I'm glad they're getting some closure, but honestly my work in this scenario is done."

"I totally get that. I really do. But you know how some people are…" He chuckled. "They just really feel like they want to shake your hand for being instrumental in finding their girl." I hesitated and he added, "It would really mean a lot to them. They live in Bellingham."

I sighed. "You're going to their house in Bellingham? What time?"

"Yes, at two o'clock."

That was only an hour from now and I was less than

five miles from Bellingham. "I'll pop in for a quick handshake but I can't stay for your reading."

"Perfect! They're going to be absolutely thrilled to death."

After we ended the call I went into a juice bar in the strip mall and got something sweet and fruity to try and quash the uneasiness in my stomach. I sipped it in my car and scrolled through my emails to kill some time. Kim had sent me my deposit and also a list of a few friends and associates of Alice and Roscoe. She'd even provided their social media links. I fired off the same message to each, telling them who I was and that I was trying to find Alice's body and asking them to provide me as much information about Alice and Roscoe as they could, and also let me know of any spots they may have visited that needed checking. I was careful not to mention that I was doing this in order to hopefully free Roscoe. I assumed a lot of their friends thought he was guilty and I wanted them to think I was more about finding the body and putting Alice to rest.

This was true. She'd been a fellow sufferer of child abuse. It might be the only connection we had besides this small city, but it was enough for me to feel compelled to find her body. She deserved to be properly buried.

At the Wu's home, Ray Hughes's small white car was already parked in the driveway. I parked on the street in front of the small blue ranch house and made my way to the door. Mrs. Wu answered my knock and Mr. Wu joined at her side a second later. Both began enthusiastically pumping my hand and repeating thank you over and over, while dabbing their damp eyes.

"Come in!" Mrs. Wu stepped aside.

"I really can't stay," I said.

"Please." Mrs. Wu pointed behind her. "I baked cake and there's tea."

"Just for a minute then," I offered.

I kicked off my shoes in the foyer and stepped through to the living room. The room held a few bouquets of flowers. Family and friends had been busy expressing their sympathies. On the fireplace mantel was a large framed picture of Rachel. It was her high school prom picture and her smile was as bright as her fuchsia gown. It was nice to put a smiling face to the body I'd found.

"She probably never should've been behind the wheel of her car," Mr. Wu said as he motioned for me to come to the dining room table. "Who knows how much longer she would've been down in that ditch if it weren't for you finding her."

A strangled sob escaped Mrs. Wu's lips, and she put a hand to her mouth as she sat at the table next to where Ray was already sitting. He offered me a wide smile as I sat opposite him. There was a pot of tea on the table and a platter of sliced coffee cake. Mrs. Wu filled a china cup with the tea and slid it in front of me, then plated a piece of cake and pushed that toward me as well.

"I'm so sorry for your loss." My voice was low and sympathetic.

"We were just about to begin our readings," Ray announced brightly. He took off his glasses and cleaned them with a napkin on the table.

My eyebrows went up in question because I thought

I'd been clear when I told Ray I didn't want to stay for whatever show he planned on doing for these folks.

"You'll stay, yes?" Mrs. Wu said. "Ray said it will only take a few minutes."

"I don't want to intrude…" I picked up my cup of tea and took a large sip. It scalded my tongue and I took a large bite of the cake, wanting to get these niceties over.

"It'll be quick," Ray said, smiling brightly.

Before I knew it, he was taking Mr. Wu's hands in both of his, closing his eyes and making a hmm noise.

"I see you working with a hammer and wood," Ray began.

Mr. Wu gasped. "Yes! I was a framing carpenter."

I watched with skeptical curiosity as it continued. Ray talked about other small details, and with each revelation both Mr. and Mrs. Wu grew more enthusiastic. He ended Mr. Wu's reading by talking about a hobby that had to do with spoons and telling the man that he sees the hobby as making him some money in the future.

Mr. Wu got up from his chair and hustled into another room. He came back to show an array of sculptures he'd made using melted and bent spoons.

"I only started this a few months ago," Mr. Wu said, his voice laced with amazement. "I've been selling them at craft fairs."

Next it was Mrs. Wu's turn. She specifically wanted to know about her daughter. Ray said that he could see Rachel doing some kind of knitting or crocheting while sitting next to her mom.

"Yes!" Mrs. Wu exclaimed. "I taught her how to crochet when she was about ten. She hated it at first, but she was even teaching her roommate at university how to do it up until…" Her voice trailed off and she pressed her lips together. "Is she happy now? Is she… is she in heaven?"

Ray looked momentarily pained but he assured the mother that her daughter was at peace and looked forward to seeing them in the afterlife.

Once Mrs. Wu's reading was over, Ray reached for my hand and I yanked it back as if he'd burned me.

"I'm good. Thanks."

The tea and cake began to turn in my stomach, and the cloying smell of the flowers made me feel lightheaded. I got to my feet.

"Mr. and Mrs. Wu, thank you for your hospitality but unfortunately I have to get back to work."

They walked me to the door, continuing to thank me profusely, and once I had my shoes back on, Mrs. Wu grabbed me in a tight hug and whimpered softly against my shoulder.

"Thank you so much for taking our case," she murmured. "We're so grateful to Ray for suggesting you. I will send you the rest of your payment tonight."

"No hurry," I assured her as I broke myself from her tight hug. "Take your time."

Outside, I gulped in the clean air and almost ran to my car, only to be surprised to find Ray right on my heels.

"Hey, sorry about that back there," he said to my back. "As soon as I got there they asked if I could start the readings. I guess they were anxious."

"That's okay." I took in another deep breath, then turned to him. "You're quite good with your readings."

I gave him a quick smile. "I'm just not ready to get one myself."

"No worries." He held up his hand. "Thank you for the compliment. You can see why I think that we'd work well together. I mean, between your dowsing rods to find the bodies and my being able to give loved ones readings, we might be able to do so much more, don't you think?"

I could see his point so I found myself nodding in agreement.

"I'm thrilled that you agree! So what do you think?" His face brightened with enthusiasm. "Want to give it a go? We could be Julie and Ray, Paranormal Extraordinaires!" He had his hands up as if putting the title on a marquee.

I felt revolted at the thought. "Sounds a bit like we're sideshow freaks, doesn't it?" The hurt look that followed made me continue with a gentler comment. "Sure, maybe one day you and I could work together. You never know, right?" I opened the door to my Jeep and climbed inside. "Nice to see you again, Ray. I've gotta go."

"Before you leave, I heard that you're taking on trying to find Alice Ebert's body. I could totally start doing readings of everyone involved. Maybe I can pick up on where her body is for you."

"Sure." I just wanted to leave now but I quickly added, "Just be careful, Ray. I mean if Roscoe turns out to be innocent, there's still a killer on the loose, right?"

"Absolutely." He made a cross over his heart. "I'll get to work immediately and keep you posted on anything I find out."

"You do that." I closed my car door then and drove off.

Just over an hour later I pulled into my own driveway, thrilled to see Garrett's dark sedan there. I walked inside and found him in the kitchen chopping vegetables. Wookie greeted me first so I gave him a quick pat on the head and then I went to Garrett, wrapped my arms around his waist from behind, and pressed my cheek between his shoulder blades.

"This is a nice surprise."

"A short one." He turned to face me and kissed me on the top of the head. "I'm heading back out tomorrow."

"I'll take what I can get." I stood on tiptoe and kissed him on the mouth. "Whatcha making?" I glanced at the array of colorful vegetables as he tossed them into a frying pan.

"Stir-frying some vegetables. I know when I'm away you mostly eat canned soup, cereal or popcorn."

"You're far too good to me."

Then I began to wonder if he'd made a trip home to check on me because he'd been worried that I'd go drown my sorrows in wine after being in my hometown. My frown caught his eye, and he lifted my chin with the tip of his finger.

"There was a change in the case I'm working and we're heading to a new location tomorrow, so all the guys took the night off. Not just me."

I gave him a quick smile and set the table while he finished cooking. After a few minutes we sat across from each other, digging in.

"Gotta admit, this is better than popcorn for dinner anytime." I shoveled a forkful of veggies and rice in my mouth. "Maybe you should stay home and be a homemaker and just do all the cooking and cleaning."

He threw back his head and laughed and the sound filled me with joy. We'd had our tough times, but God I loved this man. I could feel words burn the tip of my tongue but I swallowed them because I wasn't ready. Instead, I told him about my day. How hard it had been being near my old home, how annoyed the city cop had been to see me in the town garden, and finally, about how enthusiastic clairvoyant Ray was about us becoming the freak show.

"You think he's the real deal?" Garrett took a drink of water. "You know, it took me a long time to believe in *your* abilities. You know it took numerous times of seeing your work firsthand before I became a believer."

"Yeah, I've gotta admit, even though my talent is real different, it feels weird to believe someone can tell your past or future just by holding your hand." His mention of Wayland Canteen sprang to my head and I shuddered. "But he seems to be the real deal. I've seen him in action, and well, I've got to admit he's got something."

"You're not really thinking of partnering up with him?"

I shook my head. "I work alone but…" I swallowed another bite of food. "I did give him permission to give people readings about this Alice Ebert case. He's going to see if he can get any leads for me, and who knows, maybe he'll pick up on something."

"Seems harmless enough. Are you sure you want to spend a lot of time in that area?" Garrett reached for my hand. "I just know how it hurts you."

"I think I'll be okay." I gave his hand a squeeze. "I'm

just going to stay away from that exact area where I grew up and focus more on other parts of the area where a body could be."

"Good idea." He leaned in and kissed me.

That night we made love in a fever of passion. Garrett fell asleep spooning me, his left arm draped across my chest. On his ring finger was a platinum band with an etched scene of mountains and sea. I touched a finger to his ring and my heart ached. We'd had matching ones. But I screwed up big-time and lost mine. Now his ring felt like a constant reminder of my failure.

I woke up to the smell of coffee and bacon. With a yawn and a stretch I rolled out of bed and padded to the kitchen in bare feet. Wookie greeted me with a shove of his thick head and I gave him a good scrub behind the ears before walking over to Garrett at the stove.

"You're already dressed and ready for your day." I wrapped my arms around his waist and kissed the back of his neck as he cracked some eggs into the fry pan.

"And I took Wookie for his walk and he and Fluffy have both been fed. I was beginning to think I'd have to leave before you rolled out of bed."

Confused, I glanced over his shoulder at the clock on the stove.

"Holy crap, it's ten o'clock?" I rubbed the back of my neck. "I never sleep this late!"

"I know, and you were snoring like a freight train."

"I don't snore!" I grabbed a dish towel and swatted his butt.

He grabbed the towel and pulled me close for a kiss.

"Well, you were snoring last night but actually it was kind of cute." He tapped the tip of my nose. "I guess after yesterday you really needed a hard sleep. I'm glad."

Later Garrett grabbed his weekend bag and told me he had to hit the road.

"I might be away three or four nights. I'm really not sure." He gave me a warm hug. "I'll call you tonight."

I watched his car back out of the driveway into the drizzling fall day, then I opened my laptop and started with my emails. I was hoping for replies to the messages I sent to the contacts of Alice and Roscoe and I wasn't disappointed. Overnight I'd received a number of messages. Apparently, everyone had an opinion and wanted to share it with me. The majority of those thoughts were that Roscoe Ebert chopped her up and tossed her in the ocean. Not a single person thought he was innocent. There was also an email from Roscoe's lawyer asking if I'd like them to courier the copy of the trial transcripts. I phoned the Bellingham area law office and advised them that I'd pick up the package.

My phone rang just as I was disconnecting from that call and it was Tracey. She wanted to meet for coffee but I had other plans.

"How do you feel about boats?"

"As in cruise ships in the Mediterranean with us sipping fruity drinks, because I'm all for it if you're buying," she remarked enthusiastically.

"I was thinking more along the lines of a small fishing boat looking for a body."

# FIVE

TRACEY HESITATED ONLY briefly before agreeing to go out on a boat with me. I picked her up an hour later and she climbed into my Jeep, chatting away a mile a minute about the fact that she'd heard from her exboyfriend, Craig.

"And he brought up the time we went down to Seattle to go see a show but then we got so busy in the sheets at the hotel that we completely missed the show and didn't even come up for air until we were starved and so we ordered room service."

"You sure sound happy when you talk about him." I steered the Jeep to the exit going north on I-5.

"Yeah." She sighed.

"Do you think there's a chance you two will get back together?"

"No." She began playing with the radio until she found a rap song she liked.

"You never know…" I smiled over at her. "You only said that it didn't work out and you didn't want to talk about it. I respect that but whatever happened, maybe you can look past your differences if he makes you this happy."

"He didn't do anything wrong. Craig is a good guy with a good heart."

"Then why—"

"He wants a family. He talked about it all the time. He wants little boys running around who look just like him."

"And you don't want kids?" I passed a slow-moving car and then looked at Tracey just in time to see a curtain of pain cross her face. "Sorry, that's none of my business."

"Of course I want kids. Don't you?"

I frowned. "I'm…well… I just don't think I'd make a good mom."

"That's stupid. Of course you'd make a good mother."

Tracey was a loyal friend but she didn't live inside my head. She didn't feel the burning need for alcohol that clawed at me and all the dark thoughts of the past that whispered quicksand thoughts.

"So if you want kids and he wants kids, then what's the problem?" I asked.

"I can't have babies, Julie. I mean, physically I can but I've just decided not to. I have a genetic disease and there's a good chance I'd pass that on to my kids. I don't want that for them." She switched the radio to a new station. "I'm not saying it's wrong for other people with Ehlers-Danlos to have babies. If my mom had felt that way I wouldn't be here, right? It's just I made the decision long ago that it wasn't a journey I want to make."

"I'm sorry." The words felt weak to me but she just laughed it off.

"There's always adoption in my future so let's not get all morbid about it, okay?" She playfully punched me in the shoulder. "It's just that I saw the look on Craig's face when I told him I'd never give birth to his babies. Even though he said he'd be fine with adoption, I could tell it would kill him not to have his own. I couldn't do that to him."

I felt emotional tears prick the back of my eyes until she added, "Then I caught him sexting with some random woman on the other side of the world. I mean just some stranger! He said it wasn't the same as cheating because they both knew they'd never actually see each other in person, but the betrayal felt the same, you know? I mean, when you're with someone, the only one who should see their naked body is you. It's not cool to send nudie shots to some other person just for kicks."

"Wow. That's awful. I'm so sorry…"

Then suddenly Tracey shouted, "Oh, I love this song!" She cranked up the radio so loud my whole body vibrated with the beat.

A few minutes later we pulled into a convenience store to get drinks and snacks for the road. Tracey told the cashier that we were going out on a boat for an adventure. The bored cashier didn't reply.

"You're pretty excited about helping me find a body." I pressed the key fob to unlock the Jeep as we walked across the parking lot with our purchases.

"I've never been on a boat before. Well, I've been on a ferry, of course, but those don't really count."

"How can you live in Washington State your whole life and never go out on a boat?"

"It just never came up." She laughed as we climbed into the Jeep and settled in with our munchies.

"You're not going to freak out or throw up, are you?" I asked her.

"I dunno." She spoke around a bite of a chocolate bar. "Maybe."

"Great. March back inside that store and buy yourself some Dramamine. If you take it now it should kick in by the time we're on the boat."

She told me I was overreacting but did it anyway. Our next stop was Roscoe's lawyer's office. Tracey waited in the Jeep while I went inside and picked up a package of paperwork at least eight inches thick. I returned to the car with the bundle tucked under my arm, and Tracey's eyes grew large.

"You really going to read all that?"

I blew out an exasperated breath as I started the car. "I need to know what I'm getting into."

About forty-five minutes later we were parking at Blaine Harbor. I hefted my backpack from the back seat and we followed the directions I'd been given.

"Are you Roy?" I asked a hipster-looking guy with a bushy beard and unkempt hair.

"I am. You the dowsing girl the whole city talks about?"

"I'm Julie." I stuck out my hand and nodded to Tracey. "This is my friend, Tracey, and she's along for the ride."

"Is this the thing we're going in? It's not going to sink, is it?" The boat she indicated was a small cabin boat that looked in perfect condition.

"Sorry. She's never been on anything smaller than a ferry."

Roy snickered and helped us both aboard the vessel. Tracey had a look of panic on her face but she settled down a bit once Roy handed her a life jacket and told her she could sit in the cover of the cabin while he maneuvered the boat.

"Where do you want to go?" he asked me.

"Wherever you'd toss a body if you had one you wanted to dump."

Roy scratched his beard and gave it some thought before we headed out. When I'd called him that morning I'd told him who I was and what I was looking for. He never knew Alice or Roscoe but he knew what had happened and that most people thought Roscoe just murdered Alice then dumped her in the Pacific.

As we headed away from shore, I opened my backpack. I took out gloves and a knit cap and zipped my jacket up to my chin before taking out my dowsing rods. I took a seat near the stern, held the rods out and hoped for the best. Over the whistle of the wind in my ears I could just make out the sound of Tracey chatting nervously and nonstop to Roy.

We crisscrossed the entire Semiahmoo Bay and parts of the Strait for nearly three hours. It was the kind of fall day that made me happy I didn't live anywhere else. The sun sparked diamonds on the crest of each wave, and the icy breeze made every inch of me feel alive.

Eventually my arms got too tired from holding the rods out and I was beginning to realize the hopelessness of this search. Her body could've been washed into Canada or eaten by a frickin' orca if she'd been dumped out here. I motioned for Roy to head back. Once we were docked, I got my wallet from my pack and peeled off some bills to pay Roy for his time and fuel costs.

"Sorry it was a waste of time." He counted out the cash in front of me. "It would've been kind of cool to find a body out there."

I don't know if "cool" was the most politically correct way to describe finding a dead person but I only nodded.

"It wasn't a complete waste of time," Tracey said, pulling off her life jacket. "I think I love boating. I may even need one of my own one day."

Both Roy and I laughed as he helped us onto the dock.

"Now what?" Tracey smoothed her green-tipped hair.

We'd attracted some attention. A small crowd had gathered at the end of the pier and other boat owners were also eying us like we were performing a show just for them. I wanted to just leave, but then I thought about Alice. A fellow survivor of child abuse whose body had been tossed somewhere like trash.

They wanted a show, I'd give them a show.

"I'm going to walk the pier a little," I told her. "Just stay here."

I dropped my pack at her feet and took out my dowsing rods. Then I spent a good half hour slow walking the dock. It put on a good display for all those watching. I felt the stare of a dozen cell phone cameras filming and snapping pictures from about twenty yards away, but I ignored them and focused on the area. Blossom told me Roscoe had been lazy, and a lazy guy who'd just spent some time drinking might just toss a body right off the dock instead of even taking it out in a boat. Much to my disappointment and that of the onlookers, my rods never crossed to indicate a body.

"Let's go." I picked up my pack from Tracey's feet. "I'm hungry."

Tracey and I walked to the end of the pier where the clutch of gawkers parted like the Red Sea.

"You're like the biggest celebrity they've got around here," Tracey whispered to me as we headed to the Jeep.

"There's only about four thousand people in this city so that's not saying much."

At the Jeep I handed Tracey my rods. "Just keep those on your lap, okay, and tell me if they twitch or anything."

"You don't think we're going to drive right by a body in town without noticing, do you?" She held her hands in the air as if afraid to touch the rods.

"I don't know what to think. The cops have used a fine-tooth comb to search the city and everywhere around here but it doesn't hurt that I have a small advantage with my rods."

We drove to the retro diner near the border. Just as I parked the car, my phone rang. It was the detective I knew returning my call.

"Long time no talk," he said. "Let me guess, you want to talk to me about Roscoe Ebert."

"Hi, Larry, I appreciate you calling me back. Did you work the case?"

"I was one of the detectives working it, and I've heard you're turning the town upside down looking for her body."

"I'm not trying to get in the way of your work to find Alice's remains," I told him. "I'm sure you were very thorough looking for her."

"We were, but Washington is a big state. I know some people might get their noses out of joint if you're snooping around, but I've got no problem with it."

A couple years ago Larry had called me himself when a friend of a friend was searching for a missing hiker. I'd found the body, and at that time, Larry told me I could contact him if I ever needed anything. Now was the time to call in that favor.

"Does your gut tell you Roscoe Ebert did it?"

"Ever since my ulcer I don't trust my gut nearly as much as I used to." He chuckled. "The evidence was stacked against him and we had no other suspects."

"Not a single person who had a beef with Alice?"

"She was well liked," Detective Larry said and then he added, "Roscoe, not so much."

"Her Facebook page is still up. I'm guessing you went through her social media and didn't find anything."

"We went through everything except her phone. That was never recovered. Tried tracking it but no luck. I'm guessing wherever her body is, that's where we'd find her phone. Apparently she had a sparkly red phone case so it would be hard to miss."

"Did she store everything on her phone? Did you check to see if she had any cloud stuff?"

"Of course we did." For a second he sounded annoyed and then he cleared his throat and continued, "She had a lot of pictures. Mostly of the dog and a few selfies. Last bunch of pictures were taken on the night she was killed."

"And?"

"And more pictures of the damn dog. A couple blurry ones of the ground like she missed. We checked and had them blown up but there was nothing there."

"I'm guessing you've talked to everyone in town about her business already but I thought I'd mention Kim told me that Alice was humping everyone in town."

"That Kim…" I could visualize him slowly shaking his head. "Sometimes her mouth goes off before her brain functions."

"So she didn't tell you that Alice was cheating?"

"She'd griped about that to a few people and, yup, even to me, but you know what? We checked it out and didn't find any evidence of her cheating. Even Roscoe himself didn't believe it and said that his sister just liked to bad-mouth Alice because she may have been jealous that her own mom and dad liked Alice better."

"So you didn't find anyone else saying Alice was sleeping around?"

"Nah."

"Okay." I blew out a long breath. "Thanks again for calling me back"

"No problem. You find her, you know what to do."

"I won't touch a damn thing and I'll call you."

I ended the call and Tracey and I headed inside the diner where she gushed about the kitschy decor and begged to sit on the stools at the counter.

"We're taking a booth," I told her.

The restaurant was filled with Canadians that day and the cross-border shoppers paid me no notice as Tracey and I found an empty booth in the back.

As I'd hoped, it was Dana who came to take our order. She looked surprised to see me.

"You're back soon," she remarked. "I heard that you went and searched the community garden without any luck. Sorry for wasting your time."

"It wasn't a waste of time," I assured her. "It's just one more place where Alice isn't." I told her briefly about taking a boat out and then introduced her to Tracey.

"Are you her assistant?" Dana asked.

"Yes, I am," Tracey said with a wide grin.

"I've got a lot of tables waiting so I can't be chatting long, or I'll get in trouble." Dana glanced over her shoulder.

"We'll take coffee to start," I told her.

When Dana hurried back with our coffees Tracey ordered a tuna sandwich and I ordered my usual grilled cheese. After we were done eating and Dana returned with the bill, I asked her if she had a break coming up.

"In about half an hour it's my lunch break," she said.

"Perfect. My Jeep is parked around back so if you'd come out and give me a few minutes of your time, that would be great."

She said she would and as we got up to pay at the cash register, we walked by Barb, who managed to pour coffee for a customer and scowl at me at the same time.

"Jesus, that woman just totally gave you the stink eye," Tracey whispered.

"She thinks I'm a witch or the devil." I shrugged.

"You should tell her you'll turn her into a toad."

We both left the restaurant giggling. The back parking area for the restaurant was next to parking for the motel next door. A knot of clouds clustered overhead, but for now the rain held. We stood around waiting for Dana to get her break and come talk to us.

"So this is where you grew up, huh?" Tracey was looking around.

"Yup."

"I think it's kind of cute."

I snorted and tried to look at the place through her eyes. *Cute* was the last word that came to mind but I knew I was coloring the town with the experience of my own past.

"Most people are very happy here," I said.

"For you, it's just hard coming back."

"Yes," I admitted. "That's why I asked you to come along."

"D'awwww." She gave me a one-arm hug and I playfully pushed her away as I pointed down the block.

"That gas station was where I was working when I met Garrett."

"Wow. Can't imagine you working there." She shook her head.

I liked working there. The simple routine was what I had needed at the time.

"Do you think this waitress will really be able to give you some helpful information on where to find Alice?"

"I don't know," I admitted. "But I'm sure someone in this town knows something."

A group of young men walked out of the restaurant and headed toward a pickup truck across the lot. I recognized them as being locals and told Tracey I'd be back in a second. I asked them the same questions I'd been asking everyone and got the same answers. Alice was quiet and kept to herself. They had no idea if she was seeing someone, and if she was, they'd never seen her with a man outside of Roscoe when they were married. I handed out my business card to each of them and made my way back over to Tracey.

"Any luck?" she asked.

I heard the question but movement across the way

in the motel parking lot caught my eye. It was Blossom, leaning against her car and watching us intently.

"Wait here," I told Tracey. "If Dana comes out, give me a shout."

"But where are you—"

"I'll just be a sec."

As I walked in the direction of Blossom she saw me coming and straightened. When I was within a couple yards of her she struck a cocky pose, leaning one hip against her car and lighting a cigarette.

"Jesus, you just can't get enough of this town, huh, Beanster?" The nickname seemed to be without bite and she smiled as if glad to see me.

"I'm a sucker for punishment," I joked.

"You talk to Barb like I told you?"

"Yeah, but she wasn't much help. Apparently I'm the devil, so…" I gave a shrug.

"Ha!" She drew a hard drag on her cigarette. "Everyone's the devil to Barb."

"I just realized I forgot to ask you something last time I saw you."

"Shoot." She nodded her chin at me.

"Well, after Roscoe left that night you said you stayed at the bar and then got a ride home from some friends, right? Do you mind telling me which friends those were?"

"Nat and Jim." She blew a stream of smoke in my direction and I took a step back as the smell reached me and curdled in my stomach. "Remember them?"

"Natalie and Jim. Sure, I remember. Wow. Are they still together since high school?"

"Yup." Blossom smirked. "Nat was already knocked

up by prom. They married right after school and now they've got four rug rats. She was preggers with the third that night and so she was my designated driver. If you're going to talk to them, they're living across from the middle school in that gray two-story."

"Thanks."

She blew out smoke rings, and I suddenly remembered her being so proud of perfecting that talent in high school.

"What do you remember about Alice from school?" I asked.

She flicked ashes from her cigarette on the ground between us and screwed her face up in concentration. "She was like a stray cat that you feed once and then can't get rid of. We let her hang with us a couple times and then couldn't shake her."

By "us" Blossom was referring to the cool kids and mean girls who ruled the school. I'd avoided the group like the poison they were.

"And you didn't want her hanging with you?"

"I don't remember caring that much except that she was a bit of a drag. A chickenshit."

"How's that?"

"One night we were all down at the beach and, you know, having a few beers, right? It was hot as blazes that summer and I had the idea to go skinny dipping. Everyone was into it except Alice. She got all scared looking and just refused to go in the water. While the rest of us jumped into the waves, she just turned around and walked home."

I thought about myself at that age, covered in fresh wounds from Grandma's vicious temper, and then I remembered Alice's tendency to always wear long sleeves even in summer. Yeah, I couldn't see either one of us willing to expose our bodies for scrutiny at that age.

"Your green-haired friend is waving at you," Blossom remarked with another deep draw on her smoke.

I looked over my shoulder and saw Dana standing with Tracey.

"Okay, thanks. If you think of anything else, just—"

"Yeah, I'll send you a message but no more freebies."

"Freebies?"

"Yeah, next time it'll cost you coffee."

I laughed. She looked tired and worn down by life but her smile to me in that moment appeared genuinely friendly. Maybe scratching out an adult life had changed that inner bitch from high school.

"Coffee is on me next time," I agreed.

As I started to walk away Blossom said to my back, "Watch out for that one."

"Dana?" I asked over my shoulder.

"Yeah." She dropped her cigarette on the pavement and crushed it with the toe of her shoe. "She acts like an excited puppy, but she's an airhead and everyone says she loves to exaggerate but I just call her a liar. Just don't take anything she says as gospel."

I thanked Blossom for the warning and then joined Dana and Tracey in the neighboring parking lot.

"I don't have long for my break," Dana said, looking at the time on her phone. "And I want to grab something to eat."

"This'll be quick," I promised. "Do you know whether or not Barb still goes to see Roscoe in prison?"

She squeezed her eyes shut as if trying to remem-

ber and then slowly nodded. "Yeah, I think so. Not just
Roscoe though. She's part of some church group and
they all take turns visiting prisoners, you know, trying
to make them right with God." She snorted, then added,
"I think she goes every second Monday 'cuz I remember her saying she can't take no shifts on those days."

"The next time it comes up, could you find a way
to ask her if Roscoe ever confessed to killing Alice?"

"Oh, sure." Dana got all bright-eyed and eager then.
"I could totally do that and I'd be super casual like and
she'd never even know I was asking for you."

"I'd appreciate that," I told her.

"I'm all over it." Dana gave me two thumbs-up. "I'm
going back now before she sees me talking to you both
and gets suspicious."

She all but skipped back to the restaurant.

"She's pretty excited to help," Tracey remarked.

"Like an excited puppy," I said, repeating Blossom's
words.

We climbed in the car and as I started it up I asked
Tracey again to hold my dowsing rods. "Do you think
Dana's the type to lie for attention?"

"I dunno." Tracey shrugged. "Why do you ask?"

"Blossom mentioned people say she exaggerates and
that she lies a lot."

"She did ask me an awful lot of questions about us
looking for Alice's body and her eyes were all big like
that poor girl being dead was the best thing that ever
happened in this city." She reached over and put a hand
on my arm. "You okay? You're looking a little green."

The sandwich I'd had for lunch was suddenly not
sitting well in my gut.

"Being in this town turns my stomach." I drove out of the parking lot and took a left on D Street. "We've got one more stop to make before we can head back, okay?"

"You're the boss." Tracey gave me a mock salute.

Only three minutes later I was parking on the street in front of a gray two-story house a couple doors down and across from the middle school.

"I'm just going to go talk to the woman who drove Blossom home the night Alice was killed. Shouldn't take long so you're welcome to stay in the car."

"Yeah, I'll just hang here and see what's up on Facebook." She held up her phone.

I walked to the front door of the house and knocked. A woman in sweatpants, her hair in a messy ponytail, eventually answered the door with her T-shirt hiked up and a newborn latched on to her breast.

"Julie Hall." She smiled. "I was wondering when you'd get around to talking to me. C'mon in and don't mind the mess."

"Hi, Natalie. So you know why I'm here?" I kicked off my shoes and followed her into a cramped but tidy family room.

"Sure. Everyone knows why you're around." She laughed. "Don't put that in your mouth!" she shouted at a toddler.

I took a seat in an armchair and she sank slowly into the sofa.

"You look the same. You haven't aged a bit."

It was true. She had one of those faces that seemed to maintain the same look for decades. Her hair had fewer highlights and she wore more makeup in school, but I would've recognized her anywhere.

"I look the same except for this leech, right?" She patted the bottom of the baby happily suckling. "Number four." She sighed and pointed at the toddler. "I was about to burst with that one the night Alice died and swore I was done with babies, but Jim wanted one more."

I watched the baby latched to her breast and smiled as he began to nod off and then struggled to wake up and frantically started sucking again. I realized I was staring and looked away from Nat's breasts, feeling myself blush.

"You want something to drink? Wine was always your thing, right? I got red, white, rosé."

"I'm fine. Thanks." I thought about the wine and swallowed thickly.

"Damn. I was hoping to live vicariously through you." She pointed at her chest. "Can't drink until the baby's off the boob."

"Oh." I rubbed the crease between my eyes and gathered my thoughts. "I guess you know I want to ask about Alice. Were you close with her?"

"Not really but then I haven't been close to anyone since I've been pumping out kids. Once a week we get a sitter and go to the pub. Pathetic as it may seem, that's the highlight of my life. Not everyone can live in the big city with an FBI boyfriend and have as glamorous a job as you."

"Ha! My life is far from glam." I laughed at the thought.

Nat took the sleeping baby off her breast and got up to place him gently into a playpen. When she straightened and walked back to the couch, her breast still hung naked from her T-shirt but eventually she readjusted herself.

"So tell me about that night."

"Not much to say that you probably don't already know. We were at the pub and met up with the usual people. Blossom and Roscoe came over and joined our table. Blossom went outside for a smoke and when she came back in she just casually as anything tells Roscoe that Jet was inside Alice's car across the street."

"And how did Roscoe react?"

"He lost his mind." Nat tucked a strand of hair behind her ear. "Everyone knew Roscoe and Alice had been fighting over the damn mutt, so I don't know why Blossom had to throw it in Roscoe's face and get him all worked up about it." She rolled her eyes. "But you know what she's like. If she can add fuel to a fire she'll do that. That girl has always been about the drama."

"I remember that," I admitted.

"I bet you do." She laughed a little and then tilted her head. "Didn't she have some kind of nickname for you in school?"

"Beanster," I said.

"Oh, yeah." She smirked. "That never caught on except with her, right?"

"No. Thank God."

"Someone had started calling her Beanpole on account of her being so freakishly tall and it pissed her off to no end. Pretty sure that's why she started calling you Beanster. To take the name away from her."

That actually made a strange kind of sense, but I didn't want to think about those high school days. The toddler waddled over to me on unsteady legs and handed me a wet cookie he'd been chewing on.

"Oh. Thanks." I awkwardly held the cookie in my

palm and wondered what to do with it until Nat told me I could give it to her. She popped it into her mouth like eating a slobbery baby cookie was no big deal.

"So after Blossom came into the pub and told Roscoe about the dog, he got really angry and then what?"

She told the same story as everyone else. Roscoe had gone outside, broken into Alice's car, taken the dog and then a public argument had ensued.

"How much did he have to drink that night?"

"Oh God, I don't know. He was already drunk when we got there." She shrugged. "I was pregnant and sipping pop while Jim slammed a few back to catch up with Roscoe."

"And nobody tried to convince Roscoe not to drive home?"

"Blossom said she'd drive but he told her to screw off because nobody drives his truck but him."

"Probably Blossom was just as drunk as he was though," I surmised.

"Oh no, she was perfectly sober."

"Really?" That was new information. "So she was supposed to be the designated driver?"

"Nah, she never really cared about that. You know Blossom, she usually could drink the guys under the table, shut the place down and still look like she just stepped out of the salon but that night she was just getting over the flu and said her stomach was off."

"Who was Alice with at the coffee shop?"

"Nobody. She just liked to go there to read by herself."

This was what Roscoe said too. "When did you hear about Alice?"

"Oh gosh, I have no idea." She scrunched up her face.

"My phone just started ringing later the next morning and everyone was saying Roscoe killed Alice and he'd been arrested."

"Do you think he did it?"

"Who else?" She shrugged. "Not like Alice had a lot of enemies. I think she mostly just kept to herself after they split. I always got the impression their separation was temporary, you know? Like any minute they'd be back together like nothing happened. It's such a shame..." Her voice trailed off.

"Did you see Alice at all later that night?"

"No, her car was still across the street when we left the pub, so I figured she was still at the coffee shop. As far as I know, nobody saw her after her fight in the street with Roscoe over Jet." Suddenly she looked like an idea sprang to her mind. "Oh, hey, do you still see Katie?"

The mention of my ex best friend startled me. "No." I shook my head. "Not in a long time."

"That woman was a class A bitch." Natalie giggled. "Never in a million years did I understand why you hung out with her."

I didn't want to talk about Katie. She'd brought betrayal to a whole new level. "So if Roscoe killed Alice, where's the body?"

"Like I told your friend, that psychic guy, when he came around, I have zero clue where Alice could be, but if I had to guess, he used that sword of his to cut her up into tiny pieces then borrowed a boat and made her fish food that night. Otherwise they would've found her."

"What's that about my psychic friend?"

"That guy, um, Ray. He came and talked to me a couple hours ago too. He gave me a reading and told me I was going to be pregnant with another before the year is out and I called up Jim and told him to book that vasectomy appointment! Ray said you two were working together."

"Um. Sure."

Just then my phone vibrated in my pocket, and sure enough, it was a message from Ray.

Let's compare notes on our case later.

I didn't like him calling it *our* case. It was mine.

"You okay?" Nat asked. "You look pissed."

"Just work stuff." I folded my arms. "Did Alice have a lot of boyfriends after she split from Roscoe?"

"Far as I know she never had eyes for anyone else." She shook her head.

"Nobody she secretly had the hots for?"

"Not as far as I know."

"Kim mentioned she thought Alice was screwing around…"

"Ha!" Natalie slapped her knee. "Kim just loves to spread gossip. Nah, I can honestly say I don't think Alice would ever be the cheating type."

I got to my feet then to make my way to the door just as Natalie shrieked and ran across the room to snatch a glass snow globe from the toddler's hands.

"No!" She shook her finger in the child's face and he plopped himself down on the carpet and began to wail. "The older two never got into as much stuff as this one." She laughed.

"That's a nice snow globe." I nodded at it with my chin. "Looks fragile." And expensive.

"You know who gave that to me? Roscoe's dad. Just out of the blue. He never got me a gift for any of the other babies but he made a point of coming over here when I was pregnant with that one." She pointed to the wailing toddler. "Kim said the cancer was making him sad he didn't have any grandbabies."

As I put my shoes on, I handed her a business card. "Give me a call if you think of anything at all that relates to Alice and Roscoe, no matter how small, okay?"

"Sure."

I was halfway down the sidewalk to the Jeep when she called after me.

"Hey, Julie." I turned around and she said, "You're looking real good. I'm glad you got out of this godforsaken place."

"Thanks. Me too."

"What's wrong?" Tracey asked as I started the car. "You look like you're ready to punch a wall."

I started to say I wasn't angry but Tracey was my friend and I knew it was written all over my face. I knew she was also unaware that there was already a secret keeping a wedge between us.

A blurred image scrolled through my head.

*My head was woozy from drink. I must've pounded the drinks back fast and furious to feel this bad. I could feel myself slumping over in that dark booth in the Wayland Canteen and I was struggling to remain upright. Someone sat across from me in the booth but their face was a blur of hair and teal-green eyes. I played with the platinum band on my ring finger, turning it round and round on my finger using my thumb. I wanted that ring to remind me to get my ass back home but all it did was remind me of my shame. Suddenly I felt as though I was going to be sick and I got up to use the restroom. I stumbled and the man sitting across from me got up and caught me by the elbow...*

"A few months ago, I went on a bender at Wayland Canteen," I told Tracey, my voice as low and small as I felt at the admission.

I slid a sideways glance to see her reaction but she kept her face completely impassive.

"So you fell off the wagon." She shrugged as if it was no big deal.

"I fell off that wagon, dragged it into the woods, set it on fire and then vomited all over it." The humiliation of the admission squeezed my heart.

"It happens." She grabbed my hand and squeezed. "So, you start over."

"I—I lost my ring that night. The matching band Garrett and I chose on our Whistler getaway last year."

She winced. "Jesus…" She caught her lower lip between her teeth. "I didn't even notice you haven't been wearing it. Did you try—"

"The bar doesn't have it. I called there and even stopped in there more than once. So did Garrett. If someone found it, they didn't turn it in."

"How about getting a replacement?"

"They were one of a kind made by an artist. Even if I got another, it wouldn't be the same."

And the self-contempt washed over me again, my thumb going to the spot the ring should be. I'd found the contact name for the artist who'd sold us the rings. I'd even emailed her and sent a picture of Garrett's to see if she could do a replacement. She confirmed that she could. She even still had a record of my ring size. All I had to do was send her the payment. But the empty spot on my finger and all the disgrace that came with it was what I deserved. A replacement band would only be cheating. Covering up my screwup. I needed the daily reminder of my shame and hoped it would be enough to stop me from falling again.

"I've got an idea," Tracey said, her voice perky and bright. "You should get a tattoo on your finger. Have them do a tat of the mountain and waves that were on the ring. That way you never have to worry about losing it because, hey, it would always be with you."

"That's something to think about…" She seemed so proud of the idea that I didn't want to tell her I'd never in a million years do it. "Anyway, I'm telling you this for another reason. I told you about finding that Smart car in the ditch with that missing young woman in it?"

She nodded.

"Well, there's something I didn't tell you…" I filled her in on Raymond Hughes and how he'd given me the impromptu reading and known immediately about Wayland and then how he'd sort of convinced me to allow him in on the case to help find Alice.

"And now you're angry that he's actually going around giving people readings when you already told him that was a good idea? I don't get it." Tracey held up the rods in her lap. "You have this bizarre supernatural skill that allows you to find the dead using dowsing rods but because this guy has a different kind of talent, you're blowing him off even though he could be really helpful."

I put the Jeep into drive and pulled away from the

curb with a sigh. "You're absolutely right. I'm being an idiot."

"I did not say that, but yeah, you kind of are."

We laughed together as I drove. A few minutes later I turned the car on to a nearby street. I slowed to allow some kids to cross the street, and Tracey let out a small scream that caused me to jump.

She was frantically pointing to her lap. The dowsing rods were spinning around in unison and finally came to a stop, pointing to my right. I pulled to the curb and looked over at an old boarded-up house that looked slated for demolition.

Had I just found Alice Ebert's body?

# SIX

I snatched my dowsing rods from Tracey's lap and climbed out of the car. Her face looked pale until I told her she could just wait in the Jeep.

"Call the police," I told her. "Give them this address and tell them I've found a body."

I walked up the sidewalk and my rods pulled me forward. The house was one of those small two-bedroom homes popular fifty years ago, and by the looks of the exterior it was beyond repair. I was guessing someone planned to bulldoze the place and rebuild. I walked close to the front stoop and the rods pulled me to the right. I followed them on a crushed rock path around to the back of the house. I was nearing the back door when the rods swung and pointed inside.

The back door was old, rotted wood that sat slightly askew as if someone put a shoulder to it and not only splintered the doorjamb but took it off the bottom hinges.

"Okay. This is it."

With a deep breath I toed the door open and allowed the daylight to illuminate the kitchen area. The faded linoleum was torn up to expose the plywood beneath, and the room was littered with empty whiskey bottles and crushed beer cans. There was a pungent aroma of decay that nearly knocked me backward. I did take a step back outside then drew in a deep breath and pulled the front of my T-shirt up over my nose to try and block the smell. I walked out of the kitchen and into the first of two small bedrooms. The room was a hoard of soiled clothing and a couple torn sleeping bags in a jumbled heap. Abruptly my brain caught up with what my eyes were noticing. Jutting out from beneath the pile was someone's arm. The hand had chipped fingernail polish in bright pink. The skin was grayed and fat flies danced around the hand.

I stumbled back out of the room and then burst out of the back door. The sound of police sirens was coming close. The officers found me doubled over and vomiting in the back corner of the yard.

"You found Alice?" one officer demanded.

I straightened and gave him a nod. Unable to find my voice I just pointed to the back door of the house. I should've waited until they had looked inside but I felt lightheaded and weak. I walked to the Jeep and wordlessly climbed into the driver's seat, tossing my rods on the back seat.

"You—you found her?" Tracey asked.

I grabbed a water bottle from the cup holder and drank away the sour taste in my mouth. Before I could find my voice to answer, the cops were approaching the car. I rolled down the window.

"Not Alice," the officer said right off. "Some crackhead who probably OD'd."

"Okay." My voice cracked.

"Give your statement to my partner and then you're free to go."

The partner turned out to be the officer with the tight

ponytail who'd given me a hard time at the community garden. She was all business and fired off questions to me in a rapid succession that made it hard for me to keep up, but finally, after providing all my contact information, I was glad to be headed home.

We drove in silence for about half an hour.

"Want me to drive?" Tracey asked.

"No. I'm good."

"You're not good but—"

Whatever else she was going to say was interrupted by a call coming in. It was Ray, and I almost sent the call to voice mail but then changed my mind and put him on speaker.

"Hi, Ray."

"I was talking with Roscoe's sister, Kim, and she said that word around town was that you found a body but it wasn't Alice?"

"That's right. Probably a drug addict OD."

"That's too bad."

I didn't know if he meant it was too bad I didn't find Alice or he was sad a drug addict had met that fate. Maybe both.

"I'm headed home now so…"

"Finished here myself. I was thinking the two of us should get together and compare notes."

"I'm really not up for it," I began, but then Tracey tapped my arm and gave me a nod. I sighed. "Okay, come by my place and we can review what we know."

I fired off my address and he said he'd be there in about ninety minutes. I ended the call and gave Tracey a curious look.

"I just really want a reading," she said with a mischievous smile. "Ever since Craig and I broke up, I've been wondering if I'll ever meet someone else."

I rolled my eyes and then started laughing at the silliness of her manipulation.

When we got back to my place, I gave Wookie a good ear scratch while Tracey scooped up Fluffy and the cat purred in her arms. It felt good to be home.

"I've gotta get some air. I'm taking Wookie for a run." I snapped his leash on his collar and we went out the door.

In Wookie's favorite park I sent Garrett a text telling him I'd found a body but I was fine.

As I expected, my phone rang in my hand.

"Hey, my love, just needed to hear your voice," he said.

And I hoped it wasn't just to hear in my voice if I was sober.

*Wayland. Someone grabbed my elbow and then he whispered in my ear...*

I cleared my throat.

"I'm good." I told him about finding the body in a house set for demolition, and how the police said it looked like a drug-addicted squatter who'd most likely overdosed.

"I'm sure you were hoping it was Alice Ebert. Sorry about that."

"Yeah, it would've been nice to wrap things up just like that," I admitted.

"Are you still with Tracey?"

"I'm just walking Wookie. Tracey's back at the house preparing for a psychic reading."

"What?" He chuckled and I loved the laughter in his

voice. I explained that Ray Hughes was coming over and how he'd been interviewing people about Alice and Roscoe and doing readings.

"You've made up your mind to work with this guy."

"He definitely seems to know things. I guess two heads are better than one."

"Sounds like you've got a partner."

"Maybe… I guess he'll do his thing and I'll do mine."

"You don't sound happy. You can tell him to go away. You can both work the investigation from your own angle. There are no rules saying you have to work together."

"True. But Tracey put it in perspective for me. If I can be a dowser finding bodies, why not let a medium help me out. After all, it's about finding Alice. Not about me."

"Right." He paused. "I don't know the guy but I'm guessing you're okay with him since you invited him to the house?"

"He seems pretty harmless although a little over-enthusiastic."

"But Tracey is going to be there too?"

"Yes." I gave Wookie a pull so we could start heading back. "She's probably washing her hands right at this moment preparing for her reading." The thought made me smile. "I'll give it a try working with this guy and if it's not meshing well, I'll tell him I'm going solo."

"That sounds like a good plan." Garrett made kissing noises into the phone. "I miss you. I'll call you tonight, sweetheart."

Back at the house, Ray's car was in the driveway and I could see him about to knock on the door.

"I'm here," I called out and he turned to offer me a smile. "Sorry, I needed to take my dog for a walk."

I unleashed Wookie and the dog walked over and gave Ray a thorough sniff.

"Hello," Tracey called out, coming toward us. She smiled and waved a finger in Ray's face. "Oh my God, I know you!"

"You're my grocery girl," Ray said, sounding surprised. "Sorry, 'grocery girl' is probably not the politically correct term, is it? Grocery clerk? Grocery person?" He laughed heartily.

"You know each other?" I kicked off my shoes and waved Ray to come inside.

"He's come through my checkout a few times," Tracey said. "Did you ever find that special brand of basmati rice you were looking for?"

He said he hadn't and they took a seat at the kitchen table. Tracey played host and brought out coffee as well as cheese and crackers.

"I was just reviewing my notes before I came over." Ray held up his phone.

"It's good that we're reviewing where we're at," I said.

Wookie came over and placed his rather large head between Ray and Tracey and they both patted and praised him generously.

"I used to have two rottweilers myself." He looked wistful. "Unfortunately, they're both gone now. I often think about getting a new one."

"I never used to like dogs but Wookie's special," Tracey said.

They began to chat so I interrupted to get them on track.

"Let's compare notes." I pulled out a kitchen chair across from Ray. "Who did you give readings to today?"

"I think we talked to some of the same people…" He scrolled through his phone. "I did readings of Natalie, Barb, Kim and a couple other classmates. Unfortunately, most of the people I talked to gave me nothing of value. They believe Roscoe is guilty and that he just tossed the body in the ocean. Barb in particular thinks Roscoe did it."

"Barb let you do a reading?" I was shocked. "She basically thinks I'm the devil."

"Oh, I know her well, so…" He shrugged and pushed his glasses up his nose.

"You seem to know a lot of people," I remarked.

"Yeah, it comes in handy." A mischievous smile crossed Ray's lips as he put the cup down. "I caught Barb outside the diner on her coffee break and she asked if she could pray with me. Of course I said yes."

"That way she'd hold your hands?" I asked.

"Yup. I've got nothing against religion. I was raised pretty religious, but of course her grabbing my hands gave me a chance to read her."

"That's so-o-o sneaky!" Tracey gave him a playful punch in the shoulder and giggled.

"It was," he admitted. "It's not the usual way I like to do business though."

"I'm sure you're forgiven for this one time." Tracey actually batted her eyelashes at him and he smiled warmly back. Oh my God, they were flirting. I resisted the urge to roll my eyes.

"So you gave Barb a reading and…" I made a keep-going gesture with my hands.

"And, unfortunately, it was much too short for me to zero in on everything…" He cleared his throat. "But I did find out that she fully believes Roscoe is guilty and she thinks Alice deserved what she got."

"What?" I sat back in my chair. "Why would a supposedly good Christian woman think a nice young lady like Alice deserved to get killed by her ex-husband over a dog? Over anything for that matter?"

"It wasn't about the dog." He put his palms on the table and leaned in. "Alice had an affair when still married to Roscoe."

"Did she say that, or did you get that from your reading?" I asked. "The only person who ever mentioned that was Kim, and apparently everyone else thinks the idea of Alice screwing around is ridiculous. I wonder if Kim blabbed that bit of gossip to Barb and she's run with it." That annoyed me. "Did Roscoe tell Barb that?"

"She said it was just the impression she got from him."

"He never even hinted that to me."

"So who was she cheating with?" Tracey gushed, placing a hand briefly on Ray's arm.

"Like I said, Barb said it was a feeling she got but it could just be gossip. I'm going to try again. Next time I'll get her to talk to me longer and see about finding out more." He nodded his chin at me. "You had a busy day. You found the body of that junkie. Good for you."

"I thought it was Alice," I admitted with a small cringe. "I was really hoping it was that easy."

"It's only normal you'd assume it was Alice since

that's who you're looking for." He gave a small shrug. "Right, Tracey?"

"Sure." Tracey's eyes never left his.

Oh, brother.

"What's your opinion?" I asked Ray. "Do you think he did it?"

"Does it matter? Our job is to find Alice, right? Let the cops collect all the evidence after we find the body."

"True." I nodded.

"If I had to make a guess, I'd say that, yes, Roscoe killed her but I don't think he tossed her in the water. First, he doesn't own his own boat, and sure, he could've gone down to the marina and borrowed one, but it all seems like too much for a drunk guy. Unless, of course, it was premeditated and he thought about killing her all along."

"True." That was another bit of information I hadn't picked up. It was entirely possible that Roscoe had planned to kill Alice. Maybe he hadn't planned on doing it that night, but if he already had some ideas in place then the argument that night might have been the catalyst to put things into action. I was becoming glad that Ray was helping.

"So what's your plan now?" he asked me.

"Well…" I rubbed the back of my neck. "I think I'll go over a map of the area, make a list of everyone we know who had connections with either Roscoe or Alice and see who else I can talk to. Next time I head up that way I guess I'll do a more thorough crisscrossing of surrounding areas in my car with my rods out, just in case. And you?"

"I'll try to find out when Barb works next and schedule another prayer session." He grinned.

"I'll contact Dana. She's a coworker who seems eager to help." I covered a sudden yawn with my hand. "Once I find out Barb's schedule I'll let you know."

"Not necessary. I can work my own connections to get her schedule." He got to his feet. "You're obviously tired so I should get going."

"So soon?" Tracey shot me a pleading look.

"How about you give my friend here a reading first," I suggested. "I think she's dying for one."

"Only if you have time," Tracey rushed.

"Sure."

Ray sat back down and turned his chair toward hers next to him. She also turned to face him so they were now sitting knee-to-knee. He took both her hands in his and closed his eyes. He didn't speak for at least a couple of minutes, and when he did, his voice was low and slow.

"You've had physical difficulty. I'm afraid you have more surgeries in your future but I don't see anything soon."

"Oh my God!" Tracey squealed and Ray hushed her seriously.

"Please don't talk."

He drew in a deep breath and continued. "These surgeries will only slow you down temporarily. You worry about your friend, Julie, but I see you both staying friends a very long time. Even traveling together sometime in the next year. Somewhere warm and beachy. Something is wrong with your car. Also, you're going to get a cat in the next few months."

He released her hands and then smiled. "That's the quick version."

"That was totally amazing!" She playfully punched him in the shoulder.

I'd watched him with growing interest but kept my own hands folded in my lap so he wouldn't suddenly grab them and say something about Wayland. Or worse, reveal one other particular secret I was keeping under wraps for now.

"Oh, there was one more thing," Ray said as he got to his feet. "I see you going out to dinner with a guy you just met."

I grinned in spite of the cheesiness.

"Are you asking me out?" Tracey laughed.

"Yes."

I let Tracey walk him to the door and I stayed sitting at the kitchen table with Wookie resting on my feet. After she'd shut the door after him, Tracey returned to the table with a huge grin on her face.

"We're going out for dinner tomorrow night." She flopped down in her chair. "Can you believe how cute he is?"

"Adorable." I smiled over at my friend. "Quite the coincidence that you knew each other from the grocery store."

"Yeah." She smiled sheepishly. "I actually think he's been trying to get up the nerve to ask me out for a while. Even when the line was shorter at another clerk, he'd always stand in my line and once I saw him in his car parked close to mine when he was leaving. It's sweet that it took him so long to get up the nerve."

"Just be careful. I don't want to see you hurt."

"Yes, Mom," Tracey joked.

I was exhausted and I still wanted to dig into the trial transcript before bed so I told her I needed to drive her home. Before she got out of the Jeep she turned to me.

"In Ray's reading he said that I worry about you," Tracey said. "And I do. You just seem more…" She struggled to find the word. "Troubled than usual. Maybe this case and being in your hometown isn't the best choice."

"I knew Alice in school. We had some things in common. I just feel like I owe her, so if I find Alice it'll be something I gave the city, and then I can leave that place on a positive note and never go back." Even as I said the words, it felt like a near impossible task. "I'm going to read the information on Roscoe's trial, then if I decide to take on the case, I'm giving it a week. If I don't find Alice in that time, I'm going to close the door on the entire situation."

"Good." She reached over and gave my hand a squeeze. "I'm working tomorrow, but if something comes up and you need me, I can call in sick. It's not like the grocery store will implode if I'm not there."

"I'll be fine." But as the crease of worry deepened between her eyes I added, "But if I'm not fine, I'll call you."

After she left, I felt the fatigue of the day dragging me down. Still I opened the package of trial paperwork and stacked it next to a pad of paper and pen for jotting notes and a large cup of freshly brewed coffee. Before I knew it, hours had passed and I was sitting back in the chair frowning over everything I'd read. Garrett would be calling shortly to say goodnight. I got to my feet, scrubbed my face, brushed my teeth and climbed into bed with Wookie. I was already fast asleep when my phone rang a few minutes later and I answered with a start.

"You were asleep?"

"Just nodding off. It was a long day." I stifled a yawn. "Tell me about your day."

There was very little he could tell me, and that was the nature of his being an FBI agent, but he talked about one of the other agents, who was a practical joker, and how they'd had vegan burgers for dinner. Just the sound of his voice soothed my nerves and I found myself feeling relaxed and sinking into my pillow.

Garrett mentioned the weather had been stormy and he'd been caught in an unexpected downpour.

"It was quite the gale and—"

"What?" I sat up, my nerves on alert.

"I said the storm was quite a gale and we got wet."

But what I'd heard instead of "gale and" was "Wayland," and my stomach clenched. I faked a yawn and spoke through it so he couldn't hear the anxiety in my voice.

"Sorry, baby, I'm beat." The fake yawn triggered a real one.

We said our goodnights and I-love-yous but after I put the phone back on my bedside table, all I could think about was Wayland. I chose a calming meditation app on my phone and let it soothe me to sleep. The calming voice told me to follow my breath all the way in and all the way out, and after a while, I drifted off.

*The air in the bar was thick with beer and despair. My throat was sour from wine as I stumbled toward*

*the bathroom, hoping to throw up. My breath caught
as the stranger who was sitting in my booth grabbed
my elbow to steady me. I tried to push him away but
he held fast. He walked me toward the washrooms and
leaned in to whisper something. His thick mustache and
beard tickled my ear and his hot breath caused me to
shudder. He wore a cloying men's cologne that made
me want to retch. Whatever he said scared me to death.*

I woke up to Wookie licking my face.

"Ugh." I pushed him away. "Your breath stinks."

The sheets were tangled around my legs and I was
damp with sweat. Last night's disjointed mix of Wayland thoughts sprang to mind and I pushed them away,
feeling guilty for the craving for wine that followed.

I briefly read through the notes I'd made the night before on the trial transcript. Although it wasn't common
to convict someone of murder without a body, Roscoe
wasn't the first person to be sent to prison for murder
without a victim in the morgue. The prosecution didn't
have to work hard to prove Roscoe had motive to kill his
estranged wife. The loud argument in the center of town
provided enough witnesses to clinch that fact. It seemed
an open-and-shut case with the combination of that motive and the evidence that Roscoe's own sword had been
discovered bloody nearby, the bed of his pickup contained a sufficient amount of Alice's blood, and the rem-
nants of Alice's thumb perched inside. It was all tied up
in a little bow. A niggling in the back of my mind said
it was all a little too neat and tidy. If Roscoe had passed
out inside his trailer, how hard would it have been for
someone to set him up?

After I fed the pets, I sent off a text to Dana asking

if she could possibly let me know Barb's work schedule this week. She replied saying Barb was going to be off work both today and tomorrow at two o'clock. I replied with a thank-you and then sent a copy of that message to Ray. He called immediately and said he was going to go today and have another prayer meeting with Barb.

He laughed at his own joke.

"I'll be there right when she gets off," he added. "Not going to stay too late there because I need to get home and clean up for my date with Tracey tonight. Does she like flowers? Is it too much if I bring her roses? I don't want to come off like I'm trying too hard. Maybe flowers are too special for a first date and—"

"Tracey deserves special. I'm sure she'll like whatever flowers you get." I paused a beat and then added, "Ray, just be kind to her, okay? Don't mess with her feelings."

"I swear to God I'll be on my best behavior."

I guess I couldn't ask for more than that. It wasn't long after I hung up that Tracey began messaging me because she was excited about her date. She wanted my advice on what to wear. As if the girl whose uniform was a T-shirt and jeans was the person you went to for fashion advice.

I didn't relish the idea of making the hour drive back to my hometown but I was determined to help Alice. I'd promised to work the case for only a week and that had given me renewed determination to give it my best shot. I only wished I had more to go on. Maybe it was time to take Blossom out for coffee. I sent her a message asking what time she was done at the motel. It was almost an hour later and I was preparing my backpack to leave when she responded saying she was off today. I messaged her back asking about a coffee date. Again, she took a while to reply but finally she agreed but told me to message her later about a time since she was just getting out of bed.

The entire drive north on I-5 I played guided meditations. Generally, these put people to sleep but my goal was only to keep my nerves steady and my stomach soothed. I followed along with the deep breathing exercises as I zoomed in and out of traffic. Every once in a while I would get a flash of a vision from inside Wayland Canteen. Something bothered me about that night. Something had happened, and trying to search my head was like trying to hold water in my hands.

"It's in the past," I told myself as I zipped into the left lane to pass a slow moving minivan. "Stop obsessing and focus on Alice."

Thinking about Alice Ebert became easier as I got closer to my destination. Just because I hadn't found Alice's body in the bay didn't mean she wasn't there, but that felt wrong. Roscoe had been drunk that night. If he killed her and stashed her body it would've been nearby. I needed to check the area where he was living at the time—that trailer and farm where Kim now lived. I gave Kim a call.

"Hi, Kim, I know the police probably checked all your land for Alice's body, but I need to check it again. Just to cross it off my list."

"I guess there's no harm in that. When you thinking?"

"Today. In about half an hour."

"I'm out. I won't be back for hours."

"You don't need to be there," I assured her. "I'm just going to walk around your two acres, okay?"

"Oka-a-ay…" She seemed uncertain and added, "Like you said, the cops already checked all around there more than once, so it seems like a waste of time."

"I know but it'll put my mind at ease." I thanked her before I disconnected the call.

The drive into Kim's property immediately ramped up my nausea.

"The farm's miles away," I told myself in an attempt to calm that sick feeling. "You'll be fine."

But the land looked so similar, and the air and feel of it brought a rush of sensations from my dark and terrifying childhood. My grandmother's voice briefly snarled in my head.

*You're a stupid, worthless child.*

A comment that had usually been followed with a vicious and cruel assault.

"I'm fine. I'm safe. I'm okay." I repeated the affirmations over and over as I parked the Jeep.

Kim's two-acre plot of land was mostly just scrub of weeds and brush. Only about one-quarter acre around the trailer had been cleared. I reached inside my pack, pulled out my rods and hopped out of the Jeep. I decided to march to the back of the property and walk in rows back and forth until I reached the house and large shed. The air was damp and chilled my face as I hiked toward the property line made clear by a neighboring farmer's fence.

Once there, I held my rods out and walked. I strode to the end of the property on one side and then did an about-face and marched back to the other end of the yard. The weeds scratched my thighs through my jeans and even my arms in some places. As I walked, I tried to keep my head away from the neighborhood and away from Wayland Canteen. I thought instead about another preoccupation that I kept pushing aside.

I hummed and whistled to myself and wasn't at all surprised that by the time I'd reached the back of the trailer, the rods hadn't moved an inch. After all, it would've been the first place the cops looked. That said, if he'd buried her deep enough under the brush even the most trained investigator could've missed it. Unfortunately, Alice was nowhere around here or my rods would've said as much.

As I walked past the trailer, I pressed the fob to unlock the Jeep. Suddenly I heard a loud noise from inside the trailer. Something like glass breaking. I swung around and stared at the building. Kim's car wasn't there and she said she wouldn't be home. I glanced over at the outbuilding that had a rusted padlock on the big swinging door. The way it leaned to one side, I couldn't imagine anyone attempting to park in there.

"Damn dogs," I muttered to myself as I climbed into the Jeep. No doubt they'd knocked something on the floor. I briefly debated sending Kim a message to let her know that she might be coming home to a mess but just as I was starting my Jeep, I heard her car coming down the long driveway.

It was raining now so I waited until Kim was out of her vehicle before I climbed out of mine and joined her.

"Your muffler is busted," I pointed out, even though clearly anyone within earshot could tell the car had a problem.

"If it's not one thing it's another with this thing." She kicked a tire angrily then turned to me. "You already done?"

"Yup. Found nothing but I didn't really expect to. Just crossing my t's, know what I mean?" I shielded my eyes from the rain.

"Okay, well, I'd invite you in but I'm home early on account of I feel sick." She pointed at the trailer with a wave of a bright keychain. "Gotta hit the washroom."

"Okay. I'll keep you posted," I said and then quickly added, "By the way, I heard something break inside so be careful. Sounds like one of the dogs might have knocked something over."

She blushed to her roots and gave me a quick nod as she hustled toward her trailer. I started my car, and as she went up her steps, I noticed a large pair of muddy men's work boots outside on her stoop. Maybe it wasn't the dogs after all.

I drove off wondering about Kim having a man. She'd never mentioned it but it made me curious. I tried Blossom's phone number but it went to voice mail so I took my rods and investigated some neighborhood green areas.

A couple hours later I was coming out of Heron's Pond Park soaked to the bone after getting caught in a deluge of West Coast fall rain. My phone rang and I wiped my wet hands on my jeans before answering the call from Blossom.

"I've showered and feel almost human," she told me. "Grab me a large latte when you come over."

She rattled off her address and I told her I'd be there in fifteen minutes. I stopped to get her latte and a couple of extra-large cookies and a juice for myself. Her apartment was on F Street in a pale yellow three-level building. She buzzed me in and I took the stairs to the second floor.

She was standing with her door open as I walked down the hall, her lanky height nearly filling the space and blocking the dogs from shooting out the door.

"Nectar of the gods." She took her coffee from my hand. "Welcome to my mess."

"Thanks."

I toed off my runners and gave Jet a thorough scratch behind his ears and Chichi a pat even though the Chihuahua yipped and snarled at me. I followed Blossom across the apartment to the kitchen table. The place was a little untidy with a laundry basket on the sofa and a sink full of dishes but I wouldn't call it a mess. I could tell she'd spent quite a bit of time choosing just the right unique furniture pieces in her place.

"This is a nice apartment."

"You sound surprised."

I put the bag of cookies between us and told her to help herself. "No, you always had a good eye for fashion so I figured that would mean decorating as well."

"Not exactly a castle." She snorted. "But I guess I've done all right." She glanced around as if seeing it for the first time. "When Roscoe and I were dating, he hated coming over here. He always wanted me to come to the trailer instead."

"Really? Why is that?" I opened my bottle of juice and took a sip.

"Get this…" She sipped her coffee and smirked. "He said apartments felt like jail."

I laughed in spite of myself.

"Jesus, Beanster, you can actually laugh." Blossom reached into the bag for a cookie and broke off a small piece. "I don't think you once cracked a smile in all the years I've known you."

When she saw me every day we were in high school and I was struggling to survive under the demented rage of my grandmother.

"I smile more these days," I told her. "Things were…" I struggled to find the word and settled for "…hard. Back then, my life wasn't easy." The description was like saying a tsunami was a slight wave.

"Yeah, none of us knew about that until all the hoopla surrounding your family a few years ago." Her eyes were bright with curiosity, and I definitely didn't want to start answering questions about that time so I switched the conversation.

"If there was anyone else in the world who'd kill Alice, who do you think it would be?"

"Besides Roscoe?" She stuffed another piece of cookie in her mouth and chewed. "No idea. I mean, maybe his sister would be the only one."

"Kim?" I paused with my juice halfway to my lips and put the bottle down in stunned surprise. "Why her?"

"Oh, I don't think she really did it, I think it was Roscoe all-l-l-l the way. You asked who'd be my next thought and it would be her. She never liked Alice."

"Really? I never got that impression at all."

"It's not like she's going to start speaking ill of the dead, right?" Blossom rolled her eyes. "And Kim never walked around raging about Alice to other people but she'd make snide remarks about her being needy and whiny. I think Alice thought her and Kim could be like sisters once she married Roscoe, but Kim wasn't interested. Alice never wanted Roscoe going anywhere without her because she hated being alone. Guess she was clingy with Kim too."

I thought back to the quiet Alice I remembered from school and could see how that might be true. "Do you think Alice was really like that, or was that just Kim's opinion?"

"For sure," Blossom said with a snort. "I mean I think she had it kind of hard growing up, so when she met Roscoe she just kind of hung on for dear life. When they were out together, she always had to have her hands on him. Claiming him or something I guess, or maybe it was just she felt really insecure on account of her own life." Blossom's tone developed a superior sound when she added, "Some girls just don't know that if you're going to be like a piece of Velcro, a guy is going to look for someone who's more of a challenge."

I could tell Blossom's personal philosophy on men was that you needed to let them chase you while you played hard to get.

"Sounds like she was looking to make a family."

"Oh, sure." Blossom nodded. "And Roscoe's dad, he was all over that, right? Especially once he got the cancer. He loved Alice and was always doing stuff for her."

"Like what?"

"Like before they split up he took her to the mall and bought her a ton of clothes for no reason at all."

"That must've annoyed Kim."

"Nah." Blossom shook her head. "Kim was never interested in having a relationship with the old man."

"So you said Alice was needy. Is that why Roscoe started dating you after his marriage ended? Were you more of a challenge?"

"Ha!" Blossom barked out that bit of laughter then winked at me. "I made him work for it, that's for sure, but I knew it was never going anywhere."

"Why's that?"

"As much as he complained about Alice, he still loved her."

"Did he say that?"

"No. I could just tell."

"Where did Alice move to after they split up? I heard her mom moved to Florida and her dad passed."

"Her dad…" Blossom put her coffee cup down and stared at me. "Oh, my God you don't know."

"Know what?"

"Do you remember Lois?"

I shook my head slowly. The name didn't ring a bell.

"Lois was Alice's half sister. I guess there was no reason you'd ever know about her because Alice never mentioned her name. Maybe Alice didn't even know about her back then. Anyway, Lois returned here after high school. You were on a bender in Seattle in those days, if I remember."

I cleared my throat and looked down at the table. After school was done I'd bolted out of this godforsaken place, headed for the city and drunk myself into a near coma for months at a time. After Grandma died, I finally dried out and came home. Been struggling to keep dry ever since.

"So Alice's half sister moved here after I left. Is she still here?"

"I think she's in Bellingham."

Blossom was giving me a secretive smile like she was going to reveal something big.

"And what aren't you saying?"

"Lois killed their dad. She came here for a visit and apparently they got into drinking and brawling one night and she bashed his head in."

"You've got to be kidding me." My jaw dropped and my mind raced to catch up. "Why didn't I hear about that?"

"Far as I know, you hardly ever left your trailer unless it was to work at the gas station or go out with Katie," Blossom said.

"So what happened to Lois?"

"She did her time. As a matter of fact she just got out about a month before Alice got herself killed."

"Were they close?"

"Alice and Lois?" Blossom made a palms-up shrug. "I don't see how they could be, but I guess they might've seen each other a few times after Lois was free. I heard Alice never once visited her while she was incarcerated."

"Do you think Lois would have reason to kill Alice?"

"Got me." Blossom broke off another piece of cookie and popped it in her mouth. "I don't think they really knew each other. I'm sure Alice wouldn't want to be all touchy and feely with the person who killed her dad, so I doubt they were bonding, but what do I know?" She pointed at me. "You know way more about family dysfunction than I do."

She'd meant it as a dig but it was true so I didn't reply. I was sipping my juice and wondering about Alice's ex-con sister. Murdering someone is a lot easier the second time around.

## SEVEN

I WAS WALKING out of Blossom's building when my phone rang. It was Ray.

"I got over to the diner earlier and caught Barb on her break."

"And?"

"She was more than happy to pray with me. She's determined to save my soul, so of course I played along, right? I'm not a super religious person but I like to think I'm spiritual so I take offense to her thinking I'm the son of Satan because I'm a medium."

"Were you able to get any information?"

"Right before she took my hands in prayer, I asked her if we could also pray for Roscoe for killing Alice. It was a ploy to put Roscoe in her head when I was trying to read her and it worked."

"Really? So what information did you read off of her?"

"Nothing new, unfortunately. She believes Roscoe is guilty of killing Alice, but she still thinks she can save him from eternal damnation and still figures if Alice cheated, she probably deserved it."

"Did you get a read on who she believes Alice was having an affair with?"

"No. The only thing in her head was a vague thought about people who break the seventh commandment are

evil. I got the feeling that she's justifying Roscoe's killing of Alice based on that belief, but she's got no facts
about it. At least none I could pick up on in my reading.
Let's face it, if Barb knew the name of the person Alice
may have been stepping out with, she'd have a few evil
thoughts about that guy too. I got nothing."

I pressed the key fob on my Jeep and walked across
the parking lot, then paused with my hand on the door
to my car. "So it's all just rumor. Gossip isn't going to
help find Alice. We need to talk to more people to see
if anyone else might know for sure if Alice cheated,
and if so, who she was having an affair with. I wonder
if she had any close friends?"

"I'm on it," Ray said.

"What are you going to do?"

"I'm not really sure. Ask around I guess."

Which is really the only thing we could do. After I
hung up I started my Jeep. As I was pulling out of the
parking lot, I could see Blossom standing on her bal-
cony two floors up. She was smoking a cigarette and
staring at my car as if to make sure I was gone. I pulled
out on the front street and parked at the curb out of her
line of sight. I searched the web on my phone to try and
get information on Alice's sister, Lois. I'd been sitting
there about ten minutes when I spotted a familiar car
pulling into Blossom's parking lot. It was Kim.

Blossom hadn't mentioned Kim was coming over.
Maybe Kim was picking up the dogs even though it was
Blossom's day off? It did make me curious. I waited
a few minutes after Kim was parked and entered the
building and then I dialed Kim's number. She let it go
to voice mail and I left a message.

"I know you said you heard a rumor that Alice was having an affair while married to your brother. Could you call me back so we can talk more about that?"

I found a social media profile for Alice's half sister, Lois, and it confirmed she lived in Bellingham like Blossom had suggested. I couldn't get an exact address but searching her name did finally yield a phone number. It rang three times before being answered by a woman with a gravelly voice.

"Hello?"

"Hi, is this Lois? My name is Julie Hall."

Click.

"Hello?" I frowned at the phone and wondered if she'd hung up on me or if we'd been accidentally disconnected. I dialed again.

"Sorry, I think my call dropped there and—"

"Leave me alone."

Click.

Huh.

I decided to send a text instead.

I am trying to find Alice's body so you can lay her to rest.

Then I sent a second text.

I was her friend in high school.

Saying I was her friend was a bit of a stretch but we did have a connection.

I received a message in reply.

You're working for the enemy. Leave me alone.

So she knew I was hired by Kim and Roscoe. I guess I couldn't blame her for wanting to avoid cooperating with the person she believed killed her half sister. I didn't know how to break down that wall. I did some more online research and came across her LinkedIn page. Lois's face looked strained, with a fake and forced smile. She listed her skills as mostly clerical. Her current employer was a janitorial service.

I called the company and told them I was checking references on Lois. The call was transferred to another department and after some researching the woman there was able to find Lois's file.

The woman stated that Lois had been employed by them for six months. She worked full time cleaning an office building. I asked the name of the building and expected some resistance but she gave it to me and told me she worked three pm until eleven Monday to Friday.

Bellingham was only a fifteen-minute drive from where I was and it was barely noon. I took out my dowsing rods and placed them on my lap. I could easily kill a few hours just driving around town and the surrounding areas. If Alice's body lay in a ditch or an abandoned building around town, my rods would tell me.

The rain let up and I rolled down the windows of the Jeep to let in some air. Winding up and down the roads in town was making me feel nauseous, and the small amount of juice I had that morning added to the queasy feeling. I regretted leaving Blossom the cookies. I stopped at a corner store and picked up a couple granola bars and a banana that was slightly past its prime.

I was walking back to the Jeep and spotted Ray across the street. He had his back to me and was talking to the older man I remembered from the community garden. Ray had fisted hands on his hips and his legs spread in a look of defiance. Although I couldn't hear what was being said, the tone in Ray's voice was heated and the answering tenor in the old man's response sounded equally angry.

I climbed into the Jeep and ate the banana and one of the granola bars while watching them. Eventually, Ray stormed off, got into his car parked at the curb and sped off.

"What was that all about?" I wondered aloud.

I washed the food down with gulps from a water bottle and waited until the older guy began walking away. When he'd sauntered a couple blocks down the road and I was about to lose him from my vision, I started my car and drove up to meet him. I pulled to the curb just ahead of him, and the man stopped in his tracks and frowned.

"What do you want?"

"Just checking in," I told him. "Wondering if you have any more information on Alice."

"What is with you two?" he snarled and began to walk away.

A slight limp and his age didn't make it hard to keep up so I stepped up beside him.

"Us two?" I tried to sound innocent.

"I know you're working with that idiot, Ray." He shook his head. "The two of you going around town trying to shake every tree as if Alice is just going to fall out." He stopped walking and turned to me. "Just let the cops do their job, right? If her body is around, they'll find it. Even if they don't, it doesn't change what happened. She's dead. She ain't coming back. Sticking what's left of her in a gravesite isn't going to change that." His voice broke with emotion.

"I'm sorry. You obviously were close to Alice." My own voice grew tender. "My intention is only to pay due respect to her remains. I mean no harm at all."

"When she first started gardening her little plot, she had no clue what she was doing." He smiled. "Every day she'd come to me and ask me questions about fertilizer and how often to water and whether or not she should spray for bugs."

"So you were like her mentor. That's so nice you could help her."

But I got the feeling Alice knew that this lonely old man enjoyed her company too. Maybe all her questions were all about just making this guy feel useful.

"She was a good young woman." He shook his head and sighed. "And she had a way with plants. After she was gone the dumbass Roscoe sent over just overwatered, over-fertilized and killed all her hard work. Just like he killed her."

"If Roscoe killed her, do you have any idea where he'd bring her body?"

"From what I heard he was drunk as a skunk that night so it wouldn't have been far. I'd think he would've just buried her on his own land but I'm sure police searched there."

And so had I.

"Thank you." I reached and placed a hand on his shoulder. "I mean no disrespect to Alice."

I let him walk away then and headed back to my car. Kim called just as I was pulling away from the curb.

"You told me that Alice was messing around on Roscoe. Is that fact, or rumor?" I asked her point-blank.

"Well…" She hesitated. "There was talk that Alice had cheated. I told Roscoe that and he told me that it was all lies and to butt out."

"So Roscoe didn't believe the rumor?" If he thought Alice had cheated while they were married, it gave him motive.

"He thought the sun rose and set out of that girl's ass." Kim sighed.

"It came up at trial. The prosecution brought up there were rumors of her cheating and that was one more reason why he killed her."

"Yes but of course Roscoe's lawyer said they had no proof she was cheating."

Just because nobody had proof didn't mean that it hadn't happened. And if Roscoe still loved Alice, the thought of her with someone else could've been just one more thing, and the dog, Jet, was the final straw on the camel's back that set things in motion. Or else whoever she was having an affair with had killed her.

"Do you know the name of the guy she was supposedly seeing? If she had another boyfriend, he's a suspect."

"If I'd ever had a name, I would've given it to the cops."

"But you sound positive she cheated."

"Look, you know what this place is like; a tiny seed of gossip tossed out in the morning grows into an oak tree by noon." She exhaled loudly and then admitted, "Could be I just chose to believe it."

Another dead end. I rubbed the back of my neck and sighed.

"Hang on a second," Kim told me and then I heard her arguing with a man over a price. After a minute she came back on the line, "You won't believe how much it costs to get a damn muffler fixed. You'd think the thing was made of gold or something." She muttered a few choice curse words.

"I'm running out of options here," I told her. "What about Lois? What was their relationship like?"

"Roscoe never met Lois, as far as I know. She was locked up the entire time he was together with Alice and she only got out after he was the one behind bars."

"Good to know but I meant Alice. What was *her* relationship like with her half sister?"

"Alice didn't give a rat's ass about Lois. She was glad she was locked up." Kim sounded perturbed. "She once told me that she never even knew about Lois until just a few weeks before that girl murdered her dad. Alice was devastated when her dad was killed."

"Maybe that's why she got close to your stepdad. She was looking to have that relationship again."

"It was mutual. Dad loved Alice."

"Did that bother you?"

"Nah. He was just getting soft inside because of the cancer. The man treated me like crap for years. I had no interest in making nice-nice with him just because he was dying. Now Alice's dad was a good guy. His death bothered everyone."

"Everyone?"

"Of course! You know Alice's dad was well-liked around here. He was a stand-up guy. He started the soup kitchen for God's sake." She exhaled loudly. "The man was a friggin' saint."

"Who beat his kids," I said dryly.

"Who told you that?" Her voice sounded shrill. "God, just because you had a crappy upbringing didn't mean the entire world did!"

The venom in her voice caught me by surprise so I didn't reply right away.

"I gotta go," Kim said.

The call went dead, leaving me with a lot of questions. Mostly, I was annoyed with myself for not standing up for Alice. I should've told Kim that I knew Alice had been beaten as a child. I'd seen the marks firsthand. I'd also seen the haunted look in her eyes.

"Doesn't matter," I told myself as I drove out of town. "I believed you, Alice. Who cares what anyone else thinks. I'll settle this for you."

With new determination I got on the highway, making my way south toward Bellingham. When I arrived at the office building where Lois worked, I parked around back near the rear entrance. It was still over an hour before she was due to start her shift. I was exhausted and I lowered my seat nearly flat, closed my eyes and nodded off nearly immediately.

The sound of a car door slamming nearby woke me. For a second I had no idea where I was, and it only dawned on me as I raised my seat to the upright position and saw the back of the building. Staff were leaving and getting into their cars.

I scrolled through my phone to find the picture I'd found of Lois online. I'd taken a screenshot and now enlarged it to get a good look. Midforties, hair cut extremely short around the ears and longer and tussled on top, eyes hard like they were daring you to try something.

Almost on the nose at three an older tiny pickup truck with squealing brakes backed into a parking spot a few stalls over. A woman got out and made her way to the back of the building. Her hair was a bit longer than in the pictures. She was wearing navy cargo pants and a white polo shirt with the name of the janitorial service embroidered on the back. It was definitely Lois.

"Hey!" I hopped out of the Jeep and slammed the door shut behind me.

Lois turned, and at the sight of me, rolled her eyes so far back in her head I was sure she could see her gray matter.

"You just don't take no for an answer!" She crossed her arms and scowled. "I don't want to talk to you."

"If you ever cared at all about Alice, you will tell me what you know."

"Wow, you go straight for the jugular." She laughed mirthlessly. "Look, you are just turning this into a three-ring circus. Alice deserved better than that."

"Sorry. I don't want to do anything but find her. She was..." I stopped short of saying my friend. I had a feeling Lois would see right through that. "We had a connection in school."

"Because both of you lived in homes where you were getting the shit kicked out of you on a daily basis?" she sneered. "What do you call that? Blood sisters?" She tilted her head. "Does that make us besties too? After all, you killed your own friggin' grandpa, right? And I killed my dad. Only difference is, I went to jail."

"It was self-defense," I blurted.

"So. Was. Mine." She punctuated each word with a pointed finger at my face. "Years of him using me as a punching bag and…and worse." She swallowed. "But I hadn't seen him in years because I was the bastard kid his mistress spat out. One night I got just angry enough to find him and his family. Drove to his house to confront him for everything he'd done to me when I was a kid."

Someone walked out of the back of the building and we both became silent. The man didn't spare us even a glance as he walked to his car but we didn't speak again until he'd driven off.

"I take it that your confrontation didn't go as planned," I said quietly.

"He didn't answer the door but I could hear him beating on someone. I could hear the screams and the sound of his fists on flesh." She swallowed and her eyes looked miserable as she lowered her voice to a mere whisper. "I went around to the back of the house and the door was open. I walked inside to see him with his hands wrapped around Alice's throat. I didn't even know who she was at the time but I grabbed a beer bottle and smashed it over his head. He went down like a sack of wet cement and never got back up. I didn't mean to kill him." She ran a shaky hand through her hair. "Or maybe I did. God knows he deserved it. All I knew was I had to make him stop. I'll never forget the fear in Alice's eyes. I guess she thought I was about to kill her next. She took off running. I called 911 and tried to tell them it was self-defense but nobody bought it."

"But Alice could've testified to that."

"But she didn't. She said she was at Roscoe's all evening, and he verified that, so…" She shrugged. "I did a dime and now I'm out."

"I'm sorry."

She shifted her weight from one foot to the other. "So, as you can see, having only just briefly met Alice before going to prison, there's nothing I know about her that could help you."

"She never came to visit you?"

Something crossed her face and was gone.

"When it hit the news and she found out I was her half sister, she wrote me a couple times. Even offered to come by and visit. I didn't want her to see me locked up." She looked at her feet. "But the prison let us Skype and we scheduled a few of those. She told me how sorry she was about not standing up for me, and even thanked me for saving her. We made plans to try and be a family once I was out." Then she raised her eyes to mine. "We emailed back and forth for a bit. She was…" Lois closed her eyes. "It was a difficult time for her and Roscoe. They were scrapping in the courts and preparing for divorce. Alice said she wasn't in a good mental place to spend any sisterly time together but I told her I wanted to be there for her. I felt I owed her that. We'd seen each other in person exactly twice before that nutjob killed her over a damn dog."

"What about Alice's mom and your mother? Did they testify about the abuse?"

"Alice's mom was in the hospital having some kind of surgery the day it happened. She acted like I was insane. Said that he'd never laid a hand on her or Alice. The second that man was in the ground though, she hightailed it to Florida to shack up with some guy. My mother…" She laughed mirthlessly. "When I was twenty she died with a needle in her arm."

It must've been hard on her. No family. No one to stand by her side. I knew what that was like.

"I know you've got to get to work but—"

"I can give you another minute," she said. "Not like their trash cans are going to disappear before I get inside to empty them."

"Okay, I know you believe Roscoe's the murderer but if—and I know this is a big if—but *if* someone else did it, who would that someone be?"

She raised her palms up in the air in an elaborate shrug.

"From what I hear, everybody loved Alice. Except Roscoe because she took his damn dog. She had no enemies." The rain started up again and we stepped into the overhang of the building. "Of course, it's not like I'd known her long, right?"

"Yeah, everyone I've talked to had nice things to say about her except…" I intentionally let my voice trail off to bait her into questioning me.

"There's someone who has something negative to say?" Lois stuffed her hands into the pockets of her sweater and narrowed her eyes. "Who?"

Lois looked like the type who'd find a way to hurt someone for the wrong remark so I wasn't going to throw Kim or Barb under the bus.

"There were rumors that Alice cheated on Roscoe and that's why they split."

A shadow of worry crossed her face and was gone. "Did that asshole tell you that?"

"No." Which was weird. "Roscoe never mentioned it."

"There you go." The strange look on her face was gone as she added, "And we both know if he could've tossed her to the wolves and pointed the finger at some lover during court, he totally would've done that."

"I heard Alice didn't have any money when she died, but can you think of any way that someone could benefit from her death?"

"Nope. Like you said, she had no cash so that wasn't a motive. Roscoe's dad bought her boots and a coat the year we had all that snow. She couldn't even afford to dress herself properly."

"Sounds like she was close to his dad." That explained why he wanted to fund the finding of her body even after his death.

"Yeah, they got along. She liked both his mom and dad. They were family." Lois shook her head slowly. "I'm glad she had that kind of connection. She deserved it."

"What about Kim? She mention being close to her?"

"No, but that doesn't mean nothing." She took a step back toward the door. "Now I really gotta go."

"Thank you for talking to me." I dug out a business card and handed it to her. "I know you don't like that I'm working for Kim and Roscoe, but in reality they might be paying my bill but they aren't my true client. I'm working for Alice because she deserves to have her body found. She needs a decent burial."

Lois took the card in both hands and stared at it wordlessly.

"Please send me a message if you think of anything that could help me find her."

She gave me a sharp nod and then disappeared inside the building.

No matter what Lois said, the anxious look on her face when I brought up Alice cheating told me more than the words that left her lips.

After leaving Bellingham, I wound my way back north with the dowsing rods on my lap. Rachel Wu had been found with me just driving by, and I didn't want to take the chance that I'd go past Alice without even realizing it. There were a number of secluded areas that would make easy body dumps. Bush areas behind rest stops, trails, parks and vacant commercial buildings. Every time I racked my brain to come up with another place to try, I was disappointed with the outcome. I was no longer looking for just someplace that lazy Roscoe could've tossed Alice from the bed of his truck. There was now a possibility that some secret lover had done her in and set Roscoe up by using his pickup truck and his sword. It was nearly impossible for me to imagine where some unknown person could've dumped her. I needed to get a finger on who this person was, and unfortunately, I was getting the feeling that meant another drive to Ozette Corrections.

As I drove, I put another call in to Detective Larry. He answered on the first ring.

"Two questions. I assume you know about Alice's half sister, Lois. Was she ever a suspect?"

"We looked into her but she was working all night when Alice was killed, and went out with a coworker after her night shift. Her alibi was iron clad and she seemed pretty shook up by Alice's murder." He paused. "What's your second question?"

"I've heard rumors Alice was cheating. In all your digging did you find a lover?"

"Nope and we heard the same thing. Nobody ever saw her with a guy, there were no messages with any lover on her laptop or social media, and even more important, Roscoe was adamant she was faithful. I gotta say, I've never known someone up for murder who wouldn't throw their ex under the bus to get themselves off the hook. I'm sure Roscoe would've pointed the finger at an affair or secret lover if one existed."

He had a point. I ended the call and continued my drive.

After a couple hours I gave up crisscrossing the area in my car. Even though I'd had an impromptu nap in the car, I was suddenly bone weary. I got in the Jeep and pointed it south to home.

I had a phone call from Dr. Chen and sent it to voice mail. I'd canceled my next appointment with her and I knew she was wanting to reschedule. I was playing with fire not to see my therapist, but I needed some time to sort out everything in my head. And what was in my head was Wayland.

*The sputtering neon behind the bar read Wayland Canteen but the W was fried and no longer lit up. The stranger grabbed my elbow to keep me from faltering and whispered something in my ear that sent cold shivers down my spine. I tugged my arm from his grasp and stumbled into the ladies' room. I dropped to my knees in a filthy stall and vomited repeatedly so long and so hard that there was nothing but bile coming up. I flushed the toilet and went to the sink and stuck my head under the faucet to rinse my mouth with the tepid water, then scooped some water into my hands and washed my face. I caught a glimpse of my drunken reflection in the mirror. The room was tilting and spinning and I hardly recognized the woman looking back at me. Why? Why was I drinking? I'd been doing so good! Shame washed over me in a wave so hard it nearly buckled my knees.*

The memory was so intense I pulled the Jeep to the shoulder of the highway, climbed out and dragged cold air into my lungs to clear my head. I looked out over farm fields and my gaze rested on a distant spot that was beyond my view but still iced my veins. Even from this distance I could zero in on the area I'd been raised, and it felt like a vortex of doom that wanted to drag me back.

I needed to get back to my home and broke the speed limit to get there. My heart hurt that Garrett wasn't there because just being in his arms would take away so much sting from the day. I took care of Wookie and Fluffy, then spread out on the sofa for a nap. It felt like I'd just dozed when my phone began beeping with a flurry of texts from Tracey, who was worried about the date.

What should I wear?

Should I paint my nails?

Shave my legs?

Get a wax?

I yawned and sat up, realizing that I'd slept for over two hours. I texted a vague reply to my friend telling her she'd be fine and not to be too nervous. Then I lied and told her I was tied up and I'd have to talk to her after her date.

My stomach was demanding food so I made myself some soup. After I ate, I brought my laptop to the sofa and tried to do more research on Alice. In my gut I felt like I was missing something huge. The quicker I helped find Alice, the faster I could put the case and that entire town behind me. So far I was feeling like I'd only let Alice down.

"I'm trying," I murmured to the empty room. "I could just use a clue or two, okay?"

I pored through Alice's social media accounts, which remained active and were filled with people expressing their condolences. Beyond the pages of sympathetic friends posting comments and memories, I reached as far back as I could go but her privacy settings stopped me from seeing anything that wasn't public. I made a note to ask Roscoe if he knew her passwords. I scrolled through her list of online friends and found we had a lot of mutual acquaintances. Not surprising since we grew up in the same area. I copied all the names into a document and printed it off. The people who called themselves her online friends were as good a place as any to start a list of contacts for me to reach.

The evening wore on and I finally shut down my computer. Garrett called just as I was preparing for bed.

"You sound sad," he remarked.

"Not sad, really, just discouraged. I don't want to keep going back to that town but I feel like if I don't help find Alice, she'll never be found."

"This isn't all on you. Let law enforcement handle it. You don't have to—"

"I know I don't. I just feel like I should." I paused before adding, "I know I could sit back and let law enforcement try to find her, but it's been a couple years and I doubt it's high on their priority list since Roscoe's already in prison." I sighed. "It's just that I knew Alice in school. We weren't friends but we had similar home lives, if you know what I mean. Part of me feels I owe it to her."

"I'm sorry she had it rough," Garrett said. "But you still don't have to take on this case. This is Alice we're talking about. Not you."

"But it could've been me," I insisted. "A dozen times growing up I could've been murdered and thrown away. It was only luck and my own tenacity that I survived. I'd like to know that if I'd been killed, someone would've looked for my body. In Alice's case, I just feel like that someone has to be me."

"Okay." His voice softened. "I get that but I'd be lying if I didn't tell you that I'm worried about you."

"I'm handling it," I said. "I'm not drinking or freaking out. I'm just taking it on like any other job." I cleared my throat and pleaded, "Could we talk about something else?"

So I joked about Tracey going out with Ray and how nervous she was, and he talked about how they were wrapping things up on his case and he'd be home soon. Just the soothing sound of his voice caressed my heart in comfort and smoothed the sharp edges of my anxiety. Garrett told me how much he loved me and missed me and tears stung my eyes as I told him I missed him too. I crawled onto his side of the bed, giving up mine to Wookie, just so that I could breathe in the faint scent of my love.

I was just nodding off when Tracey called.

"Oh my God, I'm in lo-o-ove!" she shrieked.

"You are not." A smile played on my lips through my weary sigh.

"Well, maybe not love but if I'd had time to shave my legs, I would've dragged him into bed so fast it would've made his head spin."

I burst out laughing and listened while she talked about how he'd come to the door with a single rose and then they'd gone to dinner and taken a long walk in the rain afterward. How he'd asked first before taking her hand and hadn't even tried to give her another reading even though she wanted one.

"Sounds like you'll be seeing him again."

"Definitely. I was hoping for tomorrow but he said he's working on interviewing more people for this Alice thing and doesn't want to be distracted."

"That's very noble of him."

"Yeah, that's what I thought!" She sighed. "Oh! By the way, I love the website."

I thought back to checking his online presence that first time we met and didn't remember anything spectacular about it. "I saw his site but I guess I didn't take that close a look," I admitted.

"No-o-o-o, *your* site. Both of yours. The Julie and Ray site."

"The what?" I bolted upright in bed.

"Uh oh, I hope I didn't blow the surprise. He did say it wasn't live yet."

"Text me the link right now," I told her and hung up.

Seconds later her text showed up and I clicked on the website.

"You've got to be kidding me!" I growled.

Ray Hughes had taken the time to do a website that basically sold us as a team. The page opened with a split screen with his picture and bio on the left and mine on the right. He'd taken my photo and biography right off my own website. There was a tab at the top that said: Click Here for More Information. When I did, the page opened a new page with a description that read that Ray and Julie were making it their mission to help the loved ones of missing people, both alive and deceased, and to Contact Us Now for Help in bold print that pulsed with light.

I could feel a vein pulsing at my temple as I seethed at the audacity.

"Enough is enough," I snarled.

This time Ray had gone too far.

# EIGHT

I CALLED RAY'S phone number and he picked up immediately.

"You've got a very special friend there," he began without a hello. "I'm just blown away by her...her spirit and...and her joyful love of life."

"Yeah, she's terrific, but I'm not calling about Tracey." I tried to keep my voice hard but he sounded as sappy and goofy as Tracey so I could feel my anger diminish. "She told me about the website and—"

"Oh wow, I completely forgot to ask her to keep it under wraps. I was just playing around, Julie. Trust me, I would never, ever put up something like that without discussing it with you first. The site isn't live, as you can see, I was just thinking of the future, and well, I got carried away. Honestly, it's just me getting my hopes up and playing around online."

I exhaled loudly. "Look, Ray, I appreciate your help in finding Alice. Really. But I usually prefer to work entirely on my own."

"I get that, and hey, I've been the same way but don't you find it overwhelming?"

"All the requests?"

"Yeah, all the people you have to turn away because it's not possible to help everyone." He paused. "It kind of breaks my heart, you know? I just thought maybe one day, if we teamed up, we could help so many more of those people who are hurting than we do working alone."

Ugh. When he put it that way, it did make me think his idea wasn't completely horrible and that maybe I was the selfish one.

"I'm not giving you a definite no," I said slowly. "All I'm saying is let's get one case done before we go off thinking about building some kind of partnership."

"Absolutely! From now, I'll only focus on finding Alice."

"I'd appreciate that." I took a deep breath. "I'm going up to Ozette tomorrow to talk to Roscoe."

"Good idea. Although, you know you don't have to drive all the way there. You could do a Skype visitation."

"I prefer to get a feel for his reaction when he's sitting across from me."

"Sure." Ray added, "I think I'll try to find Alice's sister. You heard about her, right? She killed their dad and just got out of the pen before Alice was murdered."

"Yes, and I already talked to Lois." I thought about Ray and his overenthusiastic approach to everything. "Could you just leave her to me? It took a lot to get her to talk to me about Alice and I have a feeling that if you go to talk to her too, she's just going to spook and shut down."

"Sure. I'll leave her one hundred percent to you," he promised. "I'll cross her off my list."

I thanked him, and after the call ended, I lay in bed staring at the ceiling, trying to figure out big decisions in my life and hoping there was a magic wand that could solve it all. I tossed and turned throughout the night.

Wookie's steamy hot breath in my face dragged me from sleep land too early in the morning. I put out food for him and Fluffy, and after they ate, I snapped a leash on the dog and took him for a walk around the neighborhood. Wookie kept looking up at me, wondering when we were going to break into a run, but today that wasn't going to happen.

"Sorry, boy, I just don't have it in me today."

My body was tired and my mind even more so. When we got back, I grabbed my pack for the long drive to the Ozette Corrections Center.

I was halfway to the prison when Garrett called me.

"Hey, I'm home but you're not?"

"Awww." My heart fell just a bit because I could've used a day spent in his arms. "You're home, and meanwhile your girlfriend is on her way to prison."

I laughed and brought him up to speed on wanting to touch base with Roscoe to see if he'd heard the rumors of Alice's cheating and whether or not he could shed light on if those were true. I hoped that one look on his face would give me the answer even if he was willing to lie about it.

"And what if you find out he knew she cheated and that gave him a solid motive? Are you willing to accept he's the murderer?"

"Sure, I've always believed there's a good chance he's guilty. You can't ignore the murder weapon was his sword and the blood was in his truck. Like I told you last night, I still want to try to find her body."

"I know but I hate the idea of you continuing to tor-

ture yourself by going back there. Have you talked to
Dr. Chen about what's going on?" His tone was gentle and filled with concern for my mental health, and
I hated that all my failings as an alcoholic had placed
some of that worry in his voice.

"Kind of," I said. "I'm trying to look at it as being
cathartic. You know, a way to leave behind that place
with a positive note by helping someone I knew." When
he didn't reply right away I added, "I don't expect you
to understand but I will give myself a time limit, okay?
If I don't find Alice's remains in the next few days, I'll
return the deposit and walk away. Deal?"

"Deal."

"Did you wrap things up on your case or are you hitting the road again?"

"I'll be here for the night," he said. "Then I need to
leave in the morning to tie up a few loose ends before
taking a few days off."

"I can't wait until you're all mine for a few days,"
I told him honestly and hoped by then I could lay the
Alice mystery to rest as well.

We said goodbye and I exhaled in relief. I always
missed him when he was away doing FBI stuff, but
knowing he'd be there later today gave me something
to look forward to.

I arrived at Ozette and was impatient through the
visitor intake procedure, and by the time I was in front
of Roscoe I wasn't willing to waste any time with small
talk.

"Tell me about Alice's lover." I tugged out a chair
across from him and took a seat.

"I don't know what you're talking about." Roscoe

leaned back in his chair, rocking it onto the back legs, and gave me a cool look. "You think I'm the kind of guy who'd put up with a cheating wife?"

"Well, you didn't put up with it, did you? You kicked her out, and next thing you know, she's dead."

He was sporting a fresh black eye that was nearly swollen shut, so when he attempted to roll his eyes it looked painful.

"Roscoe, if you want me to find her body so that you have a hope in hell of getting out of here..." I leaned forward on the table. "You need to be completely straight with me. No more screwing around."

A guard walked by and tapped him on the shoulder so Roscoe brought his chair back upright and frowned at me. Beneath the frown was a flurry of other emotions I couldn't quite read. I waited a full minute before speaking again.

"I don't need this. You're lying to me and it's written all over your face. You can't expect me to find Alice when I don't have all the information." I pointed a finger at him. "Tell you what, I'll drop the case and Kim can use the money to help pay for your mother's care home, and then you can cool your jets in your cell forever for all I care."

I moved to get up from my chair, and he put up both hands and made a motion for me to take a seat.

"This is hard for me to say." Roscoe's voice was so low I had to lean in to hear him. I waited and resisted the urge to drum my fingers on the table between us. Finally, he continued, his voice even lower. "I told you she wanted kids."

"Yes." *Spit it out for God's sake.*

"Well, so did I but…" He cleared his throat. "I couldn't. I had bad swimmers so…" He shrugged. "Baby making wasn't in my equation. I suggested adoption and she wasn't completely against it, but she kept saying she wanted the pregnancy experience. She wanted to feel what it was like to have a baby grow inside her." He sighed. "I hated that look on her face when she knew it wasn't in the cards for us and it all came down to money. Made me feel even less of a man than being the entire reason she couldn't get pregnant in the first place."

He tilted his head from side to side until his neck cracked loudly, and then he finished, "So she bought some kits that would tell her exactly when she was ovulating and we agreed that she would find some dude and, you know…" He made a circle with one hand and crudely gestured with his finger in the other inserting it into the circle.

"She slept with someone with your blessing so she could get knocked up."

"Yup." He cleared his throat. "I never told a single soul about that."

"But maybe that guy is the one who killed her," I hissed. "Did you think about that?"

"Dude, of course I did, but I told her I didn't want to know nothing about the guy. Not his name, what he looked like or anything about him, so it's not like I had someone else I could point the cops to, you know?" Roscoe licked his lips. "So when she got pregnant, I thought I'd be okay, right? We could go around telling everyone it was ours and nobody would be the wiser. Except it didn't happen. She met with some guy a time or two but every month when she found out she wasn't pregnant, she got sadder and sadder, and the entire situation just made me angry. She's out doing the between-the-sheets tango with someone else and it was just killing me. I told her she had to stop and she agreed. She hated it too. So we got Jet, but of course that didn't fix things. A dog ain't a baby no matter how hard you try to make it that way."

"And you honestly know nothing about this guy? Was he local or did she travel to meet him?"

"I swear I have no idea who he is. I made her promise that the guy wasn't going to be someone from our area. Last thing I wanted was to raise my kid and constantly be wondering if the guy we just walked by on the street was his daddy, right?"

"So she stopped trying and you got the dog and…" I knew there was something else.

"She tried another time without telling me." His lips formed a thin white line of rage. "She did tell me when she peed on the stick and it came back positive. How could I be mad then? She was walking on air, yanno? But a week after the pregnancy test confirmed she was pregnant, she had a miscarriage and she just went dark after that. There was nothing left inside her but anger and resentment. Every time she looked at me, it felt like she was blaming me for not giving her what she wanted. I couldn't take it anymore so I kicked her out. It killed me."

"Who else knew?" I asked Roscoe.

"Nobody. That was part of the deal." He rubbed his hands over his jumpsuit-covered arms as if he was cold. "She had to hide it. I didn't want nobody knowing she was sleeping around."

"But people in town obviously found out, so one of you must've told someone to get those rumors started. A best friend? Your sister? It's almost impossible to be that discreet when you're in a city that size."

"I wouldn't have told anyone if you set me on fire. Jesus, how embarrassed do you think I was, letting my wife sleep around to get knocked up? And I don't think Alice would tell anyone either. We loved each other. I know that's hard to believe but it's true. We were totally on board raising a kid together and living the happily ever after. Anyone knowing would've screwed that up."

His voice was firm and I began to believe he was telling the truth. At least I knew that was what he believed, but if there were rumors going around that she cheated, those must've formulated somewhere and somehow. I asked how he thought the rumors could've started, and he only gave an elaborate shrug.

"Whoever she screwed…" Roscoe rubbed his head. "That's all I can figure. It must've been him telling people."

That's what I thought too. "Unless someone saw them together."

"She said she was careful, but sure, anything's possible, right? It's not like she was an expert at sneaking around. She promised to go out of our community and that it wouldn't be anyone I knew. She said she even used a fake name but I guess that doesn't mean somebody didn't spot her somewhere." His eyes grew hard. "I'll tell you this, if I get out of here I will find whoever killed Alice and it'll be worth it to get slammed back in here just to be able to put my hands around their throat and—"

I cut him off. "Did Alice have a best friend? Some-one she met for coffee regularly? Someone from work she got pedicures with? This was a pretty big secret to try and hide."

"Nobody. Alice kept to herself. She was all about family and she had none of her own, unless you count the half sister who killed her dad. She was friendly to people but she wasn't a girly girl, and she had trust is-sues, know what I mean?"

I knew exactly what he meant. "Maybe she arranged her meeting with this guy through social media. I know the cops probably looked through her Facebook and Instagram accounts but I wouldn't mind searching to see if anything pops up. I don't suppose you know her login and passwords."

He rattled off her email address for the login infor-mation and then added, "As for the password…" He rubbed the back of his neck with a frown. "As I told the cops when they asked, she used the same password for just about everything. I used to give her heck about that because, yanno, hackers and stuff."

"What was the password?"

"Her middle name. Jeanie."

"Okay, I'll look into her accounts and see what I can find. So there's nobody you can think of who she'd share her secrets with?"

He looked up at the ceiling as if the answer might be written up there somewhere.

"If she was gonna tell anyone…" He pointed a finger at me. "And that's a big if, she would've told my mom. I asked her not to, but at the time she said, 'Who is she gonna tell?' on account of Mom couldn't talk after her stroke. She can hear fine but just can't talk."

"She was close to your mom?"

"Yeah." Roscoe scrubbed his hands across his face, as if trying to wipe away any emotion. "My mom liked her way better than she liked me or Kim even."

I slowly nodded as I absorbed that information. Could a woman in a rest home who didn't have speech have the ability to spread gossip? There was only one way to find out.

"Which care home is your mom in?"

Roscoe gave me the name of one in Bellingham and I got to my feet.

"It's hopeless, isn't it?" His voice sounded dejected as he spoke on a long exhale.

Something in the emotional way he'd spoken about Alice screwing some guy just to get pregnant, and the venom behind the way he wanted to get his hands on whoever hurt Alice made me realize either he loved her, or he was an excellent actor. And I didn't think Roscoe was smart enough to put on this kind of a show.

"I'm going to keep trying," I told him as a goodbye.

But I had to admit that I didn't feel confident.

On the drive back I was reviewing everything I learned while focusing on getting home to Garrett. I wanted to be in his arms to cleanse away the filthy feeling I'd had in dealing with my hometown and this entire case. I was less than a mile from where I'd found Rachel Wu's body in the ditch and decided to go into a small coffee shop.

As I was paying for juice and a muffin, a hand on

my shoulder caused me to jump. I turned to see the officer who'd shown up at Rachel Wu's scene.

"I've been wanting to call you. Do you have a second?" he asked.

"Sure."

I took my food to a table and waited for him to grab a coffee and join me.

"You talked to Rachel Wu's folks."

"Yes." I nodded. "I went to their house. They wanted to thank me for finding their daughter."

"And?" he asked.

"Well, they were understandably distraught."

"Did they mention anything about drugs?"

"They know she shouldn't have been driving. Apparently she had a history of drug and alcohol abuse. Why? She had drugs in her system?"

"Yes. Heroin."

"Guess that explains why she drove off the road."

"Yeah." He took a sip from his coffee.

It felt like there was something he wasn't saying so I just nibbled on my muffin and waited for him to speak.

"Just seemed too tidy, you know?" He put his coffee cup down. "No skid marks so she didn't brake on the turn before going down the embankment. A small packet of black tar laced with fentanyl sitting prettily on the passenger seat next to her."

"You're saying the heroin with fentanyl is what killed her?"

"Yeah. A lethal dose."

"So it was the drugs that killed her, not the car wreck?"

He nodded. "Her mom and dad said she'd returned

to school after getting clean. Too bad she couldn't have stayed that way."

"Sometimes it's not that easy," I murmured. I wanted to tell him that addiction wasn't that tidy. Wine was my personal kryptonite but there wasn't a bottle of booze I wouldn't reach for when I fell off the wagon.

"Right. All it took is her to give in to temptation one last time." He rubbed the back of his neck and frowned. "Anyway, thanks for leading us to her. Appreciate it." He took another sip of his coffee. "Once a junkie always a junkie, I guess."

I really hoped not.

He left the coffee shop, leaving me to wonder about Rachel Wu and feel bad that she'd left a promising life for a quick thrill from the needle. I understood her need, but it didn't make it easier to swallow.

My heart skipped a beat of joy when I got home and saw Garrett's vehicle in the driveway, but I didn't find him inside. Wookie was also gone so he'd taken the dog for a walk. As soon as he returned, I wrapped my arms around his neck and kissed him hard.

"I missed you too," he said against my mouth as I took a breath between kisses. He held me at arm's length then and looked me in the eyes. "What's wrong?"

"Why does something have to be wrong?" I ran a hand through my hair and forced a laugh. "I've just been to prison. It shook me up a bit that's all."

"How were things at Ozette?"

We took seats at the kitchen table while I told the story of Alice and Roscoe and their unorthodox attempt to have a child. Garrett listened carefully, his soft eyes taking in everything I said and everything I didn't.

"I doubt having a baby would've saved them." Garrett shook his head. "Sounds like they already had issues."

"Yes. Babies change everything."

He briefly got that faraway look on his face. That sad, dreamy way his face got when he remembered back to when he had a wife and a child before they were torn from this planet by a drunk driver. Just as quickly, the gloomy look was gone and he was focused back on me.

"This case is taking a toll on you." He took my hand across the table. "You're no closer to finding Alice than when you started."

"Not true. I've discovered dozens of places where she is not."

He laughed, gave my hand a squeeze, then lifted it to his lips to tenderly kiss the space where my ring would've been. A shameful reminder.

"I'm starved," he announced and got up to start dinner.

He'd stopped at the grocery store on his way home and went to work browning ground beef for a pasta sauce while I chopped mushrooms and onions. I sank into the gentle domesticity of making a meal together.

If Garrett had been away at work, I would've spent the evening researching maps of the areas Alice might be and reviewing notes I'd made about things people had told me. Instead, we curled up on the sofa and watched an old movie with his arm around my shoulders. There were a hundred things I wanted to say but the words couldn't find their way from my head to my lips, so I sighed into his arms and enjoyed having my man home.

The next morning I was woken with a kiss on the cheek. When my eyelids fluttered open, Garrett was standing beside the bed smiling. He was fully clothed and had his briefcase in his hands. "I have to get to work."

I sat up, picked up my cell phone and blinked at the time. Nearly ten. "Oh my God!"

"Yeah, I didn't have the heart to wake you." He rubbed one of my shoulders. "You were tossing and turning in the night. I think you were having bad dreams."

A blurry vision crept into my mind.

*I stumbled out of the washroom, my face still damp from splashing water on it. The man was waiting for me. His face was a blur covered by his long hair and a fuzzy beard as he guided me back to our booth. I was trying so hard to sober up. I gave my head a hard shake, and the world tilted. I saw he was holding something in the palm of his hand.*

"The critters have both been fed," Garrett continued, breaking into my memory. "I took Wookie for a good hard run so you can rest. Looks like you must need it."

"Thank you, baby." I swung my legs out of bed, shaking away the dark images. "I can't believe I slept that long."

"I hope you're not coming down with something."

I got to my feet and he took me in his arms and kissed my neck.

"No fever..." He kissed me on the cheek. "I'll be back tomorrow night. Try not to overdo it while I'm gone."

I walked to the kitchen and watched his car back

out of the driveway as I poured myself a glass of water. My mind began to drift back to Wayland and I shouted, "Stop!" to halt the flood of unfocused memories. Instead, I found something happier to think about. It was one of many techniques Dr. Chen taught me to help get rid of intrusive thoughts.

I checked my phone and saw that Tracey had texted me. She had the day off and wanted to get together. I replied that I was going to visit Roscoe's mother in a seniors' home. Almost immediately she called.

"I'll come with you," she said. "I'm great with old farts."

"Probably not so great if you call them that." I laughed. "It's in Bellingham. You sure you want to go all that way?"

"I've got nothing else to do. Plus, you'll be my captive audience while I fill you in on the saga of me and Ray."

"You two are a saga now?"

"At the very least we're a kind of X-rated miniseries." She laughed and ended the call after telling me she'd be over in half an hour.

By the time I'd dressed and double-checked I had everything in my backpack, Tracey was at my door. She came inside briefly to give Fluffy some cuddles and offer Wookie some scratches behind his ears and then we were climbing into my Jeep.

"Okay, let's get this over with." I put the Jeep in reverse. "How did you and Ray go from having a romantic first date to being an X-rated miniseries?"

"It's called a booty call."

She said it with such a straight face that laughter exploded from my lips.

"Who called who?"

"Well, he called me and asked if I wanted to go out for a drink last night. I told him I wasn't feeling like going out but he was more than welcome to come to my apartment. Next thing you know…" A smile lit her face.

"You hardly know each other." I didn't want to tamp down her delirious happiness so I quickly added, "I don't mean that in a prudish way. I just don't want to see you get hurt."

"You definitely do mean it in a prudish way," Tracey said with a giggle. "Because even though we're the same age, we both know that you're an old woman in a young woman's body. That's okay though." She reached over and patted my arm. "I know you worry about me. It's not like we're running off to get married. Right now I'm just having fun. And also having really good sex."

I laughed even harder, but then I stopped mid giggle. "There's no one else around, so why does this guy have to ride my tail?"

A blue van with tinted windows was following so close on I-5 that I couldn't even catch his license plate number in my rearview mirror. I moved to the left lane and he followed. I accelerated and the van did also. Finally, I took an exit off I-5 and the van kept going.

"What a jerk," Tracey snarled. Then her phone chimed and she was giggling and texting.

I pulled into a convenience store and bought a snack. When I returned to the vehicle, Tracey was still smiling at her phone and sending messages.

"Still texting lover boy?"

Tracey sighed dreamily when her phone again chimed an incoming text.

"Yes, that's Ray again." She tapped away on her phone. "We might see each other again this evening," she said as she tucked her phone into her purse. "He's going to interview a few more people today up in Blaine."

"Okay."

"He said you weren't thrilled about the website. Sorry about that. I should've let him explain it to you."

"I was just—" furious "—surprised, I guess. I'm not exactly into a partnership at this point, but…" I quickly added, "If I change my mind, he'd definitely be someone I'd consider teaming up with. I just don't think we need to rush it. Let's at least find Alice before we start declaring to the world what an excellent team we are."

"I can see your point," Tracey said. "The way Ray talks about you, I can tell he's in awe of your dowsing abilities. Guess he's got some fanboy worshipping going on because he gets to work with the great Julie Hall."

"Ha!" I rolled my eyes at that.

The location of the care home was a few blocks down the road from a large shopping mall. Cross-border shoppers looking for bargains created gridlock until we were past the mall area.

I pulled into the parking lot of the care home. It was a modern gray stucco building tucked behind a sculpted cedar hedge.

"What's the plan?" Tracey asked.

"We're going to see Margaret Ebert. Roscoe's mother. Apparently she was quite close with Alice but unfortunately she had a stroke and can't talk."

"How are we going to get any information out of her if she can't talk?"

"I have no idea."

We walked into the building, and I told the front desk receptionist who we were wanting to see. We waited a few minutes until someone came to get us.

"Margaret doesn't get many visitors," the young woman told us as she led us down a hallway. "Are you family?"

"Friends of the family," I replied, which was almost true.

"Then you know her stroke left her unable to speak. She doesn't have the ability to write either, but her mind is still pretty sharp."

The facility shone with the glow of bright artificial lighting and smelled sharply of floor cleaner and urine. Some of the residents were out shuffling around and others were slumped in chairs. We were brought into a semiprivate room and passed a woman curled on her side in her bed. Beyond the room divider we found Margaret Ebert sitting belted into a chair next to the window, staring up at a television.

"Margaret, these nice women are here to visit," the employee said.

Margaret had short-cropped white hair, a sunken face, and wore flannel pajamas and a thick housecoat. One side of her face was slack and her right hand hung limply off the side of the chair. She looked away from the television to scrape her eyes over me and Tracey and then returned her gaze to the TV.

"How about we get your teeth in?" the woman suggested. "You always feel better that way."

The worker disappeared into a washroom and returned with Margaret's teeth. She installed them in Margaret's mouth and pronounced her ready to receive company.

The worker walked over to a counter and picked up a large board that had dozens of picture squares. One corner of the square had *yes* in large letters and the other corner had *no*. The rest of the squares were pictures of things like a bed, a plate of food, a drink, many pictures representing things like pain, family as well as emotions from tired, sad or lonely to angry, bored or happy.

"Try to ask her questions she can answer with her board," the worker told me. She pulled a small table in front of Margaret and placed the board on the table. Tracey and I took seats on either side of the old woman.

"I'm Julie Hall," I told her. "Kim told me that you and your deceased husband are the ones paying me to try and find Alice."

That got Margaret's attention. She made a clacking sound with her dentures as she regarded me with sharp eyes. Her hand was a gnarled knot but it moved slowly and deliberately to tap the board in the corner that had the word *yes*.

Maybe this wouldn't be as bad as I thought.

"I haven't had much luck finding Alice's body," I told her.

Margaret selected a box that had a picture of a teary face and the word *sad* under it.

"Yes, it's sad. I know you believe Roscoe is innocent, but honestly all I'm trying to do is find Alice. Hopefully if I can find her body, that will prove the identity of the killer."

Again, Margaret tapped the box that said *yes*.

Tracey's phone began ringing and she dug it out of her purse.

"Just a sec, sweetie," Tracey said into the phone and then she got to her feet and said to me, "I'll wait for you in the entranceway, okay?"

"Sure."

Margaret looked at Tracey and then at me and rolled her eyes and I smiled.

"Yeah, she's all about some guy right now."

Margaret tapped a box that had a laughing face that said *funny*.

"She's a riot," I admitted. "Now about Alice…" I brought my chair in a little closer. "I understand you two were close."

Margaret's knotted fist tapped *yes* then a box for *family* and then one for *sad*.

"She came to visit you sometimes?"

Margaret indicated *yes* and again *sad*.

"Did you know about her trying to get pregnant?" I asked.

Margaret clicked her dentures and hesitated before again pointing to *yes* and *sad* and then, lastly, one that said *baby*.

"I understand from Roscoe that he was not able to get Alice pregnant and before they separated they'd decided to get her pregnant in a different kind of way." I paused before adding, "With someone else." I watched her face. "Roscoe said they told nobody, but I wonder if Alice might have shared that with you?"

The lines between Margaret's eyebrows deepened with worry and she began to rock back and forth as she clicked her dentures. Finally, she selected *yes* on the board and then *mad* followed by *food*.

"I'm confused…"

Margaret quickly pointed to the boxes for *yes*, *mad* and *food* again.

Was she angry because she was hungry? I tried to refocus her attention with a yes or no question.

"So Alice *did* tell you about sleeping with someone else to try and get pregnant?"

Margaret chose *yes*.

"Did she tell you who that was?"

Margaret hit *food food food* and grunted with agitation.

"Okay, um, are you hungry? Do you want me to tell someone?"

Margaret smacked the board hard at *no* but then pounded on *food food food*. She was getting more and more frantic.

Maybe she was trying to send me a message.

"The person who Alice was sleeping with to try and get pregnant, was it someone who worked at the diner? With food?"

Margaret smacked the *no* on the board but then again hit *food food food*. Spittle flew from her mouth as she began making groaning noises and pounding her fist against the board. Obviously, the conversation was horribly traumatizing for her, and I felt devastated for making her so anxious.

"Thank you for your time, Mrs. Ebert. I'm sorry to have upset you."

She all but growled then knocked the entire board to the floor. I hurriedly left the room and went in search of the worker who'd brought us to Margaret's room. I found her down the hall.

"I'm sorry, Margaret seems very agitated. Maybe visiting wasn't such a good idea."

"Really? She's usually so calm." She frowned with worry.

"She kept indicating *food* on her board," I added. "Maybe she's just hungry. I'm going to leave now."

"I'll check on her."

As I walked back down the hall in the direction we'd come I hoped that Margaret wasn't too upset by my Alice discussion. I rushed to the front foyer, where I found Tracey sitting on a corner bench scrolling through her phone. She looked up as I got close.

"Any luck?"

"Not much. She confirmed that she knew Alice was trying to get pregnant, but she just kind of lost it when I asked her if she knew who Alice was sleeping with. She got pretty agitated. I'm not sure but she kept hitting the *food* square on her communication board. Maybe I should check back at the diner. Who knows? Maybe she was with one of the cooks there or something. I know it sounds like a reach but I don't know what else it could mean." I frowned, thinking about poor Margaret's distress. "Let's go."

It was raining hard and Tracey and I jogged across the parking lot toward the Jeep. I had my head down until I pulled the key fob from my pocket. When I pointed it at the vehicle to unlock the doors, I looked up and stopped dead in my tracks.

Tracey nearly ran right into me because I'd stopped short. Then she saw what had halted me.

"Oh my God!" Tracey shrieked.

The deluge of icy rain came sideways and thoroughly soaked me as I stood staring at my Jeep. Someone had taken red spray paint and vandalized the entire side of my vehicle with dripping red paint that read LEAVE ALICE ALONE OR YOU'RE NEXT!

# NINE

THE SPRAY-PAINTED lettering took up the entire driver side of the Jeep. The passenger side was no better with STOP LOOKING OR DIE!

"Holy smokes, you've obviously hit a sore spot with someone!" Tracey gasped.

"Definitely."

My voice was surprisingly calm, but my heart thudded painfully as we turned around and walked back into the care home to call the police. When officers arrived, they took pictures of my vehicle and asked a lot of questions. They asked the manager of the care home to take a look at the footage from their security cameras. Sadly, the security cameras in the parking lot hadn't worked in some time and there was really nothing else they could do.

"My insurance company already hates me," I moaned.

"I guess we're heading home," Tracey said. "You can't be driving around like this." She waved a hand at the Jeep.

"I'll call the insurance company and drop it off at a body shop later, but since we're almost there already, I want to go visit Kim."

"Roscoe's sister? Why?"

"She was the first person to say that Alice was cheating on Roscoe. I swear she knows more than what she's been saying."

And I wanted to see the look on her face when I shared what Roscoe told me about the arrangement he had with Alice.

I waited until I was pulling off the highway near her trailer to call Kim. "I'm close by and have a couple questions," I told her.

"I'm just on my way home from the store," Kim's voice came through the speakers of the Jeep. "Give me ten minutes."

We were at her place in five. I put the Jeep in park and we sat listening to the rain pound the Jeep.

"Jesus, how could anyone live like that? Depressing or what?" Tracey said with wonder as she stared at Kim's singlewide trailer.

I saw it through her eyes: the wooden steps leading to the door sitting askew and ready to collapse, the siding of the trailer almost completely covered in blackened streaks of West Coast algae. A power washer and a hammer would've done a lot to make it look like someone cared, but nobody did.

"It's pretty much like mine was," I murmured. "Mine was better maintained, but otherwise it could've been identical."

"I'm sorry." Tracey cringed. "I didn't mean—"

"Yes, you did, and that's okay." I looked at her and smiled. "Sometimes you can't see the awful when you're mired in it. Not that living in a trailer is bad. I loved mine. It was cozy. No annoying neighbors or street traffic…" My voice grew wistful as I looked at the mobile home. "I never let mine get covered in algae like that though. Gramps and I…" I swallowed against his name, and conflicting emotions roared in my head. "We, um, power washed every spring so…" My voice trailed off and my thumb reached to play with the platinum band on my ring finger that wasn't there.

Finally, Kim rolled up in her car and I flung the door to the Jeep open, happy to stand in the downpour rather than deal with the raging memories in my head. Tracey followed.

"What happened?" Kim held a hand up to shield her eyes from the rain and nodded a chin toward my van-dalized Jeep.

We jogged toward the trailer and Kim fumbled with her bright keychain before we got inside.

"I see somebody did a number on your car." Kim shook her head. "When did that happen?"

"Just now," Tracey said. "When we were at the care home."

"This is my friend Tracey," I told Kim.

Kim nodded hello as we all stood in the cramped entrance and toed off our shoes.

"Come in," she said. "Sorry about the mess."

The living room area looked the same as it had last time I was here, and Kim made no attempt to clear laun-dry off the sofa so we could sit. I shoved everything to one corner and Tracey and I sat hip to hip.

"So you went to the care home?" Kim asked, look-ing confused. "What did you expect to find out from a woman who can't talk?"

"It wasn't helpful," I admitted with a forced laugh. "I wanted to ask your mom if she knew that Roscoe and Alice had an arrangement."

"An arrangement?" Kim tilted her head and then leaned back to release the footrest of her recliner. "What are you talking about? What kind of arrangement?"

"The kind where she would sleep with somebody else in order to get knocked up and then they'd raise the baby as both of theirs."

Kim drummed her fingers on the armrest and guffawed. "That's the stupidest thing I ever heard. Who the hell told you that?" she scoffed.

"Roscoe. I drove up to visit him yesterday and he confirmed it." I watched her face. The shock looked genuine and was quickly replaced by anger.

"Sounds like he's just messing with your head." She snorted. "If they'd really had an arrangement like that, Roscoe would've told me. He would've told his lawyer too! The lawyer would've been able to say whoever Alice was banging was responsible for her death."

"He didn't want people to know he couldn't get Alice pregnant and that he'd given her permission to have sex with other men. It was a stupid pride thing."

"You're saying my brother went to prison to save his friggin' pride?" She rolled her eyes. "I always knew that boy's elevator didn't go to the top floor." She sat up and slammed the footrest of her chair closed as she got to her feet. "Still, that doesn't make sense."

Kim went to the kitchen counter and retrieved an electric heating pad. She moved a couple troll dolls carefully aside so that she could drape the cord over the end table and plug the heating pad in next to her chair, then placed it at her lower back. "I think he sold you a line of bull."

"Men can be pretty egotistic about that kind of thing," Tracey remarked.

Kim looked startled as if she'd completely forgotten Tracey was there. She ignored the comment.

"Plus, also," I added, "Roscoe was positive whoever she was sleeping with wasn't responsible."

"How could he possibly know that?" Kim scoffed.

"He said they had a deal it would happen out of town, with someone neither of them knew, and she'd use a fake name."

Kim pinched her lips together into a thin line and scratched at the angry, scaly rash on her neck.

"Look, you were the first to tell me Alice was messing around. You said she was humping everyone in town, remember?"

Kim closed her eyes and nodded.

"I need to know who told you that so that I can follow the thread of rumors to the source. It might be nothing, but it could be someone who knows more about who Alice slept with and possibly her killer."

"I have no idea." Kim sighed and shook her head. "I honestly can't remember if her cheating was something I just kind of latched on to myself, or if someone actually told me. I didn't like Alice—not that I want to speak ill of the dead, but she acted like she was better than me. Always sucking up to me and my stepdad like we were her new family. Worked on him, he treated her like his daughter but I wasn't buying it. Anyway maybe I just made that up. The way Roscoe was so head over heels for her and then suddenly just kicked her out, I guess I might've assumed there was somebody else."

"Okay." I got to my feet then. "Give it some thought and let me know if a name comes to mind."

"I will," Kim promised.

"Mind if I use your washroom?" I asked.

Kim nodded to the door down the short hall. The tiny bathroom was eerily identical to the one I'd had in my trailer except it was in poor shape. The cupboard door under the sink hung off-kilter because the top hinge was broken. My view from the toilet allowed me to see right inside the cabinet, and the dim bathroom light danced off something with sequins inside. I didn't want to even know what kind of sparkly objects Kim kept under her bathroom sink. I washed up using perfumed hand soap and dried my fingers on a threadbare towel.

"Thanks," I said as I left the bathroom. "I'll be in touch."

Tracey and I ran through the rain to the car and I steered back to the road. After a while the rain slowed to a drizzle and Tracey and I were silent as we drove the Jeep down the water-filled ruts on the long drive. It wasn't until we were on the highway that we spoke.

"What in the world is with those creepy troll dolls?" Tracey shuddered.

"They sure wouldn't be my choice for a collection," I admitted. "More importantly, why is she lying?"

"You think she knew Alice was stepping out on Roscoe?"

"Yeah."

"How can you tell?"

"I just feel it." I drummed my fingers on the steering wheel. "But what's in my gut isn't going to help. I need to know who Alice was sleeping with." I spoke to the voice dial feature in the Jeep and told it to call Ray. My call went to voice mail.

"Hey, I want to talk to you about what information you got from Barb. I need a name of who she thinks Alice was screwing. Failing that, I need to at least know who spread that rumor." I disconnected the call and looked over at Tracey. "Hungry? We're going to the diner."

As it happened, Barb wasn't working. According to Dana, she'd called in sick because of a migraine.

"I'm not buying it though," she leaned in to the table and whispered to us. "I heard her messed-up son is in town and she's meeting with him to try to save his soul."

"How is he messed up?" Tracey asked on a whisper. "Is it crack? Heroin?"

"I think it's a mental thing." Dana tapped her temple with her fingertip.

I really didn't care about Barb's son but I was disappointed not to get a chance to ask her about Alice. Although chances were good that she wouldn't have answered me anyway.

"Did Barb ever tell you that Alice was cheating on Roscoe?" I asked Dana.

She tapped the menus on the table and looked thoughtful.

"She's always going around blabbing about someone who's breaking one of the commandments. I usually just tune her out. Sorry." Dana handed us the menus and told us she'd be back in a minute to take our order.

"People like that really piss me off," Tracey harrumphed as she opened the menu. "That Barb should focus more on her own life and get her nose out of other people's business."

"I agree but in this particular case all we have to go on is gossip, so we're going to rake in as much of it as possible."

When Dana came back, we put in our order. I had my usual grilled cheese and Tracey ordered a burger.

"I went to visit Roscoe's mother in her care home."

"I heard she's mute since her stroke," Dana said.

"That's true but she can communicate using a board with pictures and words. As a matter of fact, when I asked her about Alice sleeping with someone she kept hitting the square for *food*. Was Alice hanging out with any men from here?"

"Not that I know of," Dana replied.

We ate mostly in silence. I was famished, and by the way Tracey devoured her burger, she was hungry too. Afterward when Dana brought the bill, I asked if she knew where Barb lived.

"Not exactly." She tapped a pen on the table. "I know her house is behind the mailbox place."

"Which one?" Since Blaine was a border city, there were a whole lot of these mailbox centers where Canadians came to pick up and mail packages.

"The one near Cost Cutters. Just look for an old blue minivan with Jesus fishes on it."

When we returned to my Jeep, we found the graffiti on the vehicle had attracted an audience. I pressed the key fob, and the gathering parted like the Red Sea and the clutch of a dozen onlookers wordlessly stared at us as we climbed into the car.

"That's kind of creepy." Tracey looked over her

shoulder at the gathering, who were now knotted to-gether and talking animatedly.

"Yeah, I'm giving this town a whole lot of mileage for things to talk about." I glanced at my gas gauge. "Damn. Need gas."

"There's a place right over—"

"Not that one," I stated emphatically.

My heart pounded at the very thought of pulling into the gas station where I used to work. I remembered Garrett picking me up from work there and driving me to go look for bodies long before he believed in me or I believed I could love a man of the law who was more than twenty years older.

"I couldn't walk in there even if you paid me." I avoided the closest station and drove a couple blocks to a different one, Tracey once again balancing the dows-ing rods on her lap.

"Seems like this entire town is one bad memory." Tracey tsked. "You don't have to take this case. I mean, you've gotta have dozens of people wanting you to find their loved ones, right?"

"It's Alice…"

She could've been me, killed in this town and body dumped somewhere after an abusive upbringing.

"I owe her," I added.

"But—"

"I'm giving it just a few more days, okay?" My tone was sharper than I intended so I softened my words. "If I can't find her within the week, I'm packing it in."

"I hope Ray can help you. He's really talented, you know? When we were out for dinner, he shook hands with the waiter and told me later that the guy didn't know it yet, but he had a serious liver disease." She looked at me sadly. "It must be a real challenge to try and stay out of it when you get vibrations giving you info on just about everyone."

"Yeah. That must be a tough gig." I was suddenly grateful for my own talent, which I could stuff in a backpack when I didn't want the dead calling to me.

We arrived near the strip mall that contained the mailbox place as well as the Cost Cutters grocery store. Up the hill and across the way was a cul-de-sac. I pulled on to the road. There were four small houses on the street but two were boarded up and looked ready for demolition. I drove slowly around to look for the blue van but didn't spot it.

"Hang on, that's Ray's car!"

Tracey pointed down one driveway to a white car parked in front of a tidy yellow house. I turned into the drive, and just as I was pulling up behind his car, Ray was walking down the sidewalk from the house. He approached my Jeep with his mouth open, and I rolled down my window when he got close.

"Oh my God, what happened to your Jeep?"

"Someone attacked Julie's car while we were interviewing Roscoe's mom at the care home," Tracey exclaimed excitedly.

"That's horrible." Ray took a step back, looked down the length of the car and whistled. "I can't believe someone would do that!"

"It sucks," I agreed.

"Did you call the police? The care home must have cameras in their lot, right?"

"Tried that but apparently the cameras at the care

home were out of order so we're out of luck." I nodded my chin to the house ahead. "Did you talk to Barb?"

"No." Ray leaned his elbows on the edge of my open window. "She's not home. Left a note in her mailbox for her to call me once she's back. Do you want me to let you know once I hear from her?"

I told him yes and he smiled around me to Tracey and gave her a wink. She replied with a giggle.

"Honestly, I think you should leave Barb to me," Ray added seriously. "She really doesn't like you." He cleared his throat. "Not that it's you, she's just, you know, is really against what she considers to be voo-doo shit. You're not going to get anything out of her."

"Okay. Surprised she'll talk to you," I remarked.

"Only because she doesn't know I'm reading her, re-member?" He wagged a finger at me and then pushed his glasses up his nose. "She just thinks she's holding my hands to pray over me."

"Yeah, I know." I nodded but it irked me.

"Sorry," Ray told me with a wave of his hand. "You've blocked me in and I really need to get going." He leaned to the side and said to Tracey, "I'll call you later."

We said our goodbyes and I backed out of the drive-way and watched Ray hurriedly drive off in a differ-ent direction.

I turned around in the cul-de-sac and got back on the main road.

"Could you pull into a store?" Tracey nodded to the strip mall across the way. "I need to use the washroom."

I turned the corner and entered the parking lot, find-ing a spot beside the shopping cart return area in front of the large grocery store. The Jeep was quite the sight with the red graffiti all over it, and people turned and openly stared.

"While I'm in there I might as well pick up a few things. Need anything?"

"No, I'm good. I'll just stay here feeding the gossip mill and letting the locals find some entertainment to discuss over dinner."

I offered a tight smile and wave to a nearby shopper, who'd paused to take a picture of the Jeep with her cell phone.

"Oh, brother." Tracey rolled her eyes and went off to the store.

The rain had let up and the sun warmed the interior of the vehicle. I rolled down the windows, leaned back in my seat and closed my eyes, trying to think of what to do next to find Alice. The slam of a shopping cart being thrust into another next to me startled me. I glanced over, surprised that it was Barb. I hopped out of the Jeep and followed her to her van.

"Barb!" I called out.

She looked over her shoulder as she reached the driver's door and pinched her lips together into a firm line when she saw it was me.

"I was wondering if I could ask you—"

"I have nothing to say to you," she said.

"I understand you know that Alice was cheating on Roscoe, and I was wondering if you knew who she was sleeping with?" It was a risky question because she hadn't actually told that to Ray, he'd only been able to get that information off her when he'd done a reading.

"I'm not a gossip, Ms. Hall, so I don't know who's

filling your head with lies." Barb looked around at the other shoppers walking nearby and waved to another older woman. "I'd appreciate it if you'd just leave well enough alone."

"You have a child. A son," I pushed.

"Don't talk about my—"

"If he was dead and his remains were missing, you'd want to give them a proper burial in a Christian cemetery, right? That's all I'm trying to do for Alice."

"Alice wasn't a Christian, and even if she was, it's too late for her now."

"But not for her family. They would like to see her remains found."

"Alice has no family to speak of, or hadn't you heard her father's dead and her mother took off to Florida to shack up with another adulterer? Like mother, like daughter."

"Like mother, like daughter? So you do know she was unfaithful to Roscoe. It would be so helpful to know who she was with. What if that person is the one who killed Alice and not Roscoe?"

She ignored me and when she opened the door to her van and climbed in, I stepped even closer so she couldn't close her door.

"Alice has a sister, Lois," I said, my mind racing. I hurriedly added, "Lois is a Christian. She found faith while in prison and she's looking to make things right for Alice by giving her a proper burial."

A number of emotions tripped across Barb's face. I could tell she was surprised by this revelation about Lois. Considering it was a complete fabrication on my part, she had a right to also have that skeptical look on her face.

"I heard Lois was out of prison, but I didn't know she was back in town."

"She's living in Bellingham," I said. "Working doing janitorial services and trying to live a decent life."

At least those statements were true.

"As I told you before, Ms. Hall, I have no interest in supporting you and your devil-worshipping dowsing rods." She stiffened her spine and put her hand on her door to close it. "I'm glad Lois has gotten right with the Lord but nothing I know could possibly help find Alice."

"It might though," I insisted. "If I can find out who Alice was stepping out with, that could lead me to find her body because it could connect me to her killer."

"No, it won't make one bit of difference," she said angrily. "Now, I've got groceries in my car and I need to get home to make a meal for my son."

With that, she slammed her van door shut, and I had to step out of the way or she would've backed right over me.

"She's a real piece of work, ain't she, Beanster?"

I turned to see Blossom unloading a shopping cart in the next stall.

"Don't get me wrong, she actually used to be kind of a cool lady. She even babysat me when I was younger." She opened the trunk of her car and put a couple grocery bags in it. "She'd make milk and cookies for us and stuff, but her son was such a wack job that I think she went chasing religion to try and help him. Not that it helped."

"She sure doesn't like me. All I want is to try and find Alice." I tilted my head. "Did you hear that Alice was sleeping around while she was married to Roscoe?"

"People say the stupidest things, don't they?" Blossom put her hands on her hips and smiled. "Alice loved that loser Roscoe. And Alice could not lie. If she tried to fib, she'd turn beet red. If I wanted to know if I looked good in my new jeans, I'd just ask Alice. She was too polite to say no, but if she said yes and then turned bright red, I knew she was telling a whopper."

"That doesn't answer my question, Blossom."

She sighed. "Alice didn't have it in her to have an affair. That would require being devious and secretive." She pointed a finger at me. "And, yes, I know about Roscoe giving her permission to get knocked up by somebody else."

"What? You knew that?" The look of stunned surprise on my face caused Blossom to giggle.

"Sure. She was my friend, you know. One night she told me all about how Roscoe had bad swimmers and couldn't get her pregnant. She was desperate to have a baby but even after he said she could get knocked up by someone else she said she just couldn't do it."

"But Roscoe said she *did* do it and even had a miscarriage before they split up."

"Well…" Blossom seemed to be weighing her words. "Alice knew I used to get around and she confided in me about the arrangement with Roscoe because she wanted me to fix her up with an ex or two."

"And did you?"

"I gave her a couple names and numbers of guys I

knew wouldn't have any trouble bedding her just for the fun of it."

"Do you think I could get those names?"

"Not a chance." Blossom laughed and walked around to her driver's door. "I know those guys and I know you'd only be pointing a finger their way as if they killed Alice. Which they didn't." She gave me a wave. "I've gotta go." She pointed at my Jeep. "And get yourself together, Beanster. Obviously, people are tired of you asking about Alice. You know how people say you can never come home again?" She smirked. "In your case I think that's true."

I walked back to my vandalized Jeep and watched Blossom squeal out of the lot.

"They had all their gluten-free stuff on sale," Tracey said as she opened the rear passenger door and unloaded four grocery bags. "I always feel better when I avoid gluten but it's so expensive to eat that way on a regular basis." She closed the back door and hopped into the passenger seat. "What's wrong? Why aren't you talking?"

"If it wasn't for the huge amount of blood found at the scene, I'd start to believe Alice faked her own death. Nothing about this makes sense. It's like this entire town is in on some big secret except me." I started up the Jeep and backed out of the spot. "Something about this Alice situation is all wrong."

"Well, sure, because she was killed but there's no body, and you're working for the guy who went to prison for killing her, so *everything* about this is so truly wrong."

"You're not helping."

I drove south toward home. Tracey turned on the radio and bopped along to a rap station while I seethed over everything I knew and didn't know about the case so far. When I took an exit, Tracey turned off the radio.

"We're going to Bellingham? Heading to that big mall? Because I'm always in the market for new shoes."

"We're not going to the mall. I want to talk to Alice's sister."

I accelerated to get to the office building for Alice's three o'clock start. We made it with only a few minutes to spare. I backed the Jeep into a spot behind the office building.

"This is where I met up with Lois when she was about to start her shift," I told Tracey. "She does janitorial services here."

"You've thought of different questions to ask her?"

"Same questions but I'm hoping for better answers."

An older Volkswagen Beetle pulled into the spot beside me and a forties woman climbed out. She was wearing the same blue cargo pants and white polo shirt with the logo that Lois had worn.

I jumped out of the Jeep and approached her. "Excuse me?"

"Yes?" She looked over her shoulder in my direction but kept walking. She had her hand on the door to the building before she stopped and eyed me suspiciously.

"I'm looking for Lois. Do you know if she's working today?"

"Who are you?" She let go of the door and folded her arms. She stole a glance at the Jeep and then shook her head. "I shouldn't be talking to you."

When she moved to open the door again, I pleaded with her.

"Wait! Please," I begged. "I'm just trying to help find her sister and I want to talk to Lois so that—"

"You ain't going to get nothing out of Lois," the woman said, exhaling loudly. "Someone broke into her apartment last night and sliced her to ribbons. She's barely hanging on at Bellingham Memorial."

I stood in stunned silence and could only stare after the woman's back as she disappeared inside the building. Climbing back behind the wheel of my car, I leaned forward and rested my head on the steering wheel.

"What is it?" Tracey asked.

"Someone attacked Lois last night."

"Oh my God, is she okay?"

"No." I straightened and looked at Tracey with my eyebrows drawn together in concern. "She's in the hospital. Someone broke into her apartment and cut her up. Lois's coworker there said she was barely hanging on. I don't know if she's conscious, but I'd like to go see. There's a chance that whoever killed Alice also tried to kill Lois."

"Don't you think that's up to the police?"

I backed out of the spot and exited to the main road.

"Definitely." I looked at Tracey. "But we're still going to see her."

We made a stop at the flower shop on the main floor of the hospital because Tracey said it was bad form to visit empty-handed. When we entered Lois's hospital room, I drew in a sharp breath at the sight of her. She was asleep or unconscious, her head and arms were completely wrapped in gauze, and in a few locations patches of blood seeped through. A young man was sitting in a chair next to the bed with a black purse on his lap. He got to his feet when we approached the bed.

"Isn't it awful?" He looked distraught. "Who would do such a thing?"

"It's horrible," I said. "I'm Julie and this is Tracey. And you are?"

"Bill." He nodded to Lois. "I'm her landlord and also her friend. She lives in my basement suite. This morning the alarm on her phone was going off nonstop so I went downstairs to check on her and I—" He choked on his words. "I found her all cut up. I thought she was dead. They said she would've been if I had found her a few minutes later."

"Did you hear anyone break in?" Tracey asked. She walked over and placed the bouquet on a bedside table.

He shook his head. "I work third shift. When I was walking in my house this morning that's when I could hear her alarm. She likes to get up early and is usually going out for a run when I'm coming home. When her alarm kept going off I figured maybe she went out for a jog and forgot her phone. I was beat and wanted to sleep so I let myself into her place to turn off her alarm so it wouldn't keep me awake. I got my key and let myself in…" His shaky hand gestured vaguely to Lois. "She was already unconscious. There was so much blood." He swallowed and closed his eyes. "I brought her purse." He pointed to the black bag he'd put on his chair when he got up. "I thought she might need it for, you know, insurance and stuff."

"Good idea," I told him. "You must be exhausted after working all night. Why don't you go home and rest? I'll make sure the nurses put her handbag in a locker or something."

"Okay. Thank you so much."

He looked immensely relieved to turn responsibility of the handbag over to someone else. I took the purse from him and he ran a hand through his hair.

"Do you think she'll be okay?"

"I hope so," I told him. I asked for his phone number. "That way if I hear of any updates on her condition, I'll pass them along."

"Good idea."

He gave me his number and then hurried out. As soon as he was gone, I took his seat and began going through Lois's purse.

"He didn't even ask how we know Lois," Tracey said.

"The poor guy's a mess. Definitely in shock."

Lois's handbag contained all the usual things. I unzipped the various compartments checking for anything that might be helpful.

"You're not going to hand that in to the nurses, are you?" Tracey whispered.

"Of course I am." I unzipped an outside pocket and took out Lois's keys and cell phone. "I'm just going to keep these for safekeeping."

"Really? Oh wow." Tracey's eyes were huge and she frantically looked left and right to make sure there weren't witnesses to my crime. "Do you think that's such a good idea? I mean…"

I hushed Tracey and placed Lois's keys and phone into my own purse. Then I walked to the head of the hospital bed and placed a gentle hand on Lois's shoulder, one of the few places not bandaged. I leaned in and whispered in her ear, "I'm so sorry you got hurt. I'm going to do my best to figure out who did this to you," I promised. "You just keep fighting, okay?"

I left her purse with the nurses, who promised to lock it away. I also gave the nurse my name and number and told her I was as close to family as she had. Which was probably true.

"Could you please call me if she wakes up?"

The nurse promised she would.

Once we were back in the car I called my insurance company and made arrangements to drop the Jeep off.

"You're wasting no time, huh?" Tracey said. "I understand. Driving around in this thing is like driving a neon billboard of weirdness."

"It sure is." I exited the onramp and merged on to the highway. "Also, Garrett is coming home tonight and I don't want him to see it."

"You're not going to tell him what happened?"

"I will," I told her. "But telling him and him seeing it in our driveway are two different things. He worries."

"Yeah, I worry about you too. I even worry about Ray. I mean, what if he actually ends up interviewing the murderer? He could grab their hands to do a reading and totally figure out that they're the ones that did it." She visibly shuddered. "I wish he'd back off."

I hadn't thought about how much risk he was in. "I'm sure that if he does come across the killer and gives that person a reading, he'll play it perfectly cool until he's safe."

"I hope so."

I let Tracey turn up the radio so she could sing along and be distracted.

Just as we got close to the body shop where I'd be leaving the Jeep, Tracey began messaging on her phone. A big smile played on her lips as she texted.

"I don't even want to know what you two are messaging," I said with a smile. The rain slapped the windshield and I turned the wipers up to high. "I do know that things between you two are moving pretty fast."

"There's nothing wrong with fast." Tracey tucked her phone between her knees and looked over at me. "You and Garrett got together pretty quickly too, right?"

"That was…different." I frowned, remembering how we came together. A mess of need and desire while I was helping find bodies hidden by a serial killer. The case had thrown us together and ripped my entire world apart.

"Sorry." Tracey leaned over and put a hand on my arm. "I know that wasn't a good time for you, but look how it ended, right? You and Garrett are like a big happily ever after romance novel or something."

"I wouldn't go that far."

I thought about the wedge that had grown between us since my night at Wayland Canteen. Garrett acted like everything was fine, but everything was wrong and I didn't know how to make up for that fiasco. "Garrett and I aren't perfect. We have issues."

*My* issues.

"That just makes you normal," Tracey said and I hoped she was right.

I pulled into the body shop parking lot. It was just a couple miles from home and only half a block down from Wayland Canteen. Being this close to that place caused my hands to sweat.

After the paperwork was done, the shop gave me a loaner car and before long we were on our way. I slowed the car down as I drove past Wayland Canteen and my heart pounded painfully.

Tracey followed my gaze out the window and noticed the pub. "It's okay. You need to forgive yourself."

*I was coming out of the bathroom and the guy with the beard and mustache had me in his arms. He was breathing something in my ear and holding me too close against his body.*

A few blocks later I was pulling up to Tracey's apartment.

"I meant what I said about forgiveness." Tracey leaned across the console to give me an awkward hug. "It was one night. You drank too much and you lost your ring. So what? It's not like you killed someone."

"That's not all. I—I didn't tell you everything," I whispered. My mouth went dry as I tried to find the words to tell her what I hadn't even shared with Dr. Chen or Garrett. "That night I—" I swallowed a thick lump in my throat. "I might have been with someone. I may have…" I shut my eyes tight and a fat tear squeezed between my lashes and tracked a line down my face. "I—I may have cheated on Garrett."

# TEN

TRACEY SAT IN stunned silence as if trying to fathom the fact that her best friend could be not only a drunk but an adulterer. I sobbed quietly until a loud jagged moan escaped my lips, and finally Tracey broke the silence.

"Look." She grabbed my hand in both of hers and squeezed. "You would never, not ever, do something to hurt Garrett. I've literally watched you run into a spray of bullets to save him."

"B-b-but…" The word came out on a hiccup of emotion.

"No buts." She squeezed my hand again. "If—and this is a huge if—you did end up with someone else briefly because you were too drunk to know better, I'm going to say that doesn't count."

"Of course it counts!" I pulled my hand from her. "I lost my ring. Maybe even I took the damn thing off because I was with someone and—"

"It doesn't count!" Tracey's voice was loud and firm. "I've never seen you drunk but I have witnessed you do your damnedest to be sober the entire time I've known you. If you had one night when things went to hell, it is nothing more than temporary insanity. Who is this guy that you think you were with?"

*His facial hair tickled my ear and I tilted my face to his to hear what he was saying. His eyes were an im-*

*possible shade of teal green and seemed to look right into me.*

"I don't know." The shameful answer came out on a hoarse whisper. "He had long, thick, dark hair and a bushy beard and mustache and bright green eyes and—"

"There you go." Tracey clapped her hands together gleefully. "Are you telling me you'd go off with some guy who sounds like a Sasquatch when you have your clean-cut FBI man at home? Not in a million years, my friend."

I desperately wanted to believe that was true, but more I wanted to claw inside my own head and pull out the putrid truth of that night so I could shine the light of day on it and know how to punish myself.

"Come inside," Tracey said. "I have some rocky road ice cream that is screaming to be eaten."

"I can't." I sat up and cleared my throat and scrubbed away the damp tears on my cheeks. "I'm going home to be with Garrett. He'll worry and…" I closed my eyes tight and drew in a jagged breath. "I just don't want him to wonder where I am."

I'd put so much worry in that man's heart already, I couldn't stand to be anything except perfect from here on out. Except…

"Okay." Tracey reached over and patted my hand. "Everything is going to be okay. Text or call me anytime, okay?"

Garrett's car wasn't yet in the driveway and I felt guilty for the relieved exhale. Wookie was seriously excited to see me, as always, and Fluffy flicked his tail in annoyance.

I logged into Alice's social media using the email and

password Roscoe gave me. After half an hour scrolling through her private messages and pages I had to admit it was a dead end. If she'd been arranging any intimate hookups, it wasn't through her social media accounts, and if it was, those conversations had been deleted.

Lastly, I used the email and password to log in to Alice's online cloud account. As Detective Larry indicated, there were a ton of pictures on there. The usual selfies as well as hundreds of photos of Jet. The pictures were dated and time stamped. The night of her death there were five pictures taken: three of Jet obviously riding in the car with her and the last two were just blurred pictures of the ground. One had something fuzzy in the lower corner of the picture that could've been Jet's fur. The dog probably moved as she was trying to take pictures of him. No doubt, had she lived, Alice would've deleted those last two. Just in case there was something I was missing I used a ton of ink and printed off the five pictures taken on her last day. Right after I hit Print, Wookie began to whimper at the door.

"Okay, let's go," I told the dog as I threw on a light jacket.

The rain had lightened to a drizzle. I took a tennis ball with me and brought Wookie on a walk to an off-leash dog park. I tossed the ball for him and he brought it back joyfully covered in slobber, and I repeated the throw until my arm was tired. On the way home I took him the long way and ran him hard.

When we got back home, we were both panting. Garrett's dark sedan was parked behind my rental car and I steeled myself to answer his pointed questions with a casualness I didn't feel.

"Hey, sweetheart," I called out as I bent to unhook Wookie's leash.

Garrett came out from the hallway that led from his home office. He was carrying some papers in his hand. He smiled as he walked toward me and pulled me into a hug.

"Welcome home." He handed me the pictures I'd sent to the printer. "I take it these are yours."

"Yeah."

We kissed and he tilted my chin and scrutinized my face.

"You okay? Looks like you were crying."

That look in his eyes...the dark worry, the deepened creases at the corners... I'd put that there, and it bit me like a snake.

"What?" I looked through the pictures I'd printed out from Alice's cloud account. "No, my face is red and wet because it's cold and rainy. I was just giving Wookie a good run for the first time in a while so you're confusing my out-of-shape sweat with sadness." I hooked my thumb in the direction of the driveway. "You noticed the rental car?"

"Of course. What happened?"

I unlaced my shoes and stepped inside. Walking toward the kitchen, I could feel Garrett's gaze boring into me and the tension in the room.

"Not a big deal," I told him. "Tracey and I went to visit Roscoe's mother in a care home in Bellingham, and when we came out vandals had spray-painted the Jeep." I folded my arms and shook my head with a look of irritation. "Probably stupid teens with nothing better to do. Anyway, I called the cops of course and they checked the care home's security cameras, but unfortunately the ones in the parking lot aren't working." I reached into the cupboard for a glass and filled it with water at the sink. "I dropped it at the body shop on my way home."

Garrett waited for me to say more but when I didn't, he simply nodded and said, "I'm just glad you're okay."

"Tell me about your case. All wrapped up?"

"I have to go into the office over the next couple days just to sort through the paperwork but I'll be coming home at night."

"Hmm." I pulled him into my arms and kissed his neck. "That's what I like to hear. Wookie loves to take your place in our bed but he isn't as much fun to snuggle."

"Tell me about what's happening with your search for Alice. I take it those pictures you printed have to do with her?"

We sat down at the kitchen table and I filled him in on everything I'd been able to uncover. Specifically, how Roscoe had given permission to Alice so she could go get knocked up by someone else and how there were a lot of rumors about it. I got to the part about Lois ending up in hospital, and his jaw tightened and the worry lines around his eyes deepened.

"I don't like that someone went after Lois," Garrett said.

"I don't think she liked it much either," I joked. "But hopefully she'll make a full recovery."

"What I mean is that someone could very well have gone after her because she talked to you."

"Doubtful," I said with a slow shake of my head. "I

didn't even tell anyone I was going to talk to her and there was nobody around to witness us and—"

"She could've told someone. The wrong someone. Maybe even Alice's killer." He rubbed the back of his neck. "This guy…whoever he is…could've wanted more than just to be a sperm donor. He might've felt used and gone after her because of it."

"So I'm not the only one who thinks that maybe Roscoe wasn't Alice's killer?"

"I'm not ruling out that the right guy is behind bars. There's an argument for that too," he admitted. "Jealous about her sleeping with another guy. He wouldn't be the first man to completely lose his mind about his wife screwing around."

*I could feel the thick mustache brush against my ear. His arms wrapping around me too tight and too familiar. The cloying scent of his cologne wrapped around me, making my stomach turn.*

"But he was the one who told her she should try and get pregnant," I said, my voice coming out a little shaky.

"Sure, and that sounds very loving in theory, doesn't it? To save his marriage and give his wife everything she wants, he tells her go get pregnant and then come home and we'll raise this kid together like one big happy family." He snorted with derision. "That spelled disaster right from the beginning. I mean he actually gave his wife permission to screw around. What kind of husband does that? Even if it did work, every time he looked at that baby he'd know it was the result of her infidelity."

"It's definitely a weird case," I said on a whisper.

"And I hate to break it to you, but these pictures you printed aren't going to help your case." He held them up from the table. "Unless the dog is the one who did it." He held up the pages that were pictures of Jet. "And these other two…" He waved the two blurry pictures of the ground. "Any particular reason you printed these?"

"Those five pictures were the ones taken on the evening of her death. The two blurry ones she probably would've deleted had she gotten the chance, but since they were the last two she took, I thought I'd see them enlarged." I held each one up to my face in turn. They weren't any better enlarged and printed. Two photos of the ground. Blurry pavement with something fuzzy in the background that looked like Jet's fur. "She probably snapped accidentally. You're right. They're nothing." I got to my feet with a forced smile. "I'm feeling sweaty from my run with Wookie. Just going to get into the shower."

"I'll order a pizza," Garrett said. "How about we eat in front of the TV and watch a movie."

"Perfect." I kissed the back of his neck.

I stood under the spray and sobbed quietly while the bathroom filled with steam. All Garrett knew about my night at Wayland was that I'd come home in a cab, the driver helping me to the door. The next morning he'd sat in stony silence, waiting for me to tell him what had happened but I couldn't. I'd been woozy from the hangover and still felt half-drunk most of the day. All I remembered for certain was that I'd walked into Wayland to ask questions about a different case I'd been working concerning a missing hiker. The person who contacted me said they lived near Wayland and suggested meeting there so he could give me more information before I took the case. I didn't like to frequent bars now that I was sober. Air thick with the smell of alcohol created a craving deep in my soul. But I had gone into bars on at least a dozen occasions for various cases and I'd been able to sip a soda without ever ordering a drink.

I don't know what happened that night. I had no explanation for Garrett the next morning either. All I knew was that I'd ordered a soda, talked to the waitress, and when the missing hiker's brother showed up, for some unfathomable reason I'd switched from cola to wine and tucked myself into a booth in the corner to drown myself at the bottom of a couple bottles of wine.

I'd woken near noon the next day, sprawled fully clothed across our bed, a bucket containing vomit on the floor nearby. I'd walked into the kitchen and was met with the gut-wrenching look of sorrow and disappointment on Garrett's face. I'd gushed profuse apologies, one after another, and he'd only nodded and returned stilted replies. Eventually, later in the evening while I sat on our sofa sobbing into my hands, he'd taken me into his arms and forgiven me.

"You'd been sober for a really long stretch," he'd told me.

"I know, but—" My voice had cracked.

"No buts." He'd kissed my tear-stained face. "So you fell off the wagon? Now you'll just start again."

Then he'd lifted my hand to his lips and that was when we both noticed my ring was missing. The look of anguish and heartbreak on his face in that moment would be forever etched in my mind.

I'd insisted on driving back to the bar, but of course there was no sign of it anywhere. I'd frantically searched the driveway and our yard. Dumped out my handbag and turned out the pockets of my jeans. After days of tearing the house and my mind apart, Garrett came to me and told me not to worry about it.

"What's done is done."

But it wasn't done. I didn't deserve that level of forgiveness because there was a chance that I'd betrayed him on a much larger and irreversible level that he didn't know about. Eventually, I'd have to come clean. I couldn't keep it to myself much longer. Once he knew, he'd leave me, but he'd always been much more than I deserved.

After toweling off, I dressed and picked up my cell phone from the bedside table. I noticed two missed calls from Ray and then it rang again in my hand.

"I'm taking the night off," I told him by way of a greeting.

"That's great. We all need downtime," he agreed. "I just thought it was time to discuss those left to interview and review what we know so far."

"That's a good idea but not tonight."

"It'll only take five minutes and—"

"It can take five minutes in the morning." I was firm. "Good night, Ray."

I ended the call and then turned my phone off entirely before I walked into the living room. I didn't know how many more evenings I had with Garrett. Once he found out my ring wasn't lost during an evening that just involved a careless drunken stupor but might have been taken off while I messed around with another man, he'd be walking out the door.

After the movie we made love right there on the sofa, and our desire for each other started over in our bedroom once we were under the sheets trying to sleep. He spooned against me afterward and as he softly snored against the top of my head I cursed every cell in my body that gave me the alcohol addiction that would cause me to lose this forever.

In the morning I felt nauseous and lightheaded from a night of tossing and turning. Garrett left me a note that he was making his way to the Seattle office but would be home for dinner. I turned on my cell phone to find a half dozen text messages from Ray and a couple from Tracey.

Ray's messages listed the people he'd interviewed and given readings to thus far and his gut feelings or impressions that might be important to the investigation. He'd given succinct point form notes and I got the impression he was a little ticked off that I hadn't wanted to do this over the phone the night before. I was right, because his final message told me to contact him once I was sure I still wanted to work as partners to find Alice.

"Whatever," I grumbled.

The texts from Tracey were sad. Ray was supposed to come over last night but he hadn't showed and wasn't returning her calls.

"What an ass!" I snarled.

I called Tracey but she'd already rectified the situation in her own mind.

"It was good while it lasted," she said. "Sure, I would've liked for it to keep going. That man was a magician in the sack and—"

"But you're okay?" I didn't need to hear details of Ray's lovemaking technique, thank you very much.

"I'm perfectly fine. I know it sounded like I was

head over heels for the guy, but honestly he was just a lot of fun."

"I'm glad to hear that."

"Just heading to the grocery store for my shift. I'm done at four o'clock if you feel like getting coffee."

"I'll let you know," I told her.

I felt energized with new determination. I'd accepted the two things I needed to do. The first thing was to either solve this Alice case or prepare to just let it go. I was determined to put everything I had into it for a couple more days and then, as promised to Garrett in the beginning, I'd throw my hands up and walk away.

The second thing was going to be more difficult. I needed to figure out exactly what happened at Wayland Canteen. If I'd cheated on Garrett, I needed to know. The uncertainty was killing me. If it was true, tough as it would be, I'd walk away from him too. It would be the hardest thing I'd ever done, but there was no way I would take the chance of hurting him again. There was a third thing on my list, but the first two needed to be resolved before I could even think of the last item.

The first thing I did was start up Lois's cell phone. The battery was dead but I'd used one of my own chargers on it overnight. Luckily she hadn't put a pass code on the phone so I was able to open it up.

If her phone was any indication, Lois had kept her head down and mostly worked. She had a social media profile but hadn't spent much time communicating there. She didn't have a ton of contacts in her phone and there didn't appear to be any serious friendships. Although her landlord had sent her some flirtatious messages early on, she'd kept her responses professional and he'd changed his tune when she didn't respond in kind. Any further messages with him were regarding her basement apartment: a couple of repairs that were needed and once a message to him saying she'd be a couple days late with the rent. Almost all her other messages were with colleagues at work about her shifts.

I'd been hoping to find a host of text messages between Lois and Alice, but if there'd been any they'd now been deleted. However, I hit the jackpot. I opened her email and scrolled back through dozens of older messages to reach ones that were between the time of Lois being released from prison and Alice's death.

Alice confided in her older half sister about her inability to have children and how it had become a wedge in her marriage. When she said she'd tried being with another man, at Roscoe's suggestion, she'd ended up miscarrying and now they were separating. Lois had been sympathetic. The back-and-forth email dialogue had continued every few days over the course of a few months. Whenever Lois gently suggested they meet in person, Alice shied away and said she wasn't ready and then the messages would stop for a few days.

Email seemed an archaic way for the two to send messages and I wondered if Alice might be worried about giving Lois her phone number. However, Alice did share her angst about separating from Roscoe. She claimed they still loved each other but he was pushing her away because he knew she wanted kids and he couldn't help. The dog only complicated matters. Roscoe seemed to focus all his energy on Jet instead of on her and she'd fought to keep the dog part of the time only to keep the lines of communication open between them. Alice told Lois on more than one occasion that she believed if they'd been able to have a baby they would still be together. From the emotional tone of her emails, it was obvious it was tearing her apart. She was still in love with Roscoe, and by the sounds of her messages, she believed he loved her too but was only pushing her away because he wanted her to find happiness without him. There was pressure from Roscoe's dad too. Alice mentioned that he'd offered to pay whatever it cost so that Alice could get pregnant, but Roscoe refused to let him use all his money on them when he might need it for his own medical bills.

One day Lois wrote Alice saying that she had a proposal that she would only discuss in person and Alice replied, agreeing to meet. The tone of the emails afterward was completely different. They were short messages:

Lois: I'm pregnant.

Alice: Congratulations! You must be so excited!

Lois: I am excited but not for the reason you think. I'd like to talk in person.

Alice a couple days later: I can't wait to tell Roscoe. We're going to be a family. Thank you! Thank you! Thank you!

That was the last email in the exchange. I sat back and absorbed what I knew and there was only one conclusion. Lois had made the suggestion that she would carry a baby for Alice and Roscoe. That last email from Alice thanking Lois was sent the day before her blood and thumb were found in the bed of Roscoe's pickup truck.

I put down the phone and closed my eyes. Lois had done everything she could to connect with Alice and had been even willing to give her the one thing she wanted more than anything. If I went by the messages alone, it would look as though Roscoe hadn't taken the news with the enthusiasm Alice had thought. In fact, the argument may have escalated and been the entire reason he killed her. Sadly, this seemed the most likely scenario.

With a long exhale I turned the phone off and reviewed the situation. Although all of this information didn't exactly set Roscoe free, there was still the very real possibility that the mystery man who knocked up Lois not only killed Alice but also returned to try to murder Lois. I needed to share what I knew about Lois and Alice with the cops. In my gut, I felt the cases were connected and they needed to know that Lois might still be in danger.

I rubbed the crease between my eyebrows as I thought of one major question. What happened to the baby?

Once again I picked up Lois's phone. I scrolled through her calendar settings until I found it. A few weeks after Alice was found dead, Lois had an appointment at a Bellingham health center known for performing abortions.

After feeding Wookie and Fluffy, I placed a call in to Detective Larry. He wasn't exactly thrilled that I'd helped myself to her phone in the hospital but I explained that the nurses would've just locked it up with the rest of her belongings. I shared what I'd been able to find out and my theory about it being connected to Alice's murder.

"I guess you weren't able to find any emails between Lois and Alice because it sounds like Alice deleted them on her end."

"Yeah. I need that phone, Julie."

"I'll drop it off," I promised.

ONCE I ARRIVED at the police station I only spent a few minutes with Detective Larry after handing in the phone. I'd already shared everything I'd uncovered on the device as well as my suspicions and what I knew from Roscoe.

"It does look like she planned to give Alice the baby she was carrying," the officer said as he scrolled through the phone. "We'll check with the health center to confirm she was there for an abortion. Did you read any hint about who the father would be?"

"No." I sighed. "He might be the key to everything, right? Whoever this guy is, he could've killed Alice and tried to take out Lois."

"Hopefully, Lois herself will be able to answer some questions once she regains consciousness."

"Does that look promising?"

"She lost a ton of blood. The officer responding to the scene thinks the upstairs neighbor missed confronting the person by minutes. Maybe seconds. There's a good chance it was the sound of Bill's car pulling up in the back driveway that scared the perp off. Whoever did this planned on killing her." The officer frowned. "Fingers crossed Lois can tell us herself."

AFTER I LEFT I opened up my own phone and mapped out the area between here and the town of Blaine. There was twenty miles by highway between the two cities but hundreds of farms, parks and vacant land galore available for dumping a body. Still, I took out my dowsing rods and kept them on my lap as I drove slowly north toward the border. This case was wearing on me. I fully planned to keep my promise to Garrett and end things soon. I wanted to honor Alice's memory but I'd decided that I couldn't risk my own health to do it.

Today I'd take the back roads and wind my way down highway exits and places that looked like logical places to drop Alice's body. More and more I was beginning to think that she was fish food somewhere at the bottom of the vast Pacific. Between the local law enforcement and myself, this entire portion of the state must've been already scoured. The hopelessness of it just dragged me down.

My dowsing rods never wiggled or wavered through all my investigations down both paved and gravel side roads. I was wasting my time. There was something missing and I decided to talk to Kim. When she didn't answer her phone, I drove to her trailer and I was surprised to find both Ray's and Blossom's cars parked on the gravel next to the trailer.

I knocked on the door and could hear some shuffling around inside before it was opened.

"Just wanted to talk to you about some more information I've been able to uncover," I told Kim.

Jet bounded over and jumped on me, and Chichi barked repeatedly. I gave both dogs head pats to calm them down and both followed at my feet when Kim told me to come in and sit down. There wasn't another available place to sit. Ray and Blossom were sitting next to the same pile of laundry on the sofa that was present every time I visited. I gave them a nod.

"Hiya, Beanster," Blossom grinned.

"Hi."

I walked over by the television and leaned a hip on the wall while I gave Ray a curious look. I wanted to ask what on earth he was doing here, but before I could form the words he answered.

"Kim asked if I'd mind coming by to give her a personal reading," he explained, pushing his glasses up his nose.

"I showed up to drop off the dogs and wanted in on the action." Blossom laughed. "Unfortunately, there's no tall, dark stranger in my future." She let out a theatrical sigh and placed the back of her hand to her forehead dramatically. "Story of my life."

"Maybe Ray can give you a reading too." Kim laughed but she looked nervous.

It was crowded with four people and two dogs in the small trailer, and I felt like I was interrupting something.

"Can I grab a soda?" Blossom asked, already up and opening the refrigerator. "Kim, everything in here is warm."

"Yeah, I know," Kim replied. "It's acting up again."

"You need a new one," Blossom said. "No sense spending good cash repairing this old thing."

"I'll just go out back and snatch some bills off my money tree then," she snapped.

"You're obviously busy, so maybe we should do this another time," I offered, shifting my weight from one foot to the other. "Then again, with both of us here, I guess we can share everything we've found out."

"Ray's already shared the readings he gave people and all those he talked to. Seems like you've both got a lot of nothing." Kim held up a hand. "I'm not blaming you at all. All my stepdad wanted was that we look into things to try and find Alice's body to help Roscoe if he was innocent. You've both done more than enough already so…"

She seemed to be taking my failure rather well. Then again, she wasn't the one who initially made the enquiry with me.

"I guess it's time we accept Alice might never be found and move on, right?" Kim shrugged. "No sense in continuing to throw money at you when you're coming up empty-handed. Ray told me he's done all he can. I don't blame either one of you for not being able to find Alice. Maybe there wasn't enough of her to uncover. Probably Roscoe chopped her up into small pieces and tossed her in the water."

I cringed at the visual but Kim seemed pleased about her summarization or, at the very least, relieved. I guess I wasn't the only one who was worn out by this case.

"There's some more information you should know." I moved a stack of old magazines and two creepy troll dolls to one side of the coffee table and lowered myself to sit there so I was directly across from Kim. I shared about Lois being attacked and in the hospital.

"Lois was pregnant when Alice was murdered. She planned on carrying the baby for Roscoe and Alice and then turning it over to be raised by them."

Kim covered her face with her hands as if it was all too much.

"Alice believed that once she told Roscoe about the baby, they'd get back together. Sounds like they were still in love."

Blossom slowly shook her head. "No. That doesn't sound right, Beanster. I mean, they were already apart. Roscoe was dating me, for God's sakes." Blossom seemed agitated as she got to her feet. "You telling me he still loved Alice and this baby would've fixed all that? I'm not buying it."

"I've read the email exchange between Alice and Lois. It was obvious that was their intentions. I'm not saying it would've fixed their relationship. I'm just telling you what Alice's intention was and what happened."

"It does sound pretty farfetched, doesn't it?" Ray snorted. "I mean, it doesn't even seem—"

"Let her finish," Kim snapped. "Tell me exactly what their emails said."

I described what I'd been able to uncover on Lois's phone and from emails between her and Alice.

"Obviously I don't have conclusive evidence. All I can tell you is what the email exchange was," I admitted. "Hopefully Lois will recover from her injuries and she'll be able to shed light on the definitive truth here."

"I'm sure the cops won't want to know anything about this until you have actual proof or until Lois says it herself." Blossom zipped up her hoodie and walked to the door, where she put on her shoes. "I've got stuff to do."

I didn't interrupt to say that I'd already talked to the police about it. Blossom gave us all a nod and told Kim she'd be back for the dogs in a couple hours, then headed out the door.

"I hate this," Kim mumbled with a slow shake of her head then an angry scratch at her crimson neck rash. "This entire situation is a tangled mess of garbage that just keeps stinking to high heaven, and every time I think it's gone away, it comes back."

I could tell she was overwhelmed by this latest bit of news. It must be hard not knowing for certain if Roscoe killed Alice.

"I understand," I told Kim. "It must've taken a lot to accept that Roscoe did this, and now there are extenuating circumstances that still might not be enough to clear his name. I know your stepdad wanted him out of prison, but honestly, even with all of this information, it probably won't be enough. Without Alice's body and without at least the name of the person Lois slept with…" I shrugged. "Plus this new information could just be another nail in his coffin."

"What do you mean?" Kim looked at me quizzically.

"I mean, what if Alice showed up here that night to tell Roscoe that Lois was carrying a baby for them. What if Roscoe had changed his mind and was happy with Blossom? What if the baby thing sent him over the edge?"

"That's a lot of what ifs," Kim said. "I can see how telling the police about that wouldn't help his case."

"I've gotta get back." Ray got to his feet then.

"Aren't you going to give Julie a reading since she's here?" Kim asked.

"No," both Ray and I replied simultaneously.

"I should get going too," I told Kim. "I'm sorry that I haven't been able to find Alice and put all this to rest. Seems like all I've got are more questions."

"Not your fault." Kim waved her hand. "It's time to just let sleeping dogs lie." She got up and walked me to the door. She sighed loudly like she was relieved to put all this to bed. "Send me your final bill and I'll be sure you're paid."

Once outside I followed Ray to where he was getting inside his car.

"Look, I don't know what you've got going on with your psychic medium stuff, and frankly I don't care because that's none of my business. How you treat Tracey though, that *is* my business. If you don't want to see her anymore, at least be man enough to tell her that instead of just standing her up."

"Yeah, that was a mess. I already talked to Tracey and everything's fine." He ran his fingers through his spiked hair, and his brown eyes softened as he smiled at me. "I had planned to see her, but I had a bad night, had a few too many cocktails once I got home and fell asleep."

That was something I could relate to, but it didn't make me feel good about Tracey possibly getting messed up with someone with a drinking problem.

"Anyway, I messaged Tracey to apologize. I'll say sorry to you too, since I know she's your best friend."

"Do you drink like that often?" I hated the judgy

sound in my voice that had no business being there, but for Tracey's sake I had to ask.

"No. Almost never. Just had a lot on my mind."

He got behind the wheel of his car as I added, "Don't we all."

"Yeah." He had his car door still open as he put the key in the ignition and started it up. "I know you're still worried about Wayland and the ring—"

He went to close his door and I put my hand on it to stop it from closing.

"What exactly do you know about Wayland Canteen and my ring?"

"Only the vibe I got off you that day on the side of the road when you found Rachel Wu in the ditch." He gave me a casual shrug. "That you were worried about someplace called Wayland and you were upset about losing your ring."

"You never mentioned the ring." I chewed nervously on the inside of my cheek as I absorbed what he said. Abruptly, I thrust out my hand. "You know what? Go ahead and give me a reading. Maybe you can tell me what happened that night. I need help to, you know, put together some missing pieces. I was..." I cleared my throat. "I was drunk that night and, well, it would be nice to figure some stuff out that I don't remember."

He looked at my outstretched hand and slowly shook his head.

"If we're going to do this, I'd rather do it properly." The softness in his eyes had been replaced by a look of smugness. He shoved his glasses up his nose as he added, "I know you don't think I'm as good as you, but I do have professional standards. If you want a proper reading, we'll do it right. Call me later this evening and we can arrange an appointment." He tugged on the door and I let it go. "By the way, I charge a hundred bucks an hour but, you know, I don't mind waiving that fee for my future partner."

I watched him drive off and I felt a surge of anger in my gut. It felt a lot like Ray was trying to coerce me into getting into a partnership with him. Even more than fury was the overwhelming surge of anxiety that Ray could actually help me find out what really happened that night at Wayland. Maybe he could tell me for certain whether I cheated on Garrett. My stomach soured at the thought.

As his car disappeared down the dirt road, I stopped myself just before climbing into my rental car, and instead turned around and walked back to the trailer. Kim had obviously been watching through a window because she opened the door before I knocked.

"Just one more question," I said. "Did Ray give you a good reading? Was he actually able to tell you what you wanted to know?"

She scratched the red and flaky skin on the side of her neck before answering.

"Ray is…" She searched for the words. "He isn't all that and a bag of chips, know what I mean?"

"No." I shifted my weight from one foot to the other while standing on the steps.

"I mean that in his own mind, he's an excellent psychic, but there's a reason why people aren't pounding down his door the way they do yours." She smiled sadly. "He knows *some* stuff, sure, but he just doesn't know enough. He's too vague, and no matter how hard he tries, people around here mostly just humor him. He seems to know just enough to make people think he's got the skills. I'm not saying he's a faker or a scammer. But he's not at your level." She chuckled. "Sure does piss him off that people around here don't talk about him with the same reverence they do you. Everyone in these parts was all saying, 'call Julie' and 'ask Julie to find her' when Alice was killed. He offered his services to people who knew Alice, and they all just kind of blew him off until recently, when he said he was working with you."

That was interesting, but at the same time, when he held my hand and knew immediately about Wayland, I'd known Ray had to be the real deal. Maybe Ray couldn't give people exactly what they wanted but he'd been right about me, and I'm sure he was right more often than that. It was hard to get respect in this industry so I wasn't holding that against Ray.

"At the end of the day, I'm sorry I've let you down." The wind kicked up and I stuffed my cold hands into my pockets. "Like you said, everyone around here was saying for you to call Julie and then, when you do, I'm not even able to find her."

"You didn't let me down," Kim said dryly. "I had zero expectation to start with. My stepdad was the one who wanted you. Personally, my feeling was what difference does it make if Alice's body is found? All the evidence pointed to Roscoe anyway." She sighed. "At least until this thing with Lois and Alice maybe having some lover…" She shook her head. "Anyway, his dad wanted to see if you could find Alice but now his money can go to paying for Mom's care home and maybe fixing up this dump. Alice is dead and no amount of lawyers or psychics are going to change that."

I thanked her and made my way back to my car just as it started to rain.

In the beginning Kim had made it appear like she didn't care that her stepdad had left money to try to free Roscoe, but now it sounded like she could really use that inheritance. I was walking away from this case but I wasn't going to take any more than the initial deposit from this family. They'd been through enough.

As I drove away down the rutted gravel road my gaze went west in the direction of the farm where I grew up and I shivered. I'd had cases before where I'd come up empty. That didn't mean the body wasn't around to be found, it just meant it wasn't where I was looking but I was happy to be putting this case and this town behind me.

The case might be dead but I still had my own mystery. I knew in my gut that I'd be calling up Ray to arrange an appointment, and would gladly turn over a hundred dollars or even a thousand if it would fill in the blanks of that one single night.

# ELEVEN

I WAS HEADING back in the direction of home and my phone rang. It was Dana, the waitress from the diner.

"I wanted to let you know that Barb quit. She decided to up and retire just like that. Not even any warning."

"Really? Wow. Guess she'd had enough of being on her feet all day."

"Yeah, but it's weird," Dana mused. "She's been serving here since before I was born. Now the whole staff schedule is a mess. I'm working a double today and tomorrow just to make up for us being short-staffed."

"Why do you think she left all of a sudden?"

"She told the boss she was under a lot of stress and her son needed her." She snorted. "Her child is like in his thirties or forties, you know? But the boss said her boy was never right in the head and has always needed help."

I didn't need to hear the town gossip and I told her that.

"Okay, but you told me to let you know if I heard anything that might be remotely related to Alice so…"

"I'm dropping the case." I turned the windshield wipers up high as I drove down the highway in the rain. "Unfortunately, if Alice is going to be found, it won't be by me."

"That's a real shame," Dana said and it sounded like

she meant it. "Everyone deserves a chance to be buried instead of dumped somewhere, you know?"

"Yeah. I know." I winced with guilt. "Is there anything else, Dana?"

"Nothing really…"

I could hear in her pause she wanted to say something so I waited.

"Okay, well, this isn't about Alice, but the last time the cops were here having lunch, I was wiping down the booth beside them. I overheard one of them say something about getting ready to lay charges in the case against Lori Cox."

Something tickled my memory.

"Lori Cox," I repeated. "Why does that name sound familiar?"

"Blossom," Dana said. "That's her real name. Not that anyone ever calls her that."

"What on earth could she be getting charged with?"

"Everyone knows her secondhand store, Blossoming, was hit by insurance lightning. Guess it caught up with her."

"Lightning? As in you think she deliberately burned the place down for the insurance?"

"I'm just repeating what I heard," Dana explained. "I don't know Blossom well enough to say she woulda done something like that. You prolly know her better than me, am I right?"

This was none of my business and had nothing to do with Alice, but I thought about how wistful Blossom sounded when she talked about her little thrift store. "She loved that shop. I can't see her doing something like that."

"People do dumb stuff for money," Dana said wisely. "Like quit school to work as a waitress in a diner."

A few minutes after that call my mind was still reliving that night at the Wayland Canteen when my phone rang again and it was Garrett. I took a deep breath, wiped the tears that had filled my eyes thinking of my failure, and forced a smile before answering.

"Hi, sweetheart." I tried to make sure to keep the anxiety from my voice.

"How are things going?" he asked.

I told him that I hadn't been able to find Alice but had wrapped things up anyway.

"I know you felt you owed it to her to find her body," he said softly. "This must be hard for you."

"Yeah, but it's the right decision." I sighed. "I can't spend any more time on this case without losing my mind." I chuckled at the comment although it had more truth than either of us wanted to admit. "Besides, Kim admitted she could use the money to help pay for her mother's care home, and God knows she could use some to fix up her trailer."

"You'd think her stepdad would've left her money to pay those bills up front."

"Apparently the will says that money needs to be spent to try and find Alice and free Roscoe first, and then what's left will go to Kim and to help her mom."

"And I bet you're not going to charge her for all the work you've already put in, are you?"

"No."

"You're a good woman. That's why I love you."

"I love you too." I bit my lip. I wanted to be the good

woman he thought I was, but the kind of woman he deserved didn't get fall-down drunk and screw around.

"Wanted to let you know that I'm going to be a bit later than I wanted," he said. "I don't want to have to come back to the office tomorrow to finish this paperwork so I'm going to work into the evening. It might be nine o'clock before I'm home."

We said our I-love-yous and I hung up.

As I made my way toward home, my head was aching and my heart was sad. I was walking away from Alice like a failure, and once the truth came out about Wayland, I might be leaving my relationship the same way. I needed to take more steps to get to the truth.

I was a few minutes away from the grocery store where Tracey worked. I called and told her I'd be waiting for her when she got off work.

I found Tracey's car parked in the staff part of the lot and I pulled into an empty space beside it. When she got off work a few minutes later, she came toward me with a worried smile.

"What up, bestie? You look like you've had better days."

"I need you to come to Wayland with me."

"Why?" Her eyebrows knit together with concern.

"I've called there a couple times after that night but nobody working there could help me. The waitress who served the booth where I was sitting that night has been off recovering from a car wreck. I called there earlier and today is her first official shift back at work." I looked down at my feet. "I can't stand not knowing, Tracey, and I don't trust myself in that place after what happened."

"Then let's do this. Get in my car." She pressed the key fob to unlock the doors. "You're too nervous to be driving."

During the short drive, my fingers were laced tightly together in my lap. Tracey parked in the lot behind the bar and I fumbled nervously with my seat belt. When we walked into Wayland Canteen, the thick smell of stale beer caused my stomach to turn.

"Over here." My voice cracked as I nodded toward a back booth that was closest to the washroom, and Tracey followed me there.

"This is where I was sitting that night."

I slid into the booth on the same side I had that night, and Tracey took a seat across from me. The bar was busy with happy hour patrons guzzling cheap draft beer and munching on cheap chicken wings. Our waitress was a busty redhead who approached our booth wearing a black T-shirt with Wayland Canteen in faded orange lettering.

She listed the happy hour specials, then asked, "What can I get you?"

"Two Cokes and some information," I told her.

She tilted her head and focused her eyes on me for the first time.

"I remember you." She slowly nodded. "I'll be right back with your Cokes."

My heart thumped painfully.

"That's good that she remembers you." Tracey reached across the table and took my trembling hand in hers. "Relax. It'll all be good."

I wish I could be as positive as Tracey.

The waitress brought our drinks, placed them in

front of us, and then motioned for Tracey to scoot over in the booth before taking a seat next to her. "I'm on a break. How can I help you?"

"First of all, would you mind checking your lost and found for a ring? A platinum band with etched mountains and ocean on it? I've called here so many times but I just keep hoping it'll turn up."

"Sure." She got up and we watched her go back into the back office and then return a few minutes later, shaking her head. "Sorry, lots of random stuff in our lost and found box. Even someone's retainer, and a single shoe…" She giggled at that. "But no ring."

I sighed. "Okay. You said that you remember me." I wrapped my hands around my drink to keep my hands from shaking. "I'm afraid I don't remember much from that night, and well, I'm hoping you can fill in some answers."

"I'm not surprised you're drawing a blank," she said dryly.

"I'm an alcoholic. I was sober for a while before I came in here," I told her, feeling embarrassment color my face as I tried to explain. "But that night, for some reason, I decided to blow that all to hell."

"Not how I see it, darling." She tapped the table between us. "What exactly do you remember?"

"I came here to meet someone for…work." I cleared my throat, not wanting to get into how I find bodies using dowsing rods and was meeting a potential client. "I sat here in this booth to wait and I remember ordering a Coke. Just like now. The man I was supposed to meet showed up. He had long, thick hair, a big bushy beard and mustache and bright green eyes, and he bought wine. Well, pretty much everything afterward is a blur. He stuck around while I was stumbling around here drunk…" I squeezed my eyes shut and took in a deep breath. "I lost my ring and…" I straightened my spine and forced myself to look her right in the eye. "Do you remember the guy? Do you know if I left with him? I came home in a cab and—"

"I'll let you know what I remember from that night. I'm pretty clear about it because it was a pretty godawful night for me too. It was raining hard when I got off shift. Roads were horrible as can be, but on my way home some maniac ran me off the road. Car rolled and I was lucky to come out of it alive. Shattered my pelvis, broke an arm, but luckily the ol' noggin stayed intact." She tapped the side of her head. "If I'd had a concussion, I doubt my memory would be so clear."

"Oh my God," Tracey exclaimed. "I wonder if mercury was in retrograde that night, or something."

We both looked at Tracey and then the waitress laughed and shook her head.

"I'm so sorry that happened to you," I told her.

"Well, physical therapy is both a blessing and a curse, but it's done and I'm recovered." She smiled. "Anyway, this is how things went down that night from my point of view." She leaned forward. "You came in, sat in this same booth and ordered a Coke just like you said. You were alone and kept looking at your phone. After a while you ordered another Coke, and then some guy showed up. He orders a couple glasses of wine at the bar and then brings the glasses over to your booth and sits down. You kept drinking your Coke. I went over to ask if you wanted anything else to drink, and at that moment your phone rang. It was really loud in here because Friday evenings we have a country band that plays honkytonk crap, and they were just warming up for their set. You said you were going to take the call outside."

"That call was from me," Tracey interrupted. "I called you because my car battery died, and I was asking if you could give me a jump if you were nearby. You said you'd come by in about half an hour. You sounded perfectly sober."

"You never told me that." I looked at Tracey.

"Well, you never showed because…you know…and I didn't want to bring it up and make you feel bad."

I did feel bad and I was beginning to feel worse about going there and having my night of shame rubbed in my face, but still, I wanted to know. I *needed* to know. I loved Garrett too much to keep the truth from him. Especially now. He deserved better than a drunk who would screw someone she just met in a bar.

"I asked the guy you were with if he wanted more wine or if I could bring you another Coke, even though your second glass of soda was still half full. He'd finished his glass of wine, but the second glass of wine was still full. He asked for another two glasses of wine and said you'd be drinking yours after your Coke. You were just coming back inside as I brought the next two glasses of wine."

"Okay." I nodded. "I guess that's when I started drinking."

I'd gone over my calendar and emails a hundred times since then. A man had contacted me asking for my help in finding the body of his girlfriend, a missing hiker. He'd asked to meet at Wayland saying he lived down the street and didn't have a car. I'd tried emailing and texting him after that night. I'd been desperate to reach him, but I'd never received a phone number for him, and all emails I sent bounced back. I couldn't even remember the guy's name.

"Because afterward…" I shook my head slowly and looked down at my hands folded in my lap. "I honestly just remember snippets, like trying to walk to the bathroom."

*Wanting to leave the bar but the room was spinning. His hand on my elbow to help me and then an arm around my waist. His hot breath in my ear.*

"At least if he'd used a credit card there might be hope we could find out his name, right?" Tracey suggested.

"He paid cash and he looked like you described, just like the typical hipster guy that comes in here." She waved a hand in the air to indicate the rest of the bar. "White, maybe late twenties or early thirties. He had a full, messy beard. Long brown hair. He wore a red-and-black plaid lumberjack-style shirt with jeans and hiking boots." She shrugged.

I looked around the bar, and it did describe a lot of the men in the place.

"Did I, um…" I drew in a deep breath and felt a deep blush color my face. "Do you remember if I left with him?" I quickly added, "I know I had to come back the next day to get my Jeep, and my boyfriend said I came home in a cab that night, but I remember being really drunk and walking outside with this guy."

"Here's the thing…" The waitress leaned in on her

elbows toward me and lowered her voice. "I don't think you were drunk at all. I never saw you take a drink of that wine, and even if you did, nobody gets bombed on one glass. He drank two and there was still one full glass sitting there when you guys left. I was wondering what was going on when I saw you get up to leave and you could hardly friggin' walk. He had his arm around you to help you or I'm sure you would've fallen down." She sat back and pointed a finger at me. "I think he roofied you."

"What!" Tracey and I exclaimed simultaneously.

If he'd roofied my Coke, that would explain my drunken feeling and the way I'd looked impaired and felt sick the next day.

"Jesus." I dragged a hand through my hair. "So, he took me back to his place and...and..." I swallowed thickly as a lump formed in my throat. "Then he stuck me in a cab and sent me home after." A small sob escaped my lips. "Oh God!"

"No-o-o." The waitress reached over, took one of my hands in hers and squeezed it. "Darling, I was outside having a smoke break behind the building and saw him with his arm around your waist trying to steer you toward a car. I knew something was screwed up about that. I called out to him and said, 'Hey, dude, what the hell is going on?' I started to walk toward him and he just let you go and then took off running. He got into his car and drove away while you slowly just slumped to the ground."

"Holy shit!" Tracey exclaimed, which was exactly the shock I felt but I couldn't find the words. A tsunami wave of relief washed over me, and my eyes filled with tears. I hadn't cheated on Garrett and I hadn't even fallen off the wagon.

"I should've called the cops on the bastard," the waitress said. "But instead I opened your purse and got your home address off your driver's license. One of our regular cab drivers was parked at the curb and I helped myself to a couple twenties from your wallet, paid him, gave him your address, and told him to make sure you got safely inside your house. I should've done more. Sorry. On my way home that night I was still thinking I should call the cops but then I had my accident and..."

"Thank you." I bit my lip to stop from sobbing. "Thank you sooo much."

"Hey, no big deal." She shrugged and smiled brightly. "Us girls gotta stick together, right?"

"You are a friggin' saint." Tracey pointed to the waitress. "Wow. That guy could've been an ax murderer or a serial rapist or a—"

"We get the picture." I laughed nervously.

"Well, I've gotta get back to work. All those medical bills aren't going to pay themselves."

When she got up from the booth, I got to my feet and grabbed her into a tight hug.

"Thank you." I breathed into her red hair as tears dampened my face.

She told me just to never leave my cola unattended again, and I swore I'd learned my lesson. Then I told Tracey, "Let's go. I can't wait to get home and tell Garrett what I found out."

I paid for our colas, leaving a hefty tip before we walked out the door.

"I knew you didn't cheat on him," Tracey said as we

walked toward her car. "I bet Garrett is going to track down this asshole and rip him to shreds."

I was grinning like a fool, and as I buckled myself into the passenger seat, more fat tears began to roll down my face. Everything was going to be okay. I sent Garrett a text telling him I loved him and that I was looking forward to seeing him tonight. He replied that he was done earlier than he originally thought and would be leaving the Seattle office within the hour and would be home in time for dinner. That would give me time to stop at the grocery store on my way home and pick up some fat steaks for barbecuing, and maybe even some decadent dessert. I was still nervous about talking to him, but my anxiousness was tempered by the excitement of sharing the truth about that night, which had been a dark cloud over us for months.

Tracey pulled into the parking lot of the grocery store where I'd parked my car. I told her I was going shopping for a few things so I could make Garrett a nice dinner.

"Thanks for coming with me and for, well, just for being a friend."

"Oh hey." She squeezed me tight. "Just remember that whether you were drinking that night or not doesn't change who you are as a person, and it sure as hell doesn't change us."

We released the hug and she folded her arms across her chest.

"But if I could get my hands on that bastard, I'd…" Her face grew dark, and lost for words, she only growled.

"Yeah. I know." I sighed. "Me too."

But my anger toward some random stranger who

tried to take advantage of me was strengthened by the real knowledge that I hadn't drunk myself into a stupor that night and hopped in bed with a stranger. I couldn't wait to share that information with Garrett.

Tracey drove away, and in the grocery store I chose the thickest T-bone I could find. As I thought about the prospect of letting Garrett know the truth of my night at Wayland, my heart felt lighter than it had in weeks. Even though Garrett would lose his mind and be furious that I was almost abducted by some crazed hipster, once he got over that, I was sure there'd be a level of relief to know I hadn't screwed up.

I bought a cheesecake to finish off our meal tonight, then loaded the groceries into the trunk of the rental car and climbed behind the wheel. I was humming a happy tune as I put the key in the ignition and then glanced in my rearview mirror. My mirror was tilted up at the ceiling for some reason, and I frowned as I reached to adjust it. Suddenly, I sensed movement in my back seat.

"Pull into a parking spot around back next to the dumpster, and don't make any sudden moves."

I felt the cold metal of a gun at my neck, but it was nothing compared to the ice in my veins. The man in my back seat was Ray Hughes.

"Oh God, Ray…" I moaned. "Look, you don't have to do this. We can—"

"Shut up and do what I told you."

He pushed the muzzle of the gun deeper into the back of my neck. I backed out of my spot and slowly drove around to the back of the grocery store, and as he directed, I pulled up next to the dumpster right next to a van that I recognized as belonging to Barb because of the Jesus fish decals on the back. I thought about running, but even as the thought entered my mind, he had one hand on my shoulder and the other pressed the gun to my temple.

"Leave your purse and cell phone behind," he instructed. "I don't want anyone tracking where you are by your phone." He motioned for me to climb out of the car and into the back of the van. "Move. Now."

The normally busy parking lot had not a single person where we were parked.

"If you try to run or scream, not only will I shoot you, I will go see Tracey, and I'll shoot her too. Then I'll use your keys, break into your house and wait for your boyfriend to come home, and when he does, I'll put a hole in his head."

The calm in his voice sent chills up my spine.

I slowly climbed out of the car, hoping someone would notice but there was absolutely nobody around at this part of the back lot. Once I was seated in the back of the van Ray took out some zip ties and bound my hands and feet, then locked the seat belt around me. He slammed the door and jogged around to the driver's side.

"Why are you doing this?" I asked as he drove out of the parking lot and a few blocks until he was on the northbound ramp to I-5. "Was it you? Did you kill Alice?"

He turned on the radio and at first a preacher came on the air, which was probably Barb's usual station, but Ray switched it to some heavy metal station and blasted it so loud my seat vibrated. At one point a state trooper vehicle passed us, but there was no way the officer could see me through the dark tinted windows. Ray's driving was flawless so as not to attract attention.

My mind reeled. How could I have missed that he was the killer? Not only had I put myself in danger, he was now connected to Tracey.

*Oh God, what am I going to do?*

I sobbed quietly while racking my brain about how to escape. We were obviously heading back to Blaine. A realization caught up with me as a faint wisp of his cologne reached my nostrils. I pinched my eyes shut and visualized Ray with longer hair not spiked or blond up top. Then I imagined him with a full beard and colored contact lenses instead of glasses. The complete picture hit me like a slap across the face. It was him! He'd been the one to poison my drink in Wayland. He'd missed his opportunity then and had been toying with me ever since.

Sensing my stare, Ray met my gaze in the rearview mirror and a smirk played on his lips.

"Remember me now?"

My throat was sandpaper dry and I could only nod.

Within an hour he was pulling the van inside Barb's garage. The houses on either side were boarded up and awaiting demolition so he didn't even have to be discreet. Still, Ray waited until the garage door slid completely shut before taking me inside.

"It was you at Wayland. You had long hair, a beard, and I'm guessing colored contacts."

"I kept waiting for you to make that connection." He laughed and shook his head as he pushed me to move faster. My ankles were still bound together with zip ties so I could only shuffle. Impatient with my slow progress, he hooked his hands under my armpits and half dragged me inside the house, then pushed me on an overstuffed sofa.

"What have you done with Barb?" I demanded. "Did you kill her?"

Was her body somewhere in this house? Would he kill me and then bury me and Barb in the same place he left Alice?

"Mom was just in the way and—"

"Barb is your mother?" I couldn't keep the incredulous sound out of my voice, and Ray laughed.

"For being the brilliant Julie Hall who knows and sees all, you really are quite dense." He gave me a patronizing smile as he lowered himself to a chair across from me. "Yes, Barb's my mother. I wasn't hatched!" He giggled at his own joke, and then hissed, "And I didn't kill her. I'm not a friggin' monster, you know!"

The last was said with anger and a look that challenged me to say otherwise. All I did was stare at the gun that lay in his lap.

"Why am I here? What do you want, Ray? Why did you drug me at Wayland and…" I swallowed my fear and asked anyway, "Why did you kill Alice?"

"I didn't kill Alice. Sheesh. I'm making tea." He abruptly jumped up from the chair. "Would you like some?"

What kind of crazy social visit did he think this was? I could only stare in answer and he shrugged.

"Suit yourself."

The zip ties binding my wrists painfully dug into my flesh as I tried to wriggle my hands free. There was a bit more room around my ankles, especially for my left foot. If I could get my shoes off, I might be able to pull at least that one foot free.

Unfortunately, Ray walked back inside the room with his tea before I had a chance to manipulate my feet enough to loosen my shoes. Instead of the overstuffed chair he was in before, he grabbed a straight-backed wooden chair from the kitchen and positioned it across the coffee table from me.

"All of this could've been avoided if you'd taken me seriously last year."

"Last year?" I parroted.

"I emailed you right after I got out of Lakewood."

Lakewood was a psychiatric hospital outside of Tacoma.

"I didn't know you emailed me," I said.

"Bullshit!" he screamed, and then he squeezed his eyes shut and brought his tea to his lips with trembling hands. "I must've sent you ten emails and you didn't respond to any, but when I sent you one single message from an entirely different account complimenting you on finding that child in the well last year, you responded." He said in a singsong woman's voice that I assumed was supposed to be mine, "Oh, thank you for saying so, it was my pleasure to help the family find comfort in their child's return."

That was my standard response when I replied at all to people complimenting me on finding someone's remains, but the ten emails he insisted he sent me, those began to also tug on my memory.

"You sent messages saying you knew I was from Blaine and now living in Everett and that I was living with my FBI boyfriend."

"Yes!" He put down his tea and slowly applauded me as if I was a dumb child. "I sent you those messages so that you'd know we had a connection. We grew up in the same town...well, I was mostly in Tacoma with my dad or in the hospital when you were growing up here, but I'd come to stay here with my mom too. I wanted you to know I knew all-l-l about you so that you'd realize how good my idea was."

The stalker. All those emails from the same account that insisted he had an idea for a great business partnership. They sounded like spam or, worse, a stalker. I'd thanked him and said I worked alone, and he'd sent a flurry of more emails and made it sound like he was watching me. I'd immediately blocked the account.

I took in a slow deep breath and then exhaled it even slower. I needed to stay calm. "You—you never signed your name at the end of those emails and the email account was just a vague number." I tried to keep the panic from my voice. "I didn't know those were from you, Ray."

"That was the whole idea!" He waved his hands in exasperation. "I knew you wouldn't remember me from living here because you kept to yourself and I wasn't here much and—"

When he said "here," he'd pointed to the floor, as if indicating this room and something occurred to me then.

"So you sent those emails from here. While you were living with your mom."

"Yes-s-s."

"Is she okay, Ray?" I asked, hoping it would give him an excuse to go check on her.

"Sure. She's sleeping it off in the back room." He rolled his eyes and gave me a slow shake of his head. "Wow, Julie Hall who's so famous around here is not the wonder kid everyone thinks, huh? See, that's why you need me. As partners we'd be unstoppable."

He'd grabbed my hand on the side of the road after I found Rachel Wu's car and said I was thinking of Wayland, but of course he'd already known about Wayland because he'd drugged me there.

"Did you…" I swallowed. "Did you kill Rachel Wu just so we could meet?"

"Of course not!" He spat. "I just arranged for you to find her."

"By telling her parents about me?" I asked.

"Yes." He sat back and gave me a smug look. "When I visited Roscoe, he kept insisting he didn't need my help because his dad had hired *you*. He said any day now you would come visit him. I started visiting his old roommate there and telling him about his future, which was hard on account of I knew nothing about him. Nothing at all. I had to wing it."

That's what he did. He researched people. He had no psychic medium skills. Ray Hughes was just manipulative and insane.

"So you visited Roscoe's old cellmate with the hopes of running into me?"

"Sure and the Rachel Wu thing was easy. She was visiting her old boyfriend at Ozette. I ran into her in the parking lot the day she went missing. She told me her usual dealer wasn't available so I made a few calls and hooked her up with the black tar. I'm always thinking." He tapped the side of his head. "My connection said it had a little boost of fenny. So she OD'd. I saw her stick the needle in her arm and then get behind the wheel. When she started up her car, she was really out of it. I yelled at her to step on it, and guess what? She did! I could've stopped her, but what did I care?" He shrugged.

"You could've called the police," I murmured. "Maybe she could've been saved if someone found her earlier."

"Not my problem. Worked out anyway because we finally got to meet." He grinned madly at me then, full of pride for helping end Rachel Wu's life. "Of course, once I saw her mom on TV pleading for help finding her daughter, I reached out to the family. I told them you could find her body and I even gave them a hint that I saw her in the area around Ozette so they'd know where to send you."

"You're happy Rachel died because we got to meet." I shook my head incredulously.

"So?" he shouted. "It's not like I killed her. She was a friggin' drug addict. I gave her what she asked for and she drove the car off the road. She died because of her own stupid weakness." He lowered his voice then and gave me another maniacal smile. "You have your own weakness. Booze. Kim and Blossom, they told me all about your problem with the bottle. But take a look at me…" He proudly thumped his chest. "I am completely drug free. All those stupid pills they filled me with at Lakewood are gone. Those meds are completely out of my system. No more drugs for this guy."

Unmedicated and psychotic. Oh God, I was beginning to realize that the only way out of this would be to keep him calm and talking until I could come up with a plan.

"So you emailed me, and I stopped replying," I said.

"Yes. When you wouldn't return my emails and meet to talk about our future business, I just knew if I got you to a bar…"

"You messaged pretending to be the boyfriend of a lost hiker and asked to meet at Wayland. You looked completely different then. Did you deliberately change your appearance so I wouldn't recognize you?"

"I was planning on getting cleaned up anyway. Mom was riding my ass about getting a haircut, and she hated the beard and colored contacts." He shrugged. "Mom said if I got cleaned up maybe I'd get a job and she was kind of right, because when we met at the side of the road after Ozette, you even let me take your hand."

"You drugged me at Wayland." My eyes met his. "Would you have killed me that night if you'd been able to get me in your car?"

"I'm not a killer." He sighed elaborately. "All I wanted was a chance to explain to you in person all about our future business. My plan was to get you here and show you my plan so that Ray Hughes and Julie Hall can partner up and take this state by storm!" He was alive with excitement. "Not just the state either. That would just be a start. We'd be doing road trips and finding lost people all over this damn country. Maybe the world!"

"That's why I'm here? To talk about, um, a business deal?"

"Of course." He cleared his throat. "Let me show you something…"

He walked around the coffee table and helped me to my feet. He had his hand on my elbow to help me as my ankles were still bound. For a second I thought he was going to leave the gun on the table, but as we passed by he snatched it up and kept it pointed between my shoulder blades.

"If you loosened the ties I could walk faster," I told him.

"I'm not in any hurry."

Great.

We made our way down the hall of the older three bedroom, my feet taking tiny steps on the worn shag carpet. He stopped me outside the first bedroom and opened the door. There was a single bed, neatly made, and a corner desk with a laptop. One wall was filled with corkboard, and thumbtacks pinned newspaper articles and emails all over the board until it was completely covered.

My eyes grew wide. "Those are all about me."

"Yup. Every time you were in the news, I printed it out. I've kept a log of all your cases that you worked and how long it took you. I even followed up with some of your clients. Told them I was researching you for a future documentary."

"Holy crap," I muttered.

It began to feel hopeless. Raymond Hughes's mind was held together with a tangle of cobwebs, and I had a feeling there was no way he'd ever let me go. Still, I couldn't help but ask again.

"You've done all this research so that we can work together." I looked him in the eye and tried my best to keep my face looking interested and not terrified. "So once we work out this business agreement, you'll untie me and we'll just get together for jobs?"

"Of course. Once we work out all the details of our seventy-thirty agreement…" He winked. "I get the seventy because it's my idea."

"Sure. That sounds fair." At this point, I would've agreed to anything as long as he let me go or, at least, let down his guard long enough for me to escape. "So let's sit down and talk this out so I know exactly what you want," I said, feigning enthusiasm.

He grabbed my elbow and we began the slow, painful walk back to the living room where he lowered me back to the sofa.

"First things first," Ray began. "We've gotta get this in writing."

"That makes sense." I nodded.

"And, of course, it would be easier if you just lived here." He nodded his chin toward the hall. "We've got a spare room, and as soon as Mom gets her sewing stuff out of there, it'll be more than comfortable."

"You want me to leave my boyfriend and my home to come live here. With you." I was trying to make him see the insanity of it, but that only made him scowl.

He began pacing the room. "You make it seem unreasonable, but Garrett will understand. It's not like we're going to get married. This is strictly business." He walked fast from one end of the living room, spun on his heels and walked back in the other direction. Back and forth for a number of minutes while he mumbled unintelligibly under his breath.

"Ray, what about Alice?" I said just above a whisper. "Did you…did you arrange her, um, situation so we could meet?"

He tilted his head and looked at me like I'd grown a third eye.

"Of course not. How many times do I have to tell you I'm not a killer?" He glared at me. "Roscoe killed her. Duh! But…but…" He shook a finger in my direction. "But that was the catalyst. I went to offer Kim my help and gave her a reading. She said her stepdad only wanted you to be the one to help find the body." His hands fisted at his sides. "I've been trying to get people to take me seriously in this town, but all they could talk about was you. I knew the only way people would see that my brain was great and my psychic skills are real, was if I was partnered with Julie Hall the magnificent."

His face was alive with deranged insanity. My gut told me he murdered Alice. It didn't matter that he denied it. He'd already admitted to helping kill Rachel Wu and using that so we could meet. In his current state, he could very well believe he had nothing to do with killing Alice. I also knew that as soon as we started to really talk about his business idea, reality could break through his psychosis when he realized it wouldn't work in a million years.

When that happened, I had no doubt he'd kill me.

# TWELVE

RAY STRODE FROM one end of the living room to the other as he ranted about his great plan. One minute he was talking about our joint website and the next he was railing about national coverage and our own television show. As his voice grew more animated, he seemed to lose track of the fact that I was even there. Eventually he'd have to leave the room. He'd get tired, or hungry, or need to use the bathroom, and when he did, I'd force off my shoes and hopefully slip at least one foot from the ties so I could make a break for it.

A low moan rose from a back room, and Ray stopped pacing mid step. He tilted his head and frowned as the sound came again. It chilled me to realize the sound was Barb coming awake.

Ray spoke to me over his shoulder. "I'll be right back."

He jogged down the hall and I frantically went to work. Using the friction of the carpet, I rubbed the heels of my shoes back and forth to try and pry my shoes loose. I was sweating as I inwardly cursed the fact that my laces were so tight. Finally I was able to get one shoe pried off my foot and then the other. Unfortunately, the left plastic strap was still much too tight around my ankle but the looser one on the right offered a little give. I was wriggling and twisting my foot, but just as I thought I might work my heel through the opening loop of the zip ties, Ray returned. Quickly, I tucked my shoes and my feet under the sofa, hoping he wouldn't notice.

"She'll sleep a bit longer now." Ray pointed down the hall with his thumb. "After years as a waitress she could probably use twenty-four hours of straight sleep." He laughed at that and mumbled something under his breath that caused him to gleefully giggle. "Mom's gonna be so proud of me once we get this business going. There'll be no more of her constant bitching…" He added in a singsong voice, "Raymond, you need to take your pills or I'm sending you back to the hospital." He sighed and smiled. "She's been telling me to take my pills my whole life and what's it gotten me? Nothing. Boring jobs working at convenience stores and pumping gas."

"I worked at a gas station," I offered meekly. Anything to keep him talking.

"Yes, I know exactly the one too!" His eyes hardened. "Whenever I'd come in you were never very friendly."

"Well, I, um…"

"Doesn't matter…" He waved it away with a flick of his wrist. "You didn't know me like you do now." He walked over to a desk in the corner of the room, opened the top drawer and pulled out a legal pad and a pen.

"Before we settle our business plan we really need to be writing out our exact plan for finding Alice," he told me, his eyes freakishly bright. "Finding her body is the key to everything. Once we find her remains together, everyone will see what a great team we are, and the publicity will be amazing. We need to have a big case solved by both of us because it'll be the perfect time to launch our business."

He flopped into an overstuffed chair next to me, leaned back in his chair and waved the pen over the pad of paper. "Okay, go."

"Go?" I parroted.

He pointed the pen at me. "Yes, let's brainstorm. First list everyone you've talked to about Alice and all the key points or hints you got from them."

"Oka-a-ay." I worried my lower lip with my teeth. We'd already done this and it hadn't revealed anything. At this point all I wanted was to keep Ray from wanting to kill me, so I started talking about all the conversations I had with Kim, Dana, Blossom and even his mom.

All of a sudden he exclaimed, "Oh my God, Tracey!" He hit his forehead with the heel of his hand. "We've got a date tonight. I don't want her getting suspicious. She might even call Garrett, and I don't want him launching any kind of investigation to find you before we can get all this settled." He dug out his phone and dialed the number, pointing the pen at the gun. "You make so much as a peep or a yawn while I'm on the phone, and I'll blow a hole through your head."

I could only nod. Although muffled at his ear, I could hear the sound of Tracey's voice mail message in the background and then the telltale beep.

"Hey, sweetie, I hate to do this, but I'm going to have to cancel our plans for tonight. Something's come up on this case and it's really an emergency I need to deal with. I'll make it up to you by taking you somewhere special on the weekend. I promise." He made a kissy noise into the phone before ending the call.

"Now." He licked the tip of the pen and jotted down a note before looking back at me. "Keep talking."

I drew a blank and he sighed.

"Fine. We'll come back to you."

What should have been a fifteen-minute process of listing those we talked to turned into a couple of hours. Ray would latch on to one ridiculous scenario after another and run it into the ground before moving on to the next.

"Blossom could've definitely stuffed Alice's body into one of the rooms at the motel where she works."

"B-but wouldn't somebody have found it by now?" I countered.

He lifted the gun from his lap and seemed to take pleasure in aiming it at my face. "Julie, dear, this brainstorming process will never work if you knock down every idea in the progression. We need to think outside the box."

"All right." I swallowed. "Sorry."

A number of times he returned to Kim's name to add something else that she'd said. He talked in circles around all the details she'd given him.

"One time she said Roscoe and Alice took a drive out to Mount Baker for a weekend at some cottage. Do you think it's worth checking out that area?"

I certainly didn't want Ray stuffing me back in that van and taking me to some secluded mountain cabin. "Um. I think it would've been hard for Roscoe to drive there drunk and then get home all in the same night."

"You're absolutely right." He wrote something

down on the notepad. "This is why it's good to compare thoughts."

I wondered briefly why Kim hadn't mentioned the weekend trip to me? Obviously, like me, she knew it wasn't a plausible area for Roscoe to dump Alice or maybe she never said it to Ray at all. His mind was obviously barely held together and he was drifting in and out of psychosis.

"You seemed to spend a lot of time talking to Kim and Blossom," I said. "Did you know them well before all this started?"

"Sure." He shrugged. "We all worked at a care home in Bellingham together for a few weeks. Blossom got fired for showing up late too many times and Kim couldn't work the kitchen after her car accident, so I guess I was there the longest. It was a shitty job." He sighed. "I'm glad I won't have to do grunt work like that anymore! But I guess the three of us got to somewhat know each other during the few weeks we were all together. Not that we were best friends or anything, but we'd see each other in the lunchroom, you know?"

"What work did you do at the senior home?" Why was this the first I was hearing about them all working there?

"I did janitorial. Emptied the trash." He shrugged. "See what I mean? This…" He stabbed the notepad in front of him with the pen. "This is my real calling. Using my psychic brain…" He tapped the side of his head.

I didn't reply because he was already on to another person on the list. Eventually we exhausted the names and scenarios of every person we interviewed. Ray read the list out loud and demanded that I approve the list and assure him we hadn't missed anyone.

"That's all," I confirmed.

"Okay. Now." He'd been frantically scribbling on the paper in his lap and now he thumbed through the pages of the legal pad until he found a blank page. "Hit me with your ideas of where her body might be."

*Seriously?*

"Ray, if I knew where her body was, I would've found it by now."

"You know this town even better than me. You grew up here. Your maniac grandpa was dumping women all over this state." He offered me a smirk. "If anyone on this planet knows where a body could be hidden in this area, it will be you."

"Maybe it's like everyone has said. Could be that Roscoe borrowed a boat, cut Alice up and dumped her body in the Pacific. If he did that, we're probably not going to find her."

*Let's face it. You did it, Ray.* The motive would've been to get me working a big case so he could chime in and show everyone what great partners we were. I wanted desperately to speak that opinion out loud but there was no way his crazy mind would accept this truth.

"Oh, come on." Ray let out a childish exasperated raspberry noise. "We both know that Roscoe was too drunk and too stupid to make that kind of effort. He stabbed her with the fancy sword he kept hanging on the wall of his trailer."

Ray got up and made slashing motions in the air as

if wielding a sword himself. "And then he pushed her off the bed of his truck and into a gully somewhere."

It sounded a lot like Ray was talking from firsthand knowledge. Had he lost complete contact with reality? Was it possible he murdered Alice, dumped her body and then his mind twisted it that he was not the murderer?

I opened my mouth to speak but he held up a hand to stop me.

"I think we need fuel to keep us going. How about a ham sandwich?"

"No. I'm good." I was thinking about how easily he drugged me at Wayland and shook my head, but my stomach grumbled loudly.

"You have to keep your strength up." He got to his feet, dropping the pen and paper on the coffee table and placing the gun in the waistband of his jeans.

This was my chance. While he was busy making food, I could make a run for it.

"Could I get something hot?" I asked, offering him a small smile. "Could you heat up some canned soup or something?" My hope was that the sound of pots and pans could cover my movement and also buy me more time.

"Of course." He gave me a pleasant, neighborly grin. "Chicken noodle okay?"

"Perfect."

The kitchen was through a door only a few steps away, while the closest exit, the front door of the house, was across the room. If I waited for just the right moment, I could make it. As soon as Ray was out of view, I worked and wiggled my right foot back and forth. I could hear the whir of an electric can opener as the straps dug into the flesh of my foot, but need obliterated any pain. I looked down and saw my foot was slick with blood and that allowed it the lubricant it needed and I was able to yank it free. I jammed both feet back under the sofa just as Ray walked back into the living room.

"Want some crackers to go with your soup?"

"That would be great." I nodded.

He turned and walked back into the kitchen. I took a deep breath and the second I heard the sound of pots rattling in a cupboard, I bolted to my feet and ran for the door. My hands were still tightly bound, making it difficult to fumble with the dead bolt. Just as I finally gripped and then turned the knob in my hands and could almost taste my own freedom, I heard a *bang* and then felt fiery pain rip into my thigh.

Ray was on me then, tackling me to the ground. My head cracked against the hardwood. I saw stars from the blow to my head, but it was nothing compared to the excruciating agony radiating from my thigh.

"I tried to do this the easy way and treat you like a respected partner." Ray grunted as he grabbed me under my arms and dragged me across the hardwood floor. "Mom is going to be so pissed when she sees the mess you've made."

The blood from my leg left a smeared path of red as he dragged me through the living room and down the hall. He took me into a back room, which appeared to be used as a sewing room. There was a small uphol-stered love seat with a wooden spindle back against one wall that was draped with fabrics. I tried to get to my feet but he pushed me back to the floor, grabbed both feet and raised them in the air, then snatched a belt off a nearby table. He bound my feet together and then let them drop to the floor. A white poker of pain exploded in my thigh.

Ray stormed out of the room and I tried to wriggle back to my feet but he returned in less than a minute with duct tape and more zip ties.

"I guess we'll have to continue our brainstorming session tomorrow," he hissed as he strapped three sets of ties tightly around my ankles.

"My leg." I moaned. "There'll be no brainstorming time tomorrow if I don't see a doctor because I'm going to bleed to death!"

Ray flipped me onto my side to look at the wound and then gave it a playful slap. "It's not that bad. Only a flesh wound." He giggled. "I'll put your feet up and bandage it to stop the bleeding."

He left the room again, returning with a first aid box, which he dropped by my head. I could hear him moving stuff around on the top of the sewing desk.

"Where does that woman keep her damn scissors?" He opened and closed drawers until finally exclaiming, "Ah-ha!"

He knelt next to me with scissors in his hand. For a second I thought for certain he was going to use the scissors to finish me off. Instead, he jabbed the point of the scissors into the fabric of my jeans and efficiently cut them off me just above my wound. Then he went to work stuffing thick bandages in the bleeding, ripped flesh as I cried out in agony. He thoroughly wrapped the leg tightly in gauze.

Then he hoisted both my bound feet into the air and

dragged me across the floor so I was closer to the love seat. Using another set of zip ties, he attached my ankles to the spindle back of the love seat so that my head and shoulders were on the ground but my hips were a few inches up and my feet were far high above my head. The position was excruciating but it should definitely prevent me from bleeding out—and also stop me from escaping.

"I'm sorry, Ray. Please don't leave me like this," I began to beg. "I promise I won't try to leave again, and we can keep on talking about the case and our business."

"You blew that chance," he spat.

"How about a reading then?" I scrambled for ideas. To give me a reading he'd have to release my hands and hold them. "You promised you'd give me a reading."

He hesitated. "You don't really want one. You think you're better than me."

"No." I softened my tone. "I really do want a reading."

He lowered himself to the floor next to me and I raised my wrists that were bound together, hoping he'd take the opportunity to undo the ties.

"I don't need your hands," he said.

Disappointment filled my gut. I was hoping to get my hands free, but instead he placed the palm of his hand on my shoulder and began to talk.

"You're going to help find more bodies. A hiker and, um, someone drowned in a lake so…" He cleared his throat. "And also you're going to come back and live here. In Blaine. And we're going to have a very successful business together."

It was so obvious in his delirium he was making it all up. Like I'd ever move back to this town that held more nightmares for me than good memories. This only confirmed Ray had zero talent as a psychic. He was a sham. A shyster. He'd foraged for information to feed people with just enough truth to make them believe him. That's how he got me to think he was the real deal. Because he knew about Wayland.

"You don't believe me." His tone was taut. "I can see it in your eyes. You think I'm making everything up, just like Mom always said." Before I could reply, he snatched up the roll of duct tape and used the scissors to snip off a strip then firmly taped my mouth shut. He leaned forward and snarled into my face, "Maybe by tomorrow you'll mean those words."

As soon as he left the room, I felt a sob fill my throat but I fought against the panic, needing to focus on making my breathing even through my nose since my mouth was covered in tape. I closed my eyes and practiced some of the meditation techniques Dr. Chen had shown me over the years. Not surprising, none of them specialized on how to relax when you were bleeding from a gunshot and tied up by a maniac, waiting for death. Still, I drew in deep breaths and forced myself to relax as much as possible.

Was there any hope that between Tracey and Garrett they'd figure out I was missing yet? It had only been a few hours since Tracey dropped me at my car at the grocery store lot. She would've gone back to her apartment without giving me any more thought until maybe tomorrow. Garrett would just be leaving his Seattle office for home. Instead of walking into my preparations for a barbecue, he'd see Wookie anxious for a chance to go out. I'd been excited to tell him all about how I hadn't fallen off my wagon and share with him something bigger that I'd been sitting on, but now that talk was gone and maybe gone forever.

If I wasn't home when he arrived, Garrett would first assume I'd be home soon. He'd try my cell phone after a couple hours, and when it only rang and went to voice mail, that's when he'd start to get concerned. I could feel tears burn my eyes as I thought of him worrying that I might be on another bender. Maybe he'd even drive by Wayland to see if the rental car was there. Hopefully, he'd call Tracey to see if I was with her, and then I prayed she'd fill him in on what really happened at the bar that night. Then his FBI investigative nature would really kick in. But how much time did I have?

I thought about Barb drugged and probably also tied up in the other room. He couldn't keep her quiet forever. Would he kill his own mother? Even if Ray tried to revisit our earlier talk about finding Alice and making a business together, how long could his deranged mental state hold that thread together before he realized it was doomed to failure?

What little light had seeped through the blinds and under the door eventually grew dark. My thigh had quieted to a constant throb that pulsed in time with one ankle that felt sprained or fractured since Ray's mighty tackle at the front door. At times I could hear movement beyond the door, and the sound of Ray pacing the floors while grumbling and ranting to the air around him. At which point would his mental state allow him to come to the realization that a partnership between us was not a reality and that, at the very least, he'd be spending the rest of his life in a mental hospital or going to prison?

Lying with head, back and shoulders on the floor and hips and legs hoisted in the air was excruciating, and eventually, numbing. I could stretch my bound hands but it did little to release the pressure everywhere else. Beyond my injuries, I had no feeling at all beneath my waist, and I was in a constant battle to keep tears from clogging my throat and congesting my sinuses. With duct tape preventing me from breathing through my mouth I needed to keep my nose clear, so I alternated between meditative exercises and making lists concerning this messed-up case.

At one point in the early morning hours a thought tripped into my brain. It was the kind of idea that I almost let pass but something about it stuck like fly paper.

When I visited Roscoe's mom in the care home, she'd over and over again indicated the box for *food* on her communication board. Food and family. What if she hadn't been trying to tell me she was hungry. Maybe what she was actually saying was that the person who killed Alice was connected to food. Ray had mentioned the night before that he, Blossom and Kim had all worked at the care home. Although Ray said he worked in janitorial, maybe Mrs. Ebert thought he was part of the crew dealing with food. I chased the threads of that idea through my head and it became more and more plausible that Mrs. Ebert knew that Ray had killed Alice but she just couldn't express it. Had he confided to her when he worked there?

I thought also about how my Jeep had been vandalized when Tracey and I were inside the care home. Ray would've known from working there that the parking lot cameras weren't in service. Even though he hadn't worked there for a while, he could've still been confident they hadn't yet been repaired so he felt safe spray-painting my vehicle without getting caught.

But why would he want to warn me off the case when, according to him, he was all about finding Alice's body so we could be heroes? A frown pulled at the tape on my mouth. There were only two explanations for that behavior. Either he did it hoping to draw even more publicity to the case, or Ray was just plain insane.

The house had been quiet for the past couple of hours, but now I could hear movement again. I desperately needed to pee and even more importantly needed to have my feet lowered to get the feeling back. When there was the sound of footsteps in the hall, I raised my head and thumped it against the hardwood floor repeatedly. Finally Ray opened the door.

"Morning." His voice was low and gravelly, like he'd just woken. "I hope you're ready to be serious today."

I was serious about getting free. My life depended on it. All I could do was nod. To my dismay he turned around and left the room. A few minutes later he was back with a tray containing a first aid kit, a bottled water and a muffin. My dry throat ached at the thought of a drink.

"I'm going to check your bandages and then I'm going to move you to a different position."

I grunted against the tape.

"You want me to take the tape off?"

I blinked hard as a yes.

He pulled the gun from the waistband of his jeans.

"You scream and I'll shoot you again." He slumped

down next to me on the floor and yanked the tape from my mouth.

"Thank you." The words came out in a low hoarse voice I didn't recognize as my own. He picked up the sewing shears and cut through the plastic ties on my ankles. When my legs dropped to the floor, I felt immediate relief and then a flood of pins and needles as blood rushed to my lower limbs.

He pushed me onto my side, tore off the blood-soaked bandages, and then carefully repacked the wound. As he worked, I bit my lip to stop from crying out. Once the new bandage was on, he helped me to a sitting position with my back against the sofa.

"Could you untie my hands?" I lifted them in front of me.

"No way."

He held the bottle of water to my lips and I drank greedily even as some sloshed down my chin and dribbled down my shirt. Next, he held the muffin up to my mouth.

"I—I really need to use the washroom," I told him.

He gave a curt nod, got to his feet and then lifted me from under my arms until I was standing. My legs were still wobbly from being bound. With my first step, my thigh screeched in agony. Holding the gun to my back, he brought me across the hall.

Once inside the washroom, he turned his back but told me he had no plans on leaving the room. At this point I didn't care about modesty. I barely managed to undo the top button of my jeans with my hands clasped together and then push them down far enough to go. He turned away as I peed and then looked up at the ceiling while I fumbled to get my pants pulled somewhat up over my hips. He did the top button and zipper up for me since I couldn't manage, and a burst of rage filled my chest. At least he didn't appear interested in raping me, my inner thoughts reasoned, but that was small consideration because he seemed to have zero problem shooting me.

Ray brought me back into the sewing room, lowered me back to the floor and took out more zip ties.

"Please," I begged. "Could you leave my hands untied?" I offered him a wince of pain. "That way I'll be able to eat and drink a water bottle on my own."

He puffed out his cheeks and then tilted his head from one side then the other as if weighing the decisions.

"I'll make them looser. But don't do anything stupid or else." He waved the gun in my face.

Instead of laying me back on the floor with my ankles in the air and attached to the wooden slats of the love seat, Ray sat me on the teak bench, tied my wrists in front of me and then attached my bound ankles to the leg of the small sofa.

"We should talk about today's plans," Ray said, clearing his throat.

He left the room and returned with the notepad from the night before. He handed me a muffin and stuffed a water bottle between my knees. Although the zip ties were still tight around each wrist, he'd looped a third one between my two wrists so that there were a few inches between my hands.

Between nibbling pieces of the muffin and drinking the water, I listened to Ray read aloud from the long list he'd made. It was a deranged itemization of all the places he thought we should check for Alice's body. He must've stayed up late itemizing every green belt, park, culvert or garden shed within a twenty-mile radius. It was completely unhinged only because the places he suggested searching for Alice were places she definitely would've been found long ago or would've been searched at the time by police. Dumpsters, ditches and sheds in and around town.

My stomach rolled with nausea. The dry bran muffin I'd choked down sat like a rock in my stomach as he read the list. I needed to get out of this house if I had any hope of surviving. I couldn't trust that Ray would take me on outings to these locations without losing his cool and shooting me on the spot.

While he talked, my gaze fell on something on the desk next to the sewing machine. A long black hinged case that I recognized immediately because my grandmother had one just like it. Inside that case would be Barb's favorite, prized fabric shears. Most seamstresses kept a few pairs of scissors and the ones in that case were special and particularly sharp. I remember my grandmother once dragging the point of those scissors down my back, carving a deep, bloody groove with hardly any effort. Next to a bundle of fabric lay the other scissors Ray had used earlier. His eyes had skipped over the black case when looking for something to cut my jeans because, like most people, he wouldn't recognize that black case. I realized Ray had stopped talking and I returned my gaze to him.

"When do you want to start the search?" I asked, shaking my head to get a lock of hair off my face.

"Tonight," he said. "Daylight would be preferred, of course, but your boyfriend is on a mission at the moment to find you. So we're going to move to a different place for the day."

Garrett was searching! I closed my eyes to keep emotional tears from rolling down my face.

"Where are we going?" I asked.

"I've got a few places in mind. I'm just going to go get myself ready." He smiled and his eyes sparked with madness. "All you need to know is that I've got your dowsing rods so you're ready."

There was a low pitiful cry from across the hall. Barb was waking again.

"I'll be back."

When he left the room, I began to flex the muscles in my legs, and even though my ankle pulsed painfully, I wiggled all my toes and stretched. Wherever we were going, I had a feeling this would be my last chance to make a run at freedom, and when the time came, I was going to be ready. As I stretched, I reached for the sewing desk to see how far I was from those sewing shears, but even at my longest stretch, they were a few feet away.

Ray must have drugged Barb again because she was, once again, completely silent. I heard another door open and close across the hall and the sound of water running. There was the distinct clang of sliding shower doors opening and shutting, and I knew now was my chance. He might only shower for two minutes but it might be the only time I had.

Once again I stretched toward the sewing table, and abruptly the heavy teak love seat scraped forward. It never occurred to me that I'd be able to move the entire bench but I did so now. Every inch I dragged it across the hardwood emitted a raucous dragging sound that I hoped was covered by the sound of the shower.

Finally, I was able to lunge forward and snatch the case from the desk. I snapped the hinged case open and grabbed the shears. The heavy-duty carbon steel had been well cared for and remained razor sharp. Even with my wrists bound, I was able to cut through the straps at my ankles like they were dental floss. It took more effort to position the scissors between my knees and saw through the ties around my wrists. A bubble of panic clogged my throat as I frantically worked, dragging the ties against the blade of the scissors until finally one side was free.

Keeping the scissors in my hands, I moved to the door and tried to hear above the blood pounding in my ears to listen for the sound of Ray in the shower. The water was still running so I opened the door to the room and began to run. I reached the front door and turned the dead bolt, the door squealing on rusty hinges as I burst outside. My ankle could hardly hold my weight as I bounded down the steps, and the wound in my thigh began to bleed. Warm blood ran down my leg as I was cutting across the lawn. In the distance, I could hear sirens coming closer but if they were coming for me, I knew they wouldn't get there in time. I'd almost reached the street and heard Ray's guttural scream from inside the house.

There was nothing but wide-open street beyond his cul-de-sac. There'd be not even a tree to hide behind, so I took a sharp right and dipped against the side of the last house on the street that was under construction. I could hear him approaching at a dead run and I waited for him to round the corner. He'd expect that I'd be running through the field behind the house and heading for town but I was crouched behind a scraggly brown cedar, and when he came around the side of the house, he never saw me.

As soon as he'd taken a step beyond me I leaped out of my hiding place with the sewing shears high above my head. With both hands, I plunged the scissors into Ray's neck. He dropped to his knees and the gun in his hand tumbled forward. As he reached for the firearm, I yanked the shears from his neck, raised them again and plunged them into his hand. An animalistic howl escaped his throat but still he crawled forward toward the gun. I jumped forward and scrambled beyond him so that I got there first.

He looked up at me, his eyes wide and mouth moving but no words were coming out. Then he collapsed into the dirt and curled into a fetal position.

I could hear sirens closer now and the sound of loud voices and car doors slamming but all I could focus on was Ray Hughes.

I took a step back, closed one eye and raised the handgun, using two hands to steady it. I was aiming to shoot him in the head.

# THIRTEEN

RAY WAS UNARMED, injured and writhing on the ground in agony, but I wanted to unload the weapon into him. It was Garrett's voice calling my name that stopped me.

"Over here," I cried out.

I moved to step around Ray and he reached a hand out to grab my ankle. With all my force, I raised my good foot, and though my sore ankle screamed, I stomped on his hand and ground my heel into it before I stepped around the corner of the house. There were police cars, their lights and sirens going, and officers with guns drawn standing at Ray's door. Other officers were surrounding Ray's house but Garrett stood in the middle of the cul-de-sac by his car. The sun was shining and he held a hand up to shield his eyes as he looked toward the sound of my voice. When he spotted me, I limped toward him, dragging my sore ankle. My thigh shrieked in agony and warm blood gushed from my thigh. His long stride reached me before I could take more than a couple steps, and Garrett swept me into his arms, burying his face in my neck and squeezing my ribs so tight I could hardly breathe.

I began to cry then, sobbing wordlessly against his chest and unable to speak. Pointing in the direction of where they could locate Ray, I allowed Garrett to carry me to his car. While I sat in the passenger seat, he examined my injuries, and still the tears kept coming. When the ambulance arrived, he tried to step aside so the EMTs could examine me but I wouldn't let go of his hand.

"Can you give her something for the pain?" Garrett asked them as they prepared to put me into the ambulance.

"No!" I shouted as they strapped me to the gurney.

"You need something." Garrett released my hand and stroked my face. "Some kind of painkiller to take the edge off."

"I can't." I shook my head firmly and then I reached again for Garrett's hand and pulled him down toward me. "I'm pregnant."

His eyes registered surprise before they became bright with tears. He bent to embrace me and his entire body shook with emotion, but he couldn't find any words as they wheeled me away.

At the hospital I was immediately brought to X-ray, where they made sure they covered my pregnant belly with a lead apron before taking images. Garrett was waiting for me in the curtained area of the triage area. Immediately I began to talk, explaining to him about what really happened at Wayland, and he held the tip of his finger to my lips.

"I know. Tracey told me." He gave me a sad smile and lowered his tone to a near whisper. "That's why you didn't tell me you were pregnant? Because you thought you may have been raped?"

Fresh tears rolled down my cheeks. Not raped. I was worried I'd gone and drunkenly slept with some random guy.

He took both my hands in his, turned my palms upward and bent and kissed my wrists tenderly. With his lips he traced the abrasions from the ties on my wrists then, finally, rested his face against my hands.

"You don't need to do this," he whispered while placing more kisses on the palms of my hands. "You always said you didn't know if you wanted to have children, and just because you're now pregnant…"

"I want this baby." My voice was firm, and suddenly I was never more sure of anything in my entire life. "If my drinking was out of control… If this baby wasn't yours…" I swallowed a sob. "Then I don't think I could've brought myself to have it but…" I lifted his face from my hands so that I could look him in the eye. "I'm absolutely sure I want this because I want us. This baby is us."

There was a wave of relief and love that flooded his face as he wrapped his arms around me and kissed my mouth.

"How did you know where to find me?"

"Tracey said you parted ways at the grocery store so I went and searched the lot. When I saw your vehicle abandoned there, I demanded to see the surveillance videos of the parking lot. The video quality was poor but eventually we could enhance the license plate enough to trace the van to Barb and Ray's house."

I closed my eyes and murmured, "Thank God for cameras."

Hours later, with a freshly sutured thigh and a boot on my ankle, Garrett brought me home. Shortly after we arrived, the police showed up wanting a full statement from me. I gave them all the details I could remember, going all the way back to being drugged at Wayland and right up until me stabbing him with scissors and breaking free.

"Is he…" I couldn't finish the question.

"You didn't kill him." The officer slapped his notebook shut and got to his feet. "In fact, he's lucky because you missed all his major arteries. He's going to jail with stitches in his neck and hand but it could've been worse."

"Yeah, I could've gotten my hands on him," Garrett snarled.

"It was obviously self-defense," the officer told Garrett as he was walked to the door. "I'm certain there'll be no disputing that fact, and the community is safer now that this guy is going to be locked away."

After that was done, Garrett set me up on the sofa with an ottoman and pillows for my sore leg and a side table littered with healthy snacks. Wookie and Fluffy both took up residence nearby, keeping a watchful eye on me. After calling Tracey and asking her to come over, Garrett headed to the store saying we needed a thousand things to keep me healthy. I laughed because everything I ever needed was already here.

Tracey arrived as soon as he was gone.

"I'm going to be an aunt?" Tracey shrieked with joy and then sobbed openly. "I was so worried. When Garrett called me looking for you and then I heard they found your rental car behind the grocery store, I thought I would absolutely die. I can't believe it was Ray!" She slumped on the sofa next to me. "I screwed a murderer."

"He was pretty good at showing a different side of himself." I thought about my vague memories of him at

Wayland and compared the long-haired, bearded, teal-eyed person to the clean-cut guy I'd been working with the past few days. "I'm just glad you didn't get hurt."

"But you did," Tracey said solemnly. "I should've seen what he was capable of. My radar when it comes to men is really off." She blew out a long breath. "My mother is right. I need to stick with guys she can fix me up with."

"So you're thinking of allowing your mom to set you up on dates?" I laughed at the thought.

Tracey chatted but mostly I tuned her out and finally told her she had to leave so I could have a nap. I was tired, but really I just wanted to be able to think. After she was gone, I hobbled over to the kitchen table and opened my laptop. By the time Garrett was back home, I had my backpack by the door and was itching to leave.

"Whoa, where do you think you're going?"

"Since I can't drive with this dumb boot, you're taking me on a little drive."

"You're not going anywhere," he said firmly. "You've had a traumatic experience and you've been physically injured. What you need…" He put a hand on my flat stomach. "What you *both* need, is rest."

"I promise to rest and let you feed me kale smoothies as soon as you take me to check this one last thing." When he opened his mouth to protest I added, "I know where Alice is." I told him my idea and his face grew hard with worry. "If you don't take me, I'll ask Tracey."

Reluctantly he agreed, and minutes later I was sitting in the passenger seat of Garrett's sedan as he drove north on I-5. The closer we got to our destination, the more antsy I became. I had packed my backpack to include all the paperwork I had on Alice's case. As Garrett drove, I read through my notes and once again looked at the five pictures Alice took on her phone on that final evening. There was a tingling of an idea in the back of my mind but I pushed the thought away for now.

An hour later as Garrett drove down a rutted gravel driveway, the hairs on the back of my neck stood on end. The house where I'd been raised had long since been demolished by the new landowners, and the trailer where I'd lived as an adult on the same property had been hauled away. Even though the buildings were different, the air felt the same in my lungs.

"It's not too late to change your mind." Garrett put the car in park, then reached for my hand and gave it a squeeze. "You don't have to do this. I can have a team here within a few hours and they can search this entire property and—"

"I have to," I whispered. "I'm pretty sure Alice was dumped here because this was the last place people thought another body would be found. She was brought here to hide her from me." I looked at him and straightened my spine. "I need to finish this."

After pulling out my dowsing rods, I climbed out and hobbled on my boot around the front of the car. With my rods held outward, I began limping slowly but with determination. Starting where the house used to be, I made my way from the far left of the acreage, slowly toward the right of the land. Then I turned and began walking down another row. The land had been cleared and was hard, compact scrub weeds. Driving a pickup out there to dump a body would not have been difficult. As I struggled to walk, all the dark, quicksand evilness that occurred on this land tried to rear up and take hold of me. Dark, nasty thoughts flooded my mind. Bursts of memories of all the excruciating moments of abuse suffered at the hands of my grandmother on this very soil, and the tyranny of an even more evil grandfather threatened to weaken me. Using the power of all the positive affirmations and meditations taught to me by Dr. Chen, I continued to walk and forced thoughts of my own trauma to stay in the past where they belonged. Whenever I felt a spark of doubt, I closed my eyes to feel Garrett's concerned gaze that followed me the entire time. I knew it was nearly impossible for him to let me do this on my own, and I loved that he respected me enough not to stop me.

By the time I reached the back of the property, my ankle was screaming inside the boot, and the stitches in my thigh were a fire of punctuation with each step. When my grandmother's voice began to hiss wickedly in my mind, I shouted back, "You have no power over me, old woman!"

The horrors of this place had held my mind captive for a long time, but I'd done the necessary healing work and now I was free. The power of that allowed me to push forward.

A garden shed at the back of the property leaned precariously in on itself. Time and weather had it to the point where it was ready to collapse. As I stepped close to the shed door, my rods crossed slowly but purposely. There'd been a time I'd been locked in that shed in the cold and dark. Left to die, but I'd been able to claw myself out and live another day.

Alice had not been so lucky.

I didn't open the door to the shed to confirm what was inside. Instead, I just looked over my shoulder and made eye contact with Garrett. He jogged across the acreage toward me. He took me in his arms and we embraced for a full minute before he helped me back across the field to his car. Once he tucked me safely inside the vehicle, he returned to confirm what we both already knew. When Garrett came back to the car he was just ending a phone call to the local law, letting them know to gather their team and bring them here.

It wasn't until he'd started the car, turned on my seat warmer and handed me a bottle of water that he asked the question.

"Was it Ray?"

"No." I shook my head slowly. "I have an idea… Let's go see Kim."

I gave Garrett instructions on the short drive to Kim's trailer. She was sitting on the front porch with a light jacket pulled tight across her chest. As Garrett put his car in park, she didn't even look up.

"Hello," I said as I approached. "Can we go inside?"

She gave me a sharp nod and got wearily to her feet. Her gaze dropped briefly to Garrett but she never asked who he was or why he was there. We followed her inside and I once again looked around the old trailer but it no longer felt like my old home.

"You found Alice." Kim lowered herself into the recliner.

"Yes." To Garrett I said, "Those final pictures that Alice took on her phone? The last one with the blurry, hairy object in the corner?"

I picked up Kim's key ring from a nearby kitchen

counter and held it up for him to see. Dangling from her keys was a troll doll with black hair. "I thought the tiny bit of hair in the corner of the picture was a bit of Jet as he moved out of the shot, but it was Kim's keychain. Alice knew something was up and she snapped a picture just before Kim killed her."

Garrett removed the revolver from the shoulder holster under his jacket and aimed it steadily at Kim. She didn't even flinch at the accusation.

"Your stepdad had always helped Alice and Roscoe out financially while ignoring you."

"I wasn't blood." Kim's voice was low and hoarse. "So I was nothing. When Alice told me they were going to have a baby, I didn't know it was Lois right away. I thought Alice was saying she was pregnant with Roscoe's kid."

"So you killed her and framed your own brother."

She picked up one of the troll dolls from the end table and wordlessly stroked the bright pink hair on its knobby head without replying.

"Alice's cell phone is in the bathroom," I told Garrett. "In the cupboard under the sink."

Kim's gaze shot up in shock.

"I caught a glimpse of something under your sink when I used your washroom," I told her. "Something red with sequins. It never occurred to me until a few minutes ago that Detective Larry mentioned Alice's phone had a red sparkly case."

Kim covered her face with her hands. She knew it was over.

"Check to see if it's still there," Garrett instructed as he kept his gun pointed at Kim. "But don't touch it."

The cabinet door broke the rest of the way off as I tugged on it and there, nestled between a tampon box and a pile of toilet paper, sat Alice's cell phone with its sparkly red case.

It wasn't long before the police arrived. Garrett told me to wait in the car and I met Detective Larry just pulling up as I left. I told him Garrett was inside and then briefly informed him about the phone and the troll doll hair in the picture.

"She did it," he said.

"Yes. She had access to the sword and his truck. She killed Alice because she knew a baby would change everything. Her stepdad was already helping Alice and Roscoe out financially and ignoring Kim's needs. I'm sure if the will is checked, it will say that Kim isn't entitled to anything if there are grandchildren, and the costs of the care home were already more than she could stand."

I waited in the car while Detective Larry and a host of other local law went inside and arrested Kim without incident but when they led her out of the trailer in handcuffs, I climbed out of the car to confront her. I limped toward the officer's car and stood in front of her.

Garrett came over and put a hand on my shoulder but it was unnecessary because Kim was in cuffs held by an officer and I was a few feet away.

Kim hissed at me, "When you look at this place, you see your own prison but this is my castle." She leaned forward and screamed, "Mine! I worked this land. It was always supposed to be mine, not to share with Roscoe and some bastard kid. I gave Alice a ride here that night. She said she wanted to talk to Roscoe and tell him that soon they could get back together because they were going to have a baby. She was so excited. I told her to wait until he sobered up in the morning and put her to bed in my room." Kim rolled her eyes at that. "When Roscoe came home drunk that night, he passed out almost immediately. I took his sword off the wall, woke Alice up and brought her out to the truck. At first I was just threatening her to get off my land and leave us alone but then she said that the property would belong to her, Roscoe and their baby. It wasn't until recently, when I was thinking about how to ditch Alice's phone that I saw on there a message from Lois that she was carrying a baby for them two. Then I knew I had to get Lois too."

"Why dump her on my land?"

"My stepdad was always talking about how cool he thought it was that you found bodies. I knew he would reach out to you to find Alice but rumors around town always said you had bad PTSD about your old homestead." Kim smirked. "Never thought you'd have the balls to go back there." She shook her head. "Guess I was wrong."

I only nodded because it confirmed what I knew. Just as the officer was bending her into the back of his car, Kim began to shout toward me.

"Guess what? I knew your grandmother was abusing you. I saw all those marks when I was babysitting you. Guess I could've stopped it but I didn't give a shit!" Her screams were carried to me on a howl of wind. "Even as a kid you always acted like you were too good for the rest of us." Her face was twisted in rage as she screamed, "This is all your fault! You're nothing but a freak, Julie Hall! May you rot in hell!"

Her rant continued but it was lost as they folded her into the back of the cop car and slammed the door.

"She let her own half brother go to prison for a crime she committed," Garrett said as he climbed into the driver's seat. He shook his head sadly. "What kind of family is that?" Then, as if suddenly realizing the land we were near, he placed a hand on my leg. "Sorry."

We both knew the evil that could reside within families.

"Let's go home." Garrett started up the car.

I was suddenly more weary than I'd ever been in my life and I slept the entire drive back home. The memory of the rest of that day and all of the next were a blur of half sleep, with snippets of Garrett waking me regularly to feed me foul kale smoothies and prenatal vitamins. At Dr. Chen's recommendation and Garrett's insistence, I spent some time relaxing so my physical injuries could heal and did phone sessions with my psychiatrist to do the mental health work.

I mostly ignored my emails but I did read one from a person who contacted me through my Divine Reunions website. It was the waitress from Wayland, who thanked me profusely for helping to pay off her medical bills. Garrett had done that and told me afterward that it was a thank-you to the woman who stuck me in a cab and sent me home so that Ray couldn't abduct me.

When he had to go to work, Garrett had Tracey come stay with me, which was great except for her obsession with reciting obscure baby names.

"How about Cinema Rumi? It works for both a boy and a girl."

I just looked at her and laughed.

I'd heard from Detective Larry that Lois had been

discharged from hospital and was recovering at home. That same day I texted Lois and asked her if she was up to having company. She said she'd planned on having more people over and would love to see me.

Tracey drove but stayed in the car when I went inside Lois's apartment.

"I can't thank you enough." Lois pulled me into a tight hug.

She still had a lot of bandages covering her body, and it looked like she'd forever carry the physical scars of trying to help her sister.

"When Kim came to my door that day," Lois began, "I let her in because she'd contacted me saying that she had a few things that belonged to Alice and asked if I wanted them as keepsakes. She tossed a large sack on the counter, telling me everything was inside. I turned around to look in the bag and felt a sudden pain and… she…"

"You don't have to talk about it," I assured her. "I'm sorry you got caught up in it."

"I don't mind talking about it."

"Do you know why Kim tried to kill you?"

"The night Alice was killed I'd just met her briefly for coffee. I'd parked down the road and watched as Roscoe broke Alice's car window to free Jet. I got out of my car and was going to intervene if things got too heated but it seemed to blow over quickly. When Roscoe left with Jet and the onlookers went back about their business, I figured it was over so I got in my car. Just as I was pulling away, a woman walked by and we made eye contact. It was Kim. She looked quickly away but I'd never met her before so seeing her meant nothing to me. Obviously she figured I could place her near Alice on the night she was killed."

"Alice's car was left on the street that night. I guess Kim convinced her to leave with her."

"I owe you big-time," Lois said, lowering herself gingerly into a chair and pointing for me to do the same. "You found my sister's body and her killer." She swiped at the tears that sprung to her eyes. "If there's ever anything I can do…"

"I just want to know one thing," I said. "You got pregnant for Alice and Roscoe."

She shook her head. "No. I had a one-night stand and found out I was pregnant. I wasn't planning on having it but then I heard how bad Alice wanted a baby and I had the idea to have the baby and let them adopt it."

"That was an extremely kindhearted thing to do."

"I just knew how bad she wanted a baby."

"I'm so sorry for your loss." I gave Lois a hug before I left. I was happy to be able to return home with all the pieces of the Alice puzzle together at last.

A WEEK LATER Garrett returned home with a paper lunch sack that he placed next to me on the sofa.

"I swear if that's more kale I'm going to barf," I told him.

"Not kale. It's something that was found in Ray Hughes's home a few days ago, and I had to do a lot of wrangling to make sure it didn't get locked up with all the other evidence."

Curious now, I picked up the bag and peered inside.

"My ring!" Tears swelled in my eyes. "Oh my God! He must have taken it from me that night at Wayland."

"His bedroom had an entire corkboard filled with information on you, and a bookshelf filled with a ton of paraphernalia on psychic stuff from crystals and tarot cards to a dozen different kinds and shapes of dowsing rods, and in with all of that was a box containing your ring." Garrett lowered himself to the sofa next to me and took the ring out of the bag. "He was probably intending to use the ring to impress you with his psychic power."

"He planned on putting it somewhere and then if I was doubting his ability he'd give me a reading that brought me to the ring." And that would've worked to convince me he was the real deal, but just knowing about Wayland had been enough.

In his deranged mental state Ray had believed he was a true psychic. As much as I hated him and hoped he'd never leave the mental hospital again, I also hoped that with the right medication he could get help.

Garrett held my hand gently in his and placed the band on my finger, where it belonged. Happy tears traced their way down my face and he kissed them away.

Over the next few months my belly grew impressively large and I took a rest from finding the dead and instead increased my visits to Dr. Chen. I needed to be absolutely positive that when our baby arrived that I was in the best mental state possible. I heard that Roscoe was released from prison and had found a place to live near his mother's care home. Kim had confessed to everything and I was grateful because that spared me having to relive the case testifying in court.

The larger my belly became, the more attentive Garrett was, and there were days I complained aloud about his mothering, but the truth was I wouldn't want it any other way. While I was on hiatus from looking for the dead, my dowsing rods rested on a shelf in our living room. They waited for the day when they'd be called to action again.

The dead were much more patient than the living.

\* \* \* \* \*

# ACKNOWLEDGMENTS

Great thanks to editor Deborah Nemeth, whose tireless efforts make me a better writer.

# ABOUT THE AUTHOR

Wendy Roberts is a mystery and supernatural writer living a super-normal life. Cloak and dagger are her bread and butter. She is the author of four novels in the Bodies of Evidence series, five Ghost Dusters mysteries, as well as *Dating Can Be Deadly* and *Grounds to Kill*. She is an armchair sleuth and a fan of all things mysterious. Wendy resides in Vancouver, Canada, where she happily tends to feral cats, rogue raccoons and writes about murder. She is always working on her next novel.

Website: www.wendyroberts.com
Twitter: www.Twitter.com/authorwendy
Instagram: @wendyroberts_author
Facebook: www.Facebook.com/wendyrobertsauthor